For Justin Neal Stumbo

Praise for
THE LIGHT-YEARS
BENEATH MY FEET

"Even at its most serious, *The Light-Years Beneath My Feet* never loses its sense of fun . . . guaranteed to capture readers' interest and have them excitedly devouring this delightful story. Exotic aliens, satire and a talking dog. What's not to like?"
—*Starlog*

"Alan Dean Foster is a master of creating strange, yet understandable, alien cultures . . . A fun read."
—*The SF Site*

"Foster's trademark dry wit, colorful characters, and talented retelling of the traditional fish-out-of water story will keep readers' attention."
—*Library Journal*

"Foster is in top form here, entertainingly mixing politics, comedy, and intriguing alien anthropology."
—*Booklist*

"Readers seeking harmless fun will look forward to the further galactic travels of Marcus and friends."
—*Publishers Weekly*

"It's slick, creative, and amusing and a great follow-up to last year's *Lost and Found*."
—*SFRevu.com*

By Alan Dean Foster
Published by Ballantine Books

The Black Hole
Cachalot
Dark Star
The Metrognome and Other Stories
Midworld
Nor Crystal Tears
Sentenced to Prism
Splinter of the Mind's Eye
Star Trek® Logs One–Ten
Voyage to the City of the Dead
. . . Who Needs Enemies?
With Friends Like These . . .
Mad Amos
The Howling Stones
Parallelities

THE ICERIGGER TRILOGY

Icerigger
Mission to Moulokin
The Deluge Drivers

THE ADVENTURES OF FLINX OF THE COMMONWEALTH

For Love of Mother-Not
The Tar-Aiym-Krang
Orphan Star
The End of the Matter
Bloodhype
Flinx in Flux
Mid-Flinx
Flinx's Folly
Sliding Scales
Running from the Deity
Trouble Magnet

THE DAMNED

Book One: A Call to Arms
Book Two: The False Mirror
Book Three: The Spoils of War

THE FOUNDING OF THE COMMONWEALTH

Phylogenesis
Dirge
Diuturnity's Dawn

THE TAKEN TRILOGY

Lost and Found
The Light-years Beneath My Feet
The Candle of Distant Earth

THE LIGHT-YEARS BENEATH MY FEET

ALAN DEAN FOSTER

BALLANTINE BOOKS · NEW YORK

The Light-years Beneath My Feet is a work of fiction. Names, characters, places, and incidents are the products of the author's imagination or are used fictitiously. Any resemblance to actual events, locales, or persons, living or dead, is entirely coincidental.

2006 Del Rey Books Mass Market Edition

Copyright © 2005 by Thranx, Inc.
Excerpt from *The Candle of Distant Earth* copyright © 2006 by Thranx, Inc.

Published in the United States by Del Rey Books, an imprint of The Random House Publishing Group, a division of Random House, Inc., New York.

DEL REY is a registered trademark and the Del Rey colophon is a trademark of Random House, Inc.

Originally published in hardcover in the United States by Del Rey Books, an imprint of The Random House Publishing Group, a division of Random House, Inc., 2005.

ISBN 978-0-345-46130-8

Printed in the United States of America

www.delreybooks.com

OPM 9 8 7 6 5 4 3 2

1

Marcus Walker's khirach-tel soufflé had fallen, and couldn't get up.

But it was trying to.

Writhing, peridot-hued filaments of specially sweetened bariile as active as they were tasty twisted and coiled like a nest of worms on speed as they struggled to re-form the compact yet airy loaf Walker had initially marshaled out of ingredients coughed up by the trio of synchronized synthesizers. Adrift in the center of the spherical preparator, suspended within its energized field and shielded from its harmful effects, he strove to maintain a semblance of recipe. All around him, the aromatic components of the special dessert he had engineered emerged from the synths to steadily merge and meld, freeze or bake. If everything came off as planned, the result ought to be a last course spectacular enough to impress the supervising Sessrimathe program that was serving as his mentor and judge.

Unfortunately, everything was not going as planned.

The radiant shower of rainbow-hued geljees that were supposed to execute an iridescent, chromatic englobement of the soufflé were growing impatient. Like bees unable to agree on the location of a hive, they threatened to disperse into individual spheres and shatter themselves against the boundaries of the preparator in a spate of sugary seppuku. Though still coherent, his carefully woven whipped lavender finishing flame, frenetic with edible purple energy, was starting to dance fitfully just beyond his left hand. He could have controlled it better with the cooking wand in his right except that he needed to focus every bit of his attention and newly learned skills on taming the wild soufflé itself. As the anchorpiece of the finished dessert, it could not be ignored, lest it descend swiftly into caloric anarchy.

Matters were not made easier by the knowledge that as he fought to control the culinary chaos swirling around him, his every move was being recorded and judged by the Sessrimathe program. If he failed to control the dessert, it would not be a crisis. But he had made so much progress, had come so far in his studies, that finishing the sweet he had designed from scratch had become for him a matter not just of nourishment, but of personal pride.

He had always given his all and had never quit on the football field. He would not quit in the kitchen—even if it was a kitchen the likes of which had never been imagined on Earth. Within it, automatic perceptors might suspend gravity and spot-control temperature, but it still required a sentient supervisor to direct the process. Doing so was a long way from engaging in the mundane machinations of the Chicago Commodities Exchange. But then, he was a long way from Chicago.

Not to mention Earth.

Following his rescue and that of his new friends from their avaricious abductors the Vilenjji, he had found himself untold light-years from home, surrounded and even coddled by the citizens of a highly advanced civilization, exposed to technological wonders any scientist on Earth would have given ten years of life to experience, with ever more promised to come.

No wonder he had speedily grown bored and homesick.

For a while following that rescue, the sophisticated world of their liberators the Sessrimathe had been endlessly fascinating. Months into their new freedom, it merely seemed endless. He came to realize that a good deal of that, and his resultant boredom, was a consequence of his own individual inadequacies. The accuracy of this realization had done nothing to improve his mood.

It seemed as if every one of his companions managed to fare

better than the lone human among them. For example, their genial hosts were continually charmed by the contrast between the massive Tuuqalian Braouk's physical power and strength and the delicacy and sensitivity of his poetry and singing. Additionally, the same stentorian recitals of heroic Tuuqalian sagas and rhythmic traditional lamentations that Marc and his friends had begun to find wearisome while they had been imprisoned together aboard the Vilenjji capture vessel proved irresistible to the Sessrimathe. Remarking on this attraction, Sque commented that perhaps their hosts were not so advanced after all.

As for the ever-acerbic K'eremu Sequi'aranaqua'na'senemu, she backed up her interminable boasting with an effortless ability to master an entirely new culture and technology that astonished their hosts. Her companions were less surprised by this achievement. During their time of captivity on board the Vilenjji collecting ship she had demonstrated more than once that her galling claims of intellectual superiority were founded on reality and not empty boasting. There seemed no circumstances, no surroundings, in which she could not, given a modest amount of time in which to make a thorough study of the situation, insinuate herself as if she had been born to them.

As for George, the now casually conversant mutt from the seedy side of the Windy City seemed to have made friends with everyone in their complex. Though the towering, faux-tree living structure was home not only to Sessrimathe but to aliens other than the inhabitants of Seremathenn, it made no difference to George. No matter how outlandish in shape or uncertain of attitude, any independent intelligence was fair game for his probing curiosity. And it was a rare sentient who did not respond favorably to the dog's tail-wagging, soulful-eyed, tongue-lolling queries.

That left Walker, who was neither an intriguingly lumbering aesthete like Braouk, superior adaptive intelligence like Sque, or inherently likeable and manifestly harmless kibbitzer like George. While the four of them argued and debated possible ways and means of attempting to return to their respective homeworlds, what could he possibly do to show them, as well as their polite and courteous hosts the Sessrimathe, that there was something more to him than dead weight?

In Chicago he had been a commodities trader, and a damn good one. Plunged into the superior, sophisticated swirl of a galactic civilization no one had suspected existed, he found to his dismay that here his chosen profession was less than useless. While trade and commerce not only existed but flourished all around him, he did not have a clue how a complete outsider like himself might even begin to participate in its enormously complex and vastly accelerated ebb and flow. Rare was the day when he did not awaken in the quarters that had been assigned to him feeling useless, inadequate, and empty of purpose. If his friends noticed his funk, they were too polite to remark on it. The sensitive Braouk suspected, Marc believed, but the Tuuqalian would never venture to comment on a friend's evident distress without first being approached for consultation.

No, in the absence of readily available help it was up to him to do something about it. Could he do anything else besides engage in the trading of intangible futures? Had his entire existence back home been restricted only to the buying and selling of tanker loads of orange juice and truckloads of coltan? What else could he do? He could play football, and very well. While the games of the Sessrimathe inclined more to the intellectual, in the course of his sojourn on Seremathenn he had observed that other resident and visiting aliens often participated in contests of skill of a physical nature. Not only could he not figure out the objectives of such games, much less the rules, some of the participants were dangerously bigger than he was. While none approached in size and intimidation factor the massive Tuuqalian Braouk, it was clear that if he tried to partake he ran the real risk of permanent injury.

Besides, he wanted to make use of his mind, not brute force, if only to forestall the inevitable comments such participation would have brought forth from the caustic Sque. Her opinion of humankind being already low enough, he saw no need to provide her with additional material for her predictable stream of verbal barbs. Not that she was incapable of inventing plenty by herself.

So—what else could he try? His inadequacy troubled and nagged him for weeks, until it came to him—logically enough—during an evening meal.

George was sharing space with him. The dog was lying on the animate shag rug-thing his own living quarters had manufactured at his request. Outside the single oval window of Walker's room the soaring spires of the artificial tree urb that had become their home glowed slightly in the soft, buttery light of Seremathenn's setting sun.

As always, the small circular aperture in the center of the floor had brought forth food at precisely the time Walker had specified. While he worked his way through the purplish and brown synthesizations, George gnawed enthusiastically on an approximation of a prime rib bone. It was neither prime rib nor bone, but the dog was content with the result. One could always close one's eyes at such times, he had noted on more than one occasion, and imagine being back on Earth.

"George, we're not making much progress at getting home."

Ears cocked toward the human who was his friend, the dog looked up from his hunk of pseudo-steer. His voice and intelligence the work of Vilenjji surgeons who were as adept as they were venal, George was able to make himself perfectly understood.

"How many times do I have to remind you what a great setup we've got here? Didn't I agree to go home, too—if the rest of you could figure out how to do it?" He returned to his bone. "It'll happen, or it won't. If you let it, the worrying will kill you before the chance to try and get home arrives. Of course, that would alleviate your concerns too, wouldn't it?"

"I know it's going to take time, George." As he spoke, Walker picked listlessly at his food. "What I'm getting at is that while all the rest of you—you, Braouk, and Sque—seem to be adapting to these surroundings, I'm still pretty much at loose ends. It's hard to stay positive when you don't have anything rewarding to do."

"Yeah," the dog muttered around mouthfuls. "Having everything done for you, having intelligent machines and helpful hosts respond to your every need, not having to report for work every day: I can see where that would get old real quick."

Used to the dog's occasional sarcasm, Walker did not respond to it. "What I'm saying is that until we can find a way out of here, I need something to *do*. Something to occupy my time. Something I can, well, be proud of. So I'm going to try and build on a favorite hobby I had back home." He hesitated ever so briefly before concluding, "I'm going to become a cook."

Jaws parted halfway, the dog looked up at him. Black eyes peered out from beneath shaggy brows. "A cook. Now that's a useful ambition, on a world where your room synthesizer burps up a meal whenever you ask for it."

Having anticipated the dog's objection, Walker was ready with a response. Setting the remnants of his own meal aside and leaning forward, he tried to convey some of the enthusiasm he had felt when the idea first came to him.

"I know that, George, but I've been doing some research. Certainly most of the food consumed on Seremathenn and on many other advanced worlds of this sprawling civilization is provided by highly sophisticated nutritional-synthesization equipment. But not, I've learned, all of it. A good deal of what is referred to as natural food is still prepared by hand—or whatever type of manipulative limb happens to be involved."

Despite his initial disparagement, the dog was now interested. "You don't say? I never thought about it." One paw gestured in the direction of the room's provider. "When they have synthesization, why would they bother with a primitive activity like cooking?"

"Because," Walker told him with a touch of triumph, "it's considered a form of art."

"Ah!" George looked momentarily wistful. "That makes sense—though not much. I do remember cooking. The thick smells outside certain restaurants. The delicate bouquet of high-class garbage." He glanced again at his friend. "Wait a minute. What makes you think you can do the local kind of cooking any more than you can deal in trading local commodities? Surely the Sessrimathe version of a working kitchen isn't going to be a sink and a stove surrounded by pots and pans?"

"I've been studying the equipment and the techniques needed to operate the relevant mechanisms." He gestured at the nearest wall. "The room has been helping me. It's all new and complicated, sure. But it's not like repairing a ship's interstellar drive, either."

" 'Cooking.' " Forepaws resting on the well-masticated fake bone, George considered briefly, then shrugged. "Go for it, I guess." He returned to his gnawing, a bit more decorously this time. "Just keep one thing in mind." Strong teeth scraped across reconstituted calcium.

"What's that?" Walker pressed him.

"You'd better find somebody else to sample your initial efforts. I'm out."

Even though he'd thought he had some idea of what he was getting into, mastering just the rudiments of Sessrimathe and greater galactic culinary technology, not to mention the essential aesthetic components, had turned out to be far more challenging than Walker had anticipated. There were times, all too many times, when he wanted to quit, to admit defeat and return to a life of depending solely on boring charity. He would not. It was the same determination that had gained him a starting position as outside linebacker on a major university football team, and that had allowed him to keep it through three full seasons. He attacked the multifarious gastronomic trials with the same forcefulness with which he had thrown himself into the path of opposing tailbacks.

The more he learned, the more aware he became of his ignorance. Only one thing besides raw willpower kept him going. He *liked* to cook. Always had. When potential lady friends wavered in their desire to go out with him, he could inevitably clinch a date by declaring that he would make dinner, from scratch, all by himself. Presented with such an unexpected avowal from a member of the opposite sex, their curiosity was invariably piqued. They inevitably went out with him if only to see how badly he would fail, and were predictably surprised when the meals he prepared turned out to be not only edible, but excellent.

Surprisingly, it was not the often highly sophisticated utensils and instrumentation that gave him the most trouble and engendered the greatest degree of frustration, but the ingredients themselves. Spices that had minds of their own, sometimes literally. Synthesized tastes whose delicate flavors had to be modified directly at the molecular level. Vegetative bases that refused, on principle, to combine as required with his chosen modifiers or extenders.

Adrift in the center of the preparator, he was more captain than chef, issuing orders to utensils and synths alike, demanding to be obeyed. Food was his symphony, a galaxy of ingredients the notes, and the cooking wand his conductor's baton. Instead of sound there was smell. When things went well, wonderful aromas swirled about him. When they went badly, his work reeked, which unsavory failures the monitoring/instruction program duly and unemotionally noted.

Today was the first time in his life Walker had ever felt personal hatred toward a soufflé.

It was not a true soufflé, of course. It was a khirach-tel, from a recipe derived from a concoction made famous on a legendary world far from Seremathenn. With the aid of the instructor program he had customized its chemical structure, working to tame some of the wilder alkaloids so that the outcome would be something Sessrimathe and human digestive systems could handle. That was difficult enough. Rendering the result tasty was far simpler than making it edible.

Focus, he told himself. Keep it together. The admonition applied to himself as much as to the swirling, balletic elements of the cuisine.

Combining dexterous use of wand and synths, he gradually beat the khirach into submission. The monitoring program proffered grudging admiration. With the khirach-tel itself under control and its more anarchic components restrained, he turned his attention to the geljees. Snapping them into place, he swiftly applied the whipped flame. The end result was spectacular, with the finished khirach-tel floating in the center of its chromatic cloud of orbiting geljees while the whipped lavender flame darted in and out of both, illuminating the khirach from within and sending shivers of light from the hundreds of individual geljees. And it was all, all of it, edible.

He hoped.

There was one way to find out. His friends' quarters, together with his own and the common room they shared, lay elsewhere within the enormous structure.

"Finished," he wearily informed both the preparation chamber and the monitoring program.

The preparator apparatus shut down. As the supportive field surrounding him dissipated, he was lowered gently to the floor. Following his directions, a proper serving tray appeared and took up a supportive position beneath the khirach. Still alive with geljees and flame, it hovered just above the tray's repelling, constraining white surface. When he took possession of his creation, the tray's support field obediently deactivated, leaving him holding it in both hands.

For a long moment he stood admiring his handiwork. Months of long training, of endless study, of frustration and failure and hard work had gone into this moment. During that time he had brought forth numerous other culinary creations, but nothing as elaborate as this. Concerning the aesthetics, there was no issue. The finished khirach-tel was truly beautiful. Part sculpture, part meal, it was indeed a work of art. He could see how it looked. Now all that remained was to find out how it tasted.

He reached out with a hand, hesitated, and pulled it back. Somewhat to his surprise, he couldn't do it. Not the first taste, anyway. He would leave it to his companions to pass judgment. George first, he decided. Despite what the dog had said months ago, George would eat most anything. If the dog rejected it ...

Preferring not to ponder that awful possibility, he headed for the nearest internal transport. His hopes were boosted by the admiring comments of several Sessrimathe and one Ouralia who glimpsed the khirach-tel in passing.

The floating bonfire that hovered in the center of the common room during the night was replaced during the day, by mutual agreement, with a mist fountain in the shape of some local flowers. The spray filled the air of the room with a cheerful mix of sound and moisture before folding back in upon itself. In response to Walker's question one day, the room had tried to explain to him the mechanism whereby water could be brought forth out of empty air, its shape and direction controlled, kept from falling to the ground, and recycled with no loss to evaporation. He quickly gave up on any thought of understanding what was being explained to him. He did not have the physics for it.

But he did have the physics, and the chemistry, for cooking. So as the transport made its way through the interior of the residential complex, he insisted to his friends that they join him in the common room.

Once there, Braouk eyed the edible fantasy admiringly. "Prepared with skill, the offering awaits eating, brightly dancing." Bulbous eyes extended on the ends of stalks protruding from the upper flanks of his blocky torso, greenish blonde quills quivering, the Tuuqalian reached out toward the tray with the tip of one massive manipulating tentacle.

Walker had to pull it away. "Sorry, Braouk. I have the details of everyone's individual metabolism on file, and while you and I can share many foods, this khirach isn't one of them. I'm afraid you'll have to give it a pass."

Both eyestalks curved forward, bringing the oculars at their tips closer to the human and his tempting creation. "I am not afraid of a small upset to my stomachs. What could happen, if daintily I taste, one lick?"

"You could go blind," Walker told him somberly. "I've subdued most of the alkaloids in the dish, but your system couldn't break them all down. Your body is particularly sensitive to at least two. It's too much of a risk."

The tentacle withdrew. Vertically aligned jaws parted and closed regretfully, serrated teeth interlocking with one another. "Next time please, you will make, something for me?"

Walker smiled. It was a sign of the progress he had made since starting on his training that someone as sensitive as Braouk might actually look forward to the results of the amateur chef's efforts. Walker turned to George.

"You, on the other hand . . ."

"Oh no, not me." The dog backed away slowly. "Remember the last offering you insisted I try? Ended up giving me a touch of the mange."

Walker remembered clearly. "That was a mistake. I should have left out the craadlin seeds. They were oiled on mostly for visual appeal, anyway."

"Yeah, well, mange doesn't have much visual appeal, either." Muttering, the dog gestured with his snout. "If it's so tasty, let her try it first."

Standing half in, half out of the aqueous floral display, a comfortably moistened Sque squinted through silvery eyes as Walker came toward her. Kneeling, he held out the tray. It was very light, as was the dish itself.

"I hope you like it, Sque," he offered encouragingly. "It's suitable for your digestive system, I promise. I know that if *you* like it, it will have passed the acid test." As tentacles coiled reflexively and she flinched back, he added hastily, "I didn't mean that literally. There's no acid in it."

Droplets of water glistened on bits of the K'eremu's outrageous personal ornamentation: the strands of iridescent metal, elegant beads, and other flashy accoutrements that decorated her person. Drawing all ten limbs beneath her brought her up to her maximum height of four feet. Horizontal slits of black pupils regarded him from within deep-set eyes the color of polished steel. Her tone was typically condescending.

"Why should I subject my educated internal constitution to the misguided flailings of a gastronomic ignoramus such as yourself?"

By now, Walker was so used to the K'eremu's casually insulting manner of speech that he hardly noticed it. "Because I've been working at this for many months now. Because I've gotten damn good at it. Because like it or not, you're my friend." When she did not stir he sighed and added, "And because only your sophisticated palate, or the physiological equivalent thereof, is mature enough to render a fitting opinion on the result."

She relented. "I must admit that from sharing my company you have become marginally more adept at recognizing blatant truths." Eyes inclined toward the tray as one tendril rose from beneath her. Brushing the tip through the delicate khirach, she swept up a dash of pseudo-soufflé, a thimbleful of geljees, just a spark of lavender flame, and brought the blend back to her small mouth. A regretful Braouk and hopeful George joined the anxious Walker in awaiting the K'eremu's verdict.

After an interminable pause she blinked both eyes, inflated slightly, and emitted a pair of bubbles to punctuate her response. "While your effort founders on the edge of the barely edible and would see you thrown out of any marginally legal eating establishment on K'erem, it cannot be denied that the result is tolerable to my system." Knowing Sque's penchant for giving voice to understatement on a cosmic scale, Walker was delighted. When she added, "I believe that, in the interests of fairness to the diligent efforts of a representative of an inferior species, I should extend myself to the degree of partaking of a second sampling," and took another bite, his heart leaped.

With the object of his friend's exertions more than validated by the K'eremu, George promptly dug into the khirach-tel with all the enthusiasm of a cat in a tuna cannery. By the time dog and K'eremu had finished with it, there was barely a flicker of lavender fire and a few desultory geljees left to garnish the scattered remnants of the soufflé itself.

Lying on his right side, belly pooched out from dogged overstuffing, George looked up lazily at where his friend sat supported by a nexus of black and gold wire that passed for a chair.

"I've got to admit, Marc, that you've come a long way since you tried coagulating that jibartle."

Braouk gestured with two of his four upper tentacles. "Remember it well, something hard to forget, that meal."

"It chased us around the room." George belched softly. "It tried to eat Sque." From the vicinity of the fountain, a number of the K'eremu's tendrils gestured by way of punctuation. "Braouk had to kill it."

Walker looked up from his chair. "That was my fault. At that stage I wasn't adequately prepared to tackle such an advanced project. I'd been doing really well, and I got cocky." He shook his head at the memory of it. "Who knew there were dishes that had to be counseled psychologically before they could be served?"

The dog showed his teeth. "That khirach-tel makes up for it. Delicious! What are you going to do now?"

Walker blinked at him. "I don't follow you, George. 'Do'?"

With an effort, the dog heaved himself back onto his feet. Tail wagging, he approached his friend and placed his chin on the man's left knee. The dog's gaze was profound.

"With your new skill. You've put enough effort into it. You should do something with it."

"Actually," Walker admitted, "I hadn't thought about it in that way. Learning local methods of artistic, natural food preparation was just a means to pass the time—and to prove that I could do something more than just exist on Sessrimathe charity."

"Then give back." Sque ambled out from beneath the water blossoms. "Do some demonstrations for our hosts. They will be as amazed as I am. Though we survive nicely thanks to a reservoir of goodwill among our hosts, even a well-fashioned reservoir can leak. Show them that you are more than the underlimbed, ignorant primitive you appear to be."

"Maybe I'll do that," he told her dryly. "I suppose it wouldn't hurt to prepare some demonstration dishes for anyone who might be interested. It would be an easy, and enjoyable, way to show our thanks to our hosts for what they've done for us."

As he slid his head back off Walker's knee, George nodded agreeably. "Just try not to make anyone sick, okay? And no more dinner that tries to eat the diner."

"I'll be careful," Walker assured him. "I know what I'm doing now." He was not simply boasting. The impossible-to-please Sque's grudging validation of the khirach-tel had been the final approval he had been seeking. He fully expected his subsequent culinary efforts to be even more spectacular. Both George and the K'eremu had the right idea: whenever possible, he should use his newly won skills to ingratiate themselves even further to their hosts. He felt confident he could do that.

What he did not expect was that his exhibition preparations of aesthetic galactic cuisine would lead to a possible way home.

2

Walker spun slowly in the center of the demonstration sphere, the ingredients for the sifdd alternately hovering and zipping around him. Beyond the boundaries of the sphere's restraining field he could see the invited guests. The majority were tripodal, three-eyed, triple-armed, beige-tinted Sessrimathe, elegantly and colorfully clad, but here and there other, even more outrageous shapes could be discerned. While his efforts at culinary artistry had not made him famous, they had at least gained him a certain notoriety. If nothing else, he was certainly the best human chef on Seremathenn. He was also the only human on Seremathenn.

This unsought exclusivity did not diminish the satisfaction he felt at what he had accomplished over the course of the preceding months. His unsophisticated species notwithstanding, he knew what he could do. In the space of a couple of years he had grown more than competent: he had become good.

At his command he was enveloped by a dust storm of different spices and seasonings. A few onlookers voiced astonishment in the gentle, muted tones of the Sessrimathe while a single loud, sharp whistle was emitted by an unseen representative of the curious Kyalrand who were paying their first visit to Seremathenn. His vision momentarily obscured by the aromatic whirlwind he had called forth, Walker was not able to identify the individual whistler.

No matter. He was busy enough, trying to control the active

components of the incipient sifdd. With dexterous strokes of his cooking wand and concomitant verbal commands to the ever-alert processing instrumentation, ingredients were combed, combined, conflated, and cooked. A ring of ground flowers not unlike flour coalesced around him. Eddies of puff pastry began to take shape, rising and expanding in carefully controlled suspension. Spice flares burst in and through the emerging ring like sharks attacking a strung-out school of bait fish.

When the perfectly crisped pastry had absorbed the last of the flavorings, Walker brought forth miniature waterspouts of liqueur and fruit juice. Under his guidance, these began to twist and coil about one another, serpentine shapes already subtle of flavor that he further imbued with essence of t'mag and surrun. When all was combined, he shattered the ring of pastry into a hundred individual shapes, each slightly different from the next, so that they orbited his waist like so many miniature moons while a constrained ring of pale pink liquid swirled lazily about his vertical axis.

He paused there for effect, letting the impressed audience savor the last moments before final processing. Then, with a flourish of commands and wand, he made the final adjustments to temperature and individual constraining fields.

The arc of pink fluid splintered, prompting murmurs of appreciation from several in the audience. Attracted to the fields being generated by the individual pastries, independent drifting globules of the customized liqueur that Walker had lovingly hand-tailored to his own specifications proceeded to englobe each and every puff. When the last portion of pastry had been encased, an appropriate collection server rose from the assemblage of instrumentation behind him. Following a rising spiral course, the device proceeded to swallow each of his flaky creations one by one. Once gathering had been completed, the server returned to its charging base, the demonstration sphere powered down, and Walker settled gently to the floor. The alien equivalent of applause that ensued was notable for its enthusiasm.

In the course of the reception that followed, he readily elaborated in some detail on the intricacies of his newly honed talent to visiting Sessrimathe who had traveled from many parts of

Seremathenn. In between knowledgeable questions and casual conversation, the visitors who filled the greeting chamber in the human's home edifice were treated to samples of the very gastronomic concert they had just seen performed.

Having mastered a modest familiarity with the basics of Sessrimathen conversation, Walker participated in these discussions with verve and ease. By now he was as comfortable around the three-legged Sessrimathe as he had been with fellow boaters out for a Sunday afternoon cruise on Lake Michigan. As was often the case at such moments, he fought hard not to think of home. They were, perhaps permanently he had reluctantly come to realize, a part of his past. Of a different time on a different world—one out of sight, mind, and reach of his present location and lifestyle.

"Not bad." The mild praise arose from somewhere near his ankles. Glancing down, he saw George noshing unashamedly on a sifdd. The dog was lying on his belly, rear legs splayed out behind him, the still-warm pastry balanced between his forelegs. "I can guess how you make the booze ball hold its form instead of turning into an instant puddle, but how do you keep it from soaking into the dough?"

"Same method," Walker told him. "But different coherent charges. One compresses and maintains the liqueur's spherical shape; another repels the fluid away from the pastry. So when you bite into one, you get both a bit of baked dough and a swallow of cooling liqueur. Opposing temperatures, consistencies, tactility, and flavors all in one." He allowed himself a moment of pardonable pride. "Food as physics."

"Not to mention the way your lips and teeth tingle from the lingering charge." Unkempt floppy ears lying against the sides of his head, the dog winked up at his friend. "Maybe sometime you can electrify a bone or two for me."

"Too easy," Walker replied. "I'll show you how to do it yourself." A slight frown creased his features as his companion rose abruptly to all fours. "Something wrong with the food?" He eyed the half-eaten sifdd uncertainly.

"Nope." The dog nodded. "I think you've got company." With that, he gently picked up the remainder of the pastry in his teeth and trotted off into the crowd, exchanging occasional greetings with those Sessrimathe he recognized. A couple, Walker noted not entirely without envy, reached down with three-fingered hands to pet the dog as he ambled past.

Expecting Sessrimathe, he was mildly startled when upon turning around he found himself confronted not by one of the ubiquitous natives of Seremathenn but by an off-worlder. One of a species he did not recognize. One that was unusually tall, unusually slender, and, it had to be admitted, unusually beautiful.

With a sinuous, graceful gait that bordered on the sensuous, the alien approached on a pair of long legs half hidden, half revealed by a boldly patterned kilt or skirt. The upper portion of the body was equally exposed by a covering of furry straps that crisscrossed the proportionately narrower torso. Protected by smaller straps, both arms ended in dual opposing digits. The head was equally long and slim, equine more than feline but with several features that tended to the piscine. Slender ears a foot long emerged from either side of the hairless skull to extend stiffly upward. Though six foot four or so (notably taller if one included the ears), the creature weighed considerably less than he did. Not one but four tapering tails emerged from a point below the back of the creature's waist. They wove and twisted gracefully in and about one another like a quartet of cobras engaged in animated conversation.

Saucer-sized eyes, big and round as those of a tarsier, with massive golden pupils set against a pale yellow background, focused intently on him. Set below a slightly protruding shelf of sculpted bone that might or might not conceal nostrils, the small mouth was open as if in a perpetual "O" of surprise. He could not discern any teeth. A circular ring of pale muscle that encircled the mouth was stained with several bright colors. The effect was not unlike looking directly down at Saturn's north pole from above.

The creature's skin was smooth as silk. In the ambient light of the room it took on the hue of polished bronze. Walker could not tell if it was leathery, scalelike, or something previously unencountered. All he knew was that the effect was eyecatchingly attractive. And those eyes . . .

Abruptly, the visitor was standing before him. Of all the aliens he and his friends had encountered in their journeying, both on the Vilenjji capture ship and subsequently on Seremathenn, this was so far indisputably the most physically striking. He found himself mesmerized by the multiple switching tails, the shimmering pupils, the achingly elegant upthrust hearing organs, and legs that were as perfectly proportioned as a fractal that had been stretched out straight as a ruler. Apparently, the creature had sought him out and intended to speak to him. He waited eagerly to see if the visitor's appearance was echoed by its voice, and to learn its gender. Surely it claimed one. No species so stunning could possibly be ignorant of the splendor of sexual reproduction.

"You, human! You pretty damn good cooker, you is."

He winced inwardly. Fingernails dragging across a blackboard. Old-fashioned dentist drills preparing to bite enamel. Metal car parts dragging across a concrete roadbed. A chill ran down his spine that had nothing to do with the moderate temperature in the room.

The sound of the exquisite creature's voice was excruciating to his ears.

Eyelids like translucent lilies momentarily slid down over the spectacular oculars as the creature blinked. As it did so, an iridescent golden frill erected and flexed on the back of the alien's head and neck. "You like cook. You no like talk?"

Unless it was failing for the first time since it had been implanted in him, the Vilenjji translator was providing a faithful rendering of the creature's speech. Swallowing, Walker concentrated on the being's physical beauty while struggling manfully to overlook the sound of its voice. The latter lingered in the air, clinging to his ears like a leech to an open wound. Taking note of the external translator clipped to one slender ear, he felt confident in replying.

"No, I do like—I enjoy conversation. I'm glad you took pleasure from my little demonstration." Desperately, he looked around for someone else he knew, someone he could inform his beautiful but sandpaper-voiced questioner that he absolutely had to speak with—right there and right now. But he recognized no one else in the milling cluster, and George had wandered off somewhere out of sight.

"Enjoy?" One willowy arm reached out to encircle his shoulders, its touch more caress than grasp. "Was overwhelming! Remarkable. Never seen nothing such like it before." The exquisite face bent toward his. "You can prepare many foods suchlike?" The delicate flowerlike fragrance that emanated from the small mouth somewhat mitigated the unrivaled harshness of tone it accompanied.

Holding his ground as well as any cultured Sessrimathe, he forced himself not to turn away. "I've learned how to prepare many specialties, yes, including a few of my own devising based on recipes from my homeworld."

"Earth," the creature snapped. Issuing from that small, ornately painted mouth, the single syllable sounded like a pencil being pushed through a cheese grater. "Home of humans."

"You've been doing some research. On me." His surprise was genuine.

The tips of both ears inclined slightly forward as all four tails came up slightly. "No special research. Perused preparatory materials that accompanied your presentation. Never hear of humans before today. Never hear of Earth before today." She paused thoughtfully. "Self-centered naming. Sessrimathe say you first of your kind they ever encounter."

Walker nodded. While thoroughly entranced by the creature's physical appearance, he could not wait to escape the sound of its voice.

"I am Viyv-pym-parr of the Niyyuu, second daughter of Avur-pym, reigning regent of Kojn-umm Province on the world of Niyu, fourth world of the sun Niy."

Oh, well—royalty, he mused. He forced himself to linger awhile longer. Perhaps the alien would hire him to come to her embassy or residence and cook for her and a group of her friends. As his skills had improved, he had been doing more and more of that, fulfilling requests from the curious and those always on the lookout for such novelties. Not for the income, which he and his friends did not need, but to express himself, to have something to do, much as Braouk recited the sagas of his people. Besides, he had not yet tired of looking at those legs, or those eyes, even if they were part and parcel of something that was far from human. Knowing that the Niyyuu was female only added to her attraction—until such times as she opened her mouth.

As to her reasons for seeking him out, his guess turned out to be half-right.

"I needs good cooker in palace. Competent is good. Unique is better even. You human, be both. Only one of you."

He smiled inwardly. Despite all he had accomplished, he was still more highly esteemed for his novelty value than for the skills he had developed. Ah, well. At least he was a sovereign novelty. He responded to her proposal by gesturing in the approved Sessrimathe manner.

"I understand. You'd like me to come and prepare some dishes for you in your residence here on Seremathenn. On which continent is it located, may I ask?" Though not in need of income thanks to the continuing generosity of the charitable Sessrimathe, he would not turn down the chance to supplement it should the opportunity arise. Besides, how demanding could be the desires of a creature so lissome—albeit orally grating.

As it turned out, he had no idea.

"Prepare dishes, yes. Here on Serematheeny no." The arm around his shoulders tightened ever so slightly. The increased pressure was more suggestive than discomfiting. "Need cooker in palace of Kojn-umm. On Niyyuu." When the stunned human failed to respond, Viyv-pym rolled her extraordinary eyes upward and gestured with her other two-fingered hand. "Out there. New audience awaits you."

The offer was as unexpected as it was unprecedented. For the first time since his arrival on Seremathenn, he was being offered a way off world. Offered a chance to travel to a distant elsewhere—and at no cost to himself. Indeed, he would profit economically from the venture. If he accepted, of course. Thinking fast, he knew he could only accept if one condition was met. One condition over which his keen if somewhat crude prospective employer had no control. Looking up, he met wondrous, hopeful eyes and tried not to lose himself in them.

"This may sound strange to you, Viyv-pym-parr . . ."

The eyes came closer. They were not hypnotic—not with that garbage disposal of a voice to accompany them—but they loomed before him like twin cabochons of alien soul. "Okay from now to call me as Viyv-pym. You know me."

Slightly confused by the shift in alien nomenclature but willing to comply, he replied without hesitation. "All right, Viyv-pym." The irregular syllables slid delectably off his tongue. "This may sound strange to you, but before I can give serious consideration to your offer, it's important that I know where Niyu is located in relation to Seremathenn and the rest of the galaxy. I suppose the first thing is to access an appropriate map or schematic and then—"

"Got one right here, human Marc." Both golden-yellow eyes blinked again. Or was it a double wink, he wondered? And if so, what might it signify? Some things, he decided, he was better off not pondering for too long.

From within a hidden pocket concealed beneath the kilt-skirt she withdrew a small stylus with a brushed metallic gray surface. Entwining two long, serpentine fingers around it caused the device to generate several three-dimensional scenes in the space between them. As she cycled rapidly through the available images, he caught fleeting glimpses of life and landscapes that were as foreign to him as life on Seremathenn was to that of Earth. Despite their inherent alienness and the speed of their passing, one or two were more than a little suggestive of something at once familiar and inaccessible.

When the map of the galaxy appeared, she focused on one section and enlarged it. A pinpoint of light brightened. "Seremathenn," she rasped at him. A barely perceptible flexing of one digit caused the light to shift elsewhere. "Niyu."

He caught his breath. While his ignorance of matters astronomic prevented him from even beginning to estimate the actual distances involved, there was no denying that Viyv-pym's homeworld lay an impressive distance from Seremathenn. Furthermore, it was clearly located away from the galactic center and out along one of the galaxy's two main spiral arms. A step of cosmic dimensions toward Earth. Toward home. Although it was apparent that Viyv-pym herself knew nothing of humans or their world, it was conceivable that another of her kind more versed in astronomics or the intelligences that populated the galaxy might have some knowledge of humanity. Or perhaps there were far-ranging sentients with some faint knowledge of Earth who visited distant Niyu but never came as far in as Seremathenn. Possibilities not risked were possibilities that would never exist.

Provided Niyu lay within the *right* spiral arm—the same spiral arm as Earth. If not, by accepting her offer of employment he would only be taking himself even farther away from the world of his birth, perhaps irrevocably so. His chances of making the right choice in the galactic scheme of things were fifty-fifty. He hesitated—but not for long.

Hell, he'd bought and sold consignments and futures of raw materials worth millions of dollars on odds far worse than that. Of one thing he was 100 percent certain: remaining on Seremathenn certainly brought him no closer to home.

What were his other options? If he declined the Niyyuu's offer he might never come across another half as promising. He might very well live out his life on Seremathenn, the lone representative of his species among millions of creatures whose intrinsic courtesy rendered them no less alien. Or if he bided his time he might encounter other, similar offers—to carry him off in directions even less promising than Niyu. He had not become successful in his chosen profession through indecision. It was time to take a gamble.

"I accept, with one condition."

Eyes like polished pendants of Scythian gold stared back into his own. "You will receive treatment in accordance with you skills. Medium of exchange will be satisfying." The tips of her astonishing ears quivered, and the light of the room shimmered on her bronzed metallic epidermis. "Regency of Kojn-umm treats properly the members of its staff."

"It's not about money, or living conditions. You've researched my background. Do you know how I came to be here, on Seremathenn?"

She turned off and repocketed the compact image generator. As she reached beneath the folds of her kilt-skirt to do so, he found his eyes wandering. If she noticed the shift in attention or his subsequent confusion and embarrassment, she gave no sign.

"You was Vilenjji captive. A people harboring more than their share of clods. Is clear violation of all civilized norms to treat any sentients as goods. Cannot sell sentients." Dark circlet of mystery, the perfect painted circle of a mouth expanded slightly. "Can only rent them."

Not quite sure that she was making a joke, he held back from laughing. "During the time I spent on the Vilenjji vessel, I made three friends. Three very close friends." He took a deep breath. "If I agree to come and work for you, I would like for them to come along with me."

Again the double blink, twice this time, the lilac eyelids flashing. "You ask much."

He held his ground, much as he had when confronted by difficult decisions at his brokerage in Chicago. Trading, doing business, were skills in which he had full confidence.

"Other captives," she murmured, her voice like steel filings caught in a car's transmission. "Other uniques. Have these, you's friends, entertaining skills like you?"

Walker proceeded to enumerate the many and varied virtues of his companions. Fortunately there was no need for embellishment, unless one counted his bending of the truth when describing Sque's personality as "independent."

For a long moment he was afraid she wouldn't agree to his terms. He spent the time studying the lithe, limber alien shape while simultaneously wondering what the hell he was doing. The voice, he told himself. Concentrate on that wince-inducing gravel crusher of a voice and ignore everything else.

I have been away from Earth for far, far too long, he reflected to himself uneasily.

"I give you what you want," she finally responded. "Wanting only one, I deign to accept four." She held up both slender hands. "Count one unique for each finger." For some reason this observation caused her to emit a series of short, sharp, and decidedly unfeminine coughs that he later learned were Niyyuuan indicators of amusement.

The offer was more than he could have hoped for, Walker felt. Now all he had to do was convince his companions to go along with the deal. He was certain of only one thing: with friends or without, he was going with Viyv-pym. He was not going to pass on this, the best chance that had come along since his arrival on Seremathenn to get him a little nearer home.

But if his friends opted out, it was going to be a long and lonely journey indeed.

"Bargain is striked." One hand reached for him, approaching like an eel swimming underwater. He didn't flinch. He did not *want* to flinch.

The alien hand touched his neck, the two long flexible digits sliding around to the back. Slick, leathery, cool skin brushed the short hair near the top of his spine. He shivered slightly. *Voice,* he reasoned frantically. *Remember that awful voice.* The fingers pressed against him ever so slightly. *Good God,* he thought wildly, *surely she's not going to . . . ?*

The serpentine fingers withdrew. He didn't know whether to feel relieved or disappointed.

"I know you's living details. Transport will be provided you and you's companions. After one ten-day passing, time depart for Niyu. Is doable you?"

He nodded. "Is doable. I will be ready."

The spectacular frill on the back of her head and neck flared, catching the light and splintering it into shards of liquid gold. "Look forward you being on Niyu. I know you will enjoy." A hand and arm gestured at the room packed with the elegant assembled. "In Kojn-umm, not so many always talking. Will be smaller audience for you art, but more appreciative."

With that she turned and strode, or rather flowed, away through the crowd. For some time Walker was able to follow her progress, the slender pointed ears and frilled bronze head rising and falling above the majority of other aliens. Then she was gone. Only then did the full import of his decision hit home. Not only would he be leaving behind the civilized culture of

Seremathenn, he would be abandoning, perhaps permanently, the protection and charity that had been afforded him by the compassionate Sessrimathe.

Real profit only comes from taking real risks, he reminded himself. He began to make his own way through the crowd, absently acknowledging the compliments that came his way. More important business now pressed heavily on his mind.

He had some serious convincing to do.

It was Braouk's turn to choose the ornamentation for the center of their common room. The Tuuqalian had set the room the task of producing a series of small geysers to remind him of a favorite undeveloped region on his homeworld. The result, as installed by the building's AI, was a trio of small, geologically impeccable cones that spouted steadily from the center of the commons. How the building's intelligent response system had managed the plumbing to both deliver and recover the boiling hot water without swathing everything in sight in a sheen of condensation was a mechanical mystery Walker made no effort to try to unravel. He had long since given up marveling at or trying to comprehend the wonders of Sessrimathe science.

The four friends sat around the bubbling, spraying, simulated geysers, but they were not relaxed. Not while faced with the single most momentous decision that had confronted them since their arrival on Seremathenn. To go with Walker or to stay: each of his friends, irrespective of their own individual manner of thinking, could only come to one of two conclusions.

Braouk was uncertain but ready. "Too long here, away from my home, hearts breaking." All four massive upper tentacles curled forward to rest against the sides of his mouth. "I am prepared for whatever may come."

Suspended in his custom-built chair—which he was definitely going to miss, he knew—and with the Tuuqalian on board, Walker turned his attention to the K'eremu. Sequi'aranaqua'na'senemu sat on the floor across from him, her tendrils splayed out around her in familiar floral fashion. She would have reveled in the water from the geysers had it only been many dozens of degrees cooler. As it was, the occasional droplet that escaped the system's recovery field dripped from her maroon skin or glistened on the bits of metal and gemstone and beads that cloaked her person in a small riot of color. Somewhat to his surprise, she concurred with the Tuuqalian.

"There is still much to learn here, both from the Sessrimathe and from those other sentients who visit them. But there is much to learn anywhere that is new, and I tire of the conversation of well-meaning fools, no matter how superficially intelligent they may appear to be." A pair of tendrils rose to wave in Walker's direction. "I too am ready to move on. There is always something to learn, and one may hope, however unreasonably, that such a journey will indeed bring us nearer K'erem, the true center of advanced civilization in this or any other galaxy."

Two aboard. Only one more left to signal his agreement and, truth be told, the one whose acceptance mattered most to Walker. He glanced down at the small figure that was sprawled on the semianimate rug to his immediate left.

"George?"

The dog looked away. "I dunno, Marc. Talk about taking a leap into the unknown . . ."

"You said before that you'd leave here if the right opportunity presented itself. Well, it's presented itself. We don't even have to worry about money. In fact, not only do we get free transportation a parstep closer to home, we're getting paid for going."

Dark brown eyes looked up at him from beneath shaggy brows. "That's just it, Marc. *Are* we getting closer to home? If the other arm of the galaxy is where Earth lies, we'll be heading off down the wrong trail. With a good chance we won't be able to retrace our steps." One paw gestured to take in their surroundings. "We've got everything we could need here, and we don't have to work for it."

Having dealt with it before, Walker had anticipated the dog's reluctance. "We've been over all this, George. Seremathenn is nice, and the Sessrimathe have been very good to us. But this isn't home." He looked up, through the mist being generated by the miniature geysers. "Not for any of us." He indicated the sprawled shape of the K'eremu. "If the odds are acceptable to Sque, they should be for any of us."

"Appropriately astute of you," she observed approvingly. "You continue to exhibit a limited but commendable ability to learn, however slowly."

Wrestling with himself mentally, George held out to the last before yielding. "I said I'd go, yeah. So I'll go." He shook his head slowly. "First I had to give up real alleys. Now I'm giving up artificial ones." Once more the bushy head turned toward the expectant human. "You'd better be guessing right about this, Marc, or I swear I'll end my days chewing on your bones. These Niyyuu who've engaged your services and agreed to take us with you: what are they like?"

"I've only met one of them." Walker leaned back, and his chair leaned with him, careful to maintain his posture and its attitude. "She was very persuasive."

"Obviously," the dog replied impatiently. "I mean, what are they *like*? You, me, Braouk-boy over there, or"—he shuddered slightly—"the squid?"

Sque took no offense at the implied slight. She was far too aloof to react to insults from so lowly a type as George. Or for that matter, from anyone in the room.

Walker considered. "It's hard to say, having met only one of them. You can't judge an entire species from one individual. But she was . . . nice. Polite. Eager to engage me. Eager enough to agree to take four to get one. I can't say if it's indigenous to her kind, but her voice is a bit on the rough side. No, not rough. Grating. Annoying, even."

"No problem, since you'll be the one talking to her." Rising to his feet, the dog headed off in the direction of his own room. "I'm amenable to this, but that doesn't mean I have to be happy about it."

"Where are you going?" Walker asked concernedly.

The dog didn't look back. "There's a bone I want to commune with. Once we leave Sessrimathe, I don't know if I'll see another one again." He glanced back briefly. "Or if I do, if I'll recognize it as such."

"You worry too much about food!" Walker called after him.

"And you worry too much, period." Ducking his head, George pushed himself through the customized dog door that led to his quarters. "But in this instance, a little worrying just might be justified."

3

Going through the things he had acquired in the years since his arrival on Seremathenn, Walker was surprised at how little there was to pack. Though in possession of a fascinating assortment of devices and objects provided by the Sessrimathe and his room's own synthesizer, on examining them one at a time he found that none of them meant anything to him. They had no connection with a real home, or with the life from which he had been so brutally wrenched. Therefore there seemed little need to take them with him. Doing so would only have meant burdening himself with more to worry about. Surely the Niyyuu, if not as advanced or sophisticated as the Sessrimathe, would provide adequately for his basic needs and for those of his companions.

It developed that his friends felt similarly. Accommodating though it had been to them, Seremathenn was not their home, either. However captivating, the products of its advanced civilization had no connection to their own. Braouk saw no need to take more than the minimal necessities with him, George's kit consisted primarily of his animate rug and a few packaged foodstuffs of which he had grown particularly fond, and Sque disdained nearly everything that was not of K'eremu manufacture anyway.

The winnowing process left Walker with a small carry bag of toiletries, a couple of changes of clothing, and little else. He eyed the modest luggage as he prepared for bed. In a couple of days everything he had worked so hard to assimilate over the past years was going to be put behind him, literally as well as figuratively. There would be a new civilization to adapt to, new marvels to admire, and with luck, access to new intelligences who might at the very least have a clue as to which corner of the cosmos his tiny, out-of-the-way home lay. Directing the room to reduce the internal illumination to minimal, he watched as the walls dimmed until he could just make out shapes and spaces. Among other things, the room was its own night-light. Turning over, he tucked the faux feather pillow beneath his head and closed his eyes.

He was in his rented 4X4 again, sleepy instead of frantic this time, as he stared up at horizontally flattened eyes that flared across the lower portion of a tapering head. A membranous hearing sensor protruded from near the top of the purple conical skull. A single sucker-lined arm flap was reaching for him.

An old dream, he told himself. One that, though he relived it with less and less frequency, never lost its power to unsettle. The alien appendage touched his bare shoulder. It felt very real.

In the dream as well as the reality that had given rise to it, he had been clad in jeans and flannel shirt. His shoulder had not been bare. He blinked. Then his eyes went almost as wide as those of the creature gazing coldly down at him.

Vilenjji. In his room.

As he tried to scream, the heavy arm flap pressed down hard over his mouth. Fortunately, it did not cover his nose. Moving up rapidly behind him, a second Vilenjji easily lifted him up in the bed and despite Walker's frantic, desperate efforts, proceeded to secure his arms behind him. Something was slapped over his mouth. It adhered tightly to the flesh and drew his lips together into a thin, tight line. Eyes goggling, moaning futilely, he was lifted off the bed and found himself being carried ignominiously toward the doorway.

Out in the faintly illuminated common room, his shock was magnified threefold as his abductor set him down on the floor. At least a dozen of his former kidnappers had crowded into the high-ceilinged open space. Arrayed like the specimens they had once been and now threatened to become again, his friends were lined up alongside Braouk's softly gurgling imitation geysers.

An outraged Sque had all ten of her limbs secured beneath her while the furious, straining Tuuqalian was cocooned in enough heavy-duty bindings to secure half a dozen elephants. Next to him, a helpless George gazed across at Walker. The dog's dark brown eyes were full of fear.

With the same swaying, side-to-side gait Walker had thought never to see again, a single massive Vilenjji came toward him. With time, the commodities trader had become adept at recognizing individual alien characteristics. A chill as if a glass of ice water had been dumped down his back flowed through him. He recognized the alien.

Bending toward the securely bound human, Pret-Klob peered into much smaller, much rounder eyes that glared back up at him with a mixture of defiance, outrage, and alarm.

"Do you recall my telling you, some time ago, on board the Sessrimathe vessel that misguidedly chose to interfere in the normal course of commerce, that in the realness of time the natural order of things would be restored?" When a disoriented and increasingly panicky Walker made no move to respond, the Vilenjji commander straightened.

"You wonder at my presence. Know that I regard myself as something of a master of judicial minutiae. It took time, but with work and patience even the overweening Sessrimathe can grow bored with justice. Finally freed from their custody, having 'admitted' to my error and repented most strenuously of my ways, I was eventually able to reconstitute a small portion of my original association. As primary shareholders, we determined to commence our financial recovery by repossessing as much of our original inventory as possible. It is only business." Turning, he hissed orders to his cohorts.

Walker felt himself lifted and bundled into some sort of open, hard-sided container. He was joined by a trembling George and the stolid cephalopodian form of Sque, whereupon the container's lid was moved into place above them. They must have a separate, special container for Braouk, he thought as the container began to move. A wise decision on the part of the Vilenjji. Given half a chance, the infuriated Tuuqalian would tear every one of the Vilenjji limb from flap. As the flow of adrenaline began to ebb, Walker slumped against the soft inner wall of the container.

They were prisoners again.

Their container admitted sounds as well as voices, though not light. He could hear the Vilenjji chattering among themselves in their clipped, abrupt manner as the container holding him and his friends was hurried along. Somehow, their captors had succeeded in penetrating the residential complex's admittedly modest security. Breaking the codification that protected the travelers' common room and the individual living quarters beyond had required a higher level of skill. He was not surprised to discover that the Vilenjji were adept at breaking and entering. Antisocial activity in all its many ramifications was a celebrated specialty of theirs.

It felt as if they were moving faster now, probably via one of the complex's numerous internal transports. He struggled ineffectually. At this late hour only the building's few fully nocturnal residents would be about, and they would have no reason beyond individual curiosity to challenge the procession of Vilenjji and their attendant containers. Given the typical level of politeness displayed by the Sessrimathe and the sentients who regularly visited Seremathenn, Walker was not sanguine about anyone choosing to venture such a query. And once outside and beyond the boundaries of the complex...

The container came to an abrupt stop. Walker and George looked at one another. Off in a corner of the container, an immensely irritated Sque squatted on her bound tendrils, her silvery horizontal eyes flashing in the near darkness. With her speaking trunk fastened to her head, she was unable to give voice to the outrage she felt.

Preparing to transfer us to a mobile transport, Walker thought frantically. From there, a swift journey to the nearest port. Then to a vessel waiting in orbit that would depart as soon as they were aboard for parts beyond the reach of the disapproving Sessrimathe and central galactic civilization. Eventually to be sold.

The way things were going, he and his friends might as well never have been rescued from the Vilenjji ship.

An abrupt leap in the type and frequency of the sounds he could hear outside their prison drew his attention away from increasingly gloomy thoughts. Unexpectedly, the container gave a sharp lurch to the right. It teetered there for a moment before falling over onto its side. Muted yelps came from George as the bound and muffled dog was dumped on top of his friend. Accustomed to never losing her grip, Sque was especially unnerved by the upset.

Loud hisses reached the captives. These were interspersed with coarse, guttural exclamations in a language Walker did not recognize. Muted by distance, the barrier formed by the container, and physical disorientation, his Vilenjji implant was also unable to translate them. Overturned, the container finally steadied, with George atop Walker and Sque sputtering incoherently behind her bindings somewhere in the vicinity of his feet. With its owner stabilized, Walker's implant was finally able to make some sense of the cacophony outside the container. At the same time, he thought he recognized the second source of shouting.

Though individually distinct, the harsh, rough voices sounded very much like that of the lissome Niyyuu who had recently engaged his services.

Emitting a recalcitrant inorganic screech, the cover of their container was stripped off and pulled back. All three prisoners promptly tumbled out, not onto hard ground or paving, but onto the short blue-green ground cover that wove its way through much of the city. Light appeared, flashed in their faces, and moved considerably away. Tall, slender figures bent to apply small handheld devices to their bindings. Each of the hands that were working on them, Walker noted immediately, had only two opposing digits.

Helped to his feet, he found himself surrounded by a quartet of tall Niyyuu. In the dim light of early morning, with Seremathenn's sun still well below the horizon, he did not try to determine if the concerned Niyyuu who surrounded him exhibited sexual dimorphism. At the moment, there was no sign of the Vilenjji. Only elegant Sessrimathe landscaping, tall trees, and behind them, the flickering lights of their residence tower, itself designed and built to resemble the leafy forest giants it had replaced.

Standing next to his friend, George was licking one paw and using it to clean his mouth and face where the Vilenjji bindings had adhered. "That was close. It was other things, too, but that's the most polite description I can come up with."

"Shameful!" Nearby, Sque had spread herself out and was extending her tendrils one by one, stretching each in turn to relieve the enforced strain that had been placed on the muscles. "Really, the Vilenjji are a species that would benefit from a serious lesson in manners. I would be pleased to deliver such myself, did not circumstances prevent it."

Now provided with a direct line of sight, or rather hearing, Walker's implant effortlessly translated the words of the Niyyuu who appeared before him. "You all right, you and friends?" Walker winced slightly. If anything, this Niyyuu's voice was more of an ear-numbing screech than that of Viyv-pym. He nodded, then realized that the alien probably had no idea of the gesture's significance.

"We're fine. Thanks to you. Another time-part and it would have been too late. We'd have been hustled off world and out of reach."

A second tall, supple figure eased the speaker aside. "Sorry for delay in coming. Takes time analyze data, reach decision, move. Could have alerted Sessrimathe authority, but decided come ourselves."

While George observed the exchange with interest, a grateful Walker bowed slightly to Viyv-pym. In the dim light her huge eyes took on a faint luminosity that was beyond beguiling. Noting his friend's expression, the dog snickered. Or maybe it was just a cough caused by being muffled for so long.

"Why?" Walker stared unabashedly into those eyes, watching as the frill on the back of her head and neck bobbed up and down like a vertical metronome. "Why not call the local authority? Why risk your own lives to help us?"

"Not help you." Though affable as ever, her tone was reminiscent of a steel chisel etching glass. "Protect my asset. Promise already deliver you to Kojn-umm." Smooth metallic skin and gleaming golden eyes leaned closer. "Viyv-pym keeps her promises."

He couldn't determine—certainly not from her abrasive tone—if that last was a pledge or threat. In the end, he decided it didn't matter. Not with half a dozen hulking Vilenjji bodies strewn across the ground and in among the nearby trees. Sessrimathe authority would want to know what had happened here, he knew. Like much else, he decided to leave explanations to the Niyyuu. They were members of this same galactic civilization, while he and his friends were only visitors. Transitory ones, he continued to hope.

"If your new friend is agreeable," Sque declared with a waving of several tendrils, "I believe it would be advisable for us to leave with them now, in the security of their company, lest our barbaric tormentors return in greater strength for another attempt upon our freedom."

"Some did escape." Viyv-pym glanced to her left, her entire upper body swiveling as smoothly as if on gimbals. "As we not know what reserves of personnel or weapons they may have, recommendation of small tentacled one is practical."

"Now?" Walker looked back toward the towering marvel of Sessrimathe engineering that had been his only home for the past two years. "It's very late, and we have personal items we'd like to bring with us."

Sque peered unblinkingly up at him. "You feel in need of sleep, human? This encounter has rendered you sufficiently relaxed to re-retire?"

Walker had to confess that he was not sleepy in the least.

Viyv-pym gestured toward the complex. "Return and gather belongings. Is enough time, I think. We assist. But leave tonight, now. Scenic Niyu awaits you talents."

Braouk had no head, but the eyes on the ends of their stalks rose to gaze at the night sky. "Standing here talking, time is clearly wasted, departure awaits." Silhouetted against the stars, he was a mountain of stability in the midst of unsettled circumstances.

Was Pret-Klob among the Vilenjji dead? Walker found himself wondering as he and his friends together with a small escort of Niyyuu made their way back to the building. Or had the commander of the avaricious alien association succeeded in escaping into the landscaping? No matter, he tried to assure himself. Where they were going, it was unlikely such as the Vilenjji would follow.

This time, he told himself, he and his friends would finally go down in the ledgers of the Vilenjji as a permanent write-off to inventory.

On the way to the transfer port, their modest baggage tucked neatly in back of the large private transport, Walker tried again to thank their rescuer. In response, Viyv-pym turned in the seat that was too wide and too short for her. It might, he thought, have contributed to the irritation that underlined the words that spilled from the perfectly round mouth, though given the level of apparent prickliness that was the norm for Niyyuu speech it was difficult to tell.

"I tell you already, Marcus, no need for thanking. No one steals from a Niyyuu a contracted employee."

Disdaining the sloping seat, Sque had climbed up onto its back. From there, she could survey the entire interior of the transport, as well as enjoy a better view of the brightening terrain outside.

"While such persistence in pursuit of a mere mercantile end suggests customs aligned with the most primitive, its aptness cannot be denied. In that regard, such diligence can only be commended." Silver-gray eyes flashed with intensity. "It does inspire one to wonder at its remarkable timeliness."

Walker looked over to where the K'eremu was perched firmly on the back of the seat. "I don't follow you, Sque."

"An occurrence in habitual accord with the normal state of affairs," she informed him, with no more than the usual condescension. "I am referring to the question of how our self-confessedly unaltruistic liberators managed to conveniently appear in the necessary place at the astonishingly appropriate time to manage our rescue."

George spoke up before Walker could reply, the dog's attention focused on Viyv-pym. "Yeah. How did you know what was going on, and how to find us? The Vilenjji could have bundled us out of our complex via any one of a dozen possible exits."

Silently, Viyv-pym stretched herself across the back of the seat. As the speeding transport rocked silently from side to side, one willowy arm reached toward Walker. This time he didn't flinch at all. Both long, flexible fingers lightly stroked the back of his neck before withdrawing.

"You will remember," she rasped softly. "Our first meeting. After making agreement, I touched you then like so. At that time was conveyed from me an absorptive penetrator."

Walker gaped at her. "You put something *inside* me?"

"Liquid tracker." Suddenly that round mouth appeared much more alien than inviting. With it she could, he noted, neither smile nor frown. "Harmless, time-delineated insertion. Will be completely gone you system in few more days."

"But why?"

"I should think that intrinsically obvious." If anything, Sque was amused by his discomfiture.

"Keep track you," the Niyyuu told him without embarrassment. "Protect asset. Insure come to no harm. When alerted to unlikely movement of you person at unusual time of day/night, enables I and my staff to respond with caution." She placed the two digits of her left hand over her mouth and spoke between them. He thought he was familiar with Niyyuu laughter. Perhaps this was the species equivalent of a smile. "Good thing do so, too. You not agree?"

"We're very grateful, of course," he assured her as the transport inclined slightly to the right, turning north at high speed. "But you could have told me what you did."

"Not necessary." Radiant yellow-gold eyes enveloped him. "Would have made you feel better to know?" Amidst the aural gravel, a flicker of concern emerged.

"Of course I . . ." He hesitated. Would he have felt better knowing that some kind of alien tracking fluid was coursing through his circulatory system? Did he feel better for knowing it now? It wasn't as if she was somehow taking advantage of him.

As was sometimes the case, George was able to better articulate his friend's feelings than Walker was himself. "Makes you feel a little like property, does it? Remind you somehow of a previous situation?"

Walker glanced over at the dog, who was sitting up now and watching their Niyyuu employer intently. "This is nothing like our previous situation, George. We were prisoners of the Vilen-jji: captives. Viyv-pym is hiring us. There's a vast difference in that."

"Difference, okay," the dog conceded as he scratched at one shoulder. " 'Vast,' I'm not so sure."

As soon as she digested the full import of the dog's comments, Viyv-pym grew visibly annoyed. "Captives? Prisoners? What kind insult this? I take yous Kojn-umm because of respect yous' abilities!" One hand pointed at Walker as the tips of her slender ears quivered and her tails lashed the sides of her seat. "Unique being exhibits unique talent. That only reason I extend offer to bring yous all Niyu. You think is nothing for me to do so? Cost involved goes beyond simple hiring. I have personal reputation to maintain!"

She was truly beautiful when she was angry, Walker could not help thinking. If only she wouldn't yell quite so much. The normal Niyyuu tone of voice was discordant enough.

"Okay, okay." Grumbling but far from mollified by her ear-bending outburst, George finished scratching and stretched back out on the seat. "Don't sprain your tongue—if you've got one." He glanced up at the man seated next to him. "Touchy bitch, isn't she?"

Walker held his breath, but evidently the Vilenjji implant translated the dog's comment in a way that was consistent with good manners. At least, Viyv-pym did not respond as a human female might have. Behind them, Braouk was reciting the eighth quatrain of the *Kerelon Soliloquy*. In order to squeeze inside, the Tuuqalian had to lie flat on the empty deck at the rear of the transport. Lost in melancholy reminiscence, he paid little attention to the conversation forward.

Once Viyv-pym had calmed down, Walker was able to reflect more dispassionately on George's comments. Had the dog been out of line, or was he onto something Walker was too excited or blinded to see? Had he advanced their cause of traveling nearer to their homes, or had he simply entered into an agreement that was little different from the one the Vilenjji had intended for them all along? Ostensibly, he and his companions were free agents, able to enter into an employment contract of their own choosing. Could they also exit it if and when they wished? They would be on Niyu—not sophisticated, highly civilized Sessri-mathe—dealing with a species that, beyond their obvious physical attractiveness, neither he nor his companions knew anything about. How would Viyv-pym react, for example, if after arriving and performing his demonstrations for a few weeks he announced that he and his friends wished to leave?

Maybe he hadn't made such a smart call after all, he found himself worrying. Worse still, he had inveigled his only friends into going along with it.

Something lightly touched his shoulder. Turning, he found himself staring into black, horizontal pupils set in eyes of silver. A two-foot-long tendril was coiled lightly against his clavicle while the pinkish mouth tube that emerged from the nest of tentacles fluttered in his direction.

"I cannot read thoughts. Evolved as we are, my kind has not yet advanced to that degree. But in the time we have spent forced to endure one another's company, I have become somewhat sensitive to your moods and expressions. You fear the consequences of the decision you have made."

There was a time when such close proximity face-to-face with a creature like Sque would have sent Walker reeling in shock. It was a measure of how much he had adapted that he did not even flinch from the rubbery cephalopodian visage.

"Yes, I do." A glance in George's direction showed that the dog had laid his head down on crossed forepaws and was ignoring them both. "George always knows how to stir up my uncertainties."

"A psychological device that should not be cavalierly employed by species unsophisticated in its use. Think a moment, Marcus Walker. If a self-evidently superior being like myself did not believe that there was more to be gained by accepting the offer of these Niyyuu than by declining it, would I have agreed to come along?"

Coming as it did straight from the K'eremu, the realization boosted his spirits. "No. No, you wouldn't have. You would have stayed on Seremathenn no matter how much I urged you to come."

"Precisely. Your oafish pleadings would have had no effect on me whatsoever." The tendril withdrew. "I am here only because I believe it truly does afford me the best opportunity to journey a bit nearer my homeworld that I have been offered since our arrival on Seremathenn, however meager it may eventually turn out to be. My decision has nothing to do with any perceived affection you believe I may hold toward your quaintly primitive individual person."

Walker was more relieved than he would have thought possible. "Thanks, Sque. I needed that reassurance."

"It is unintended," the K'eremu concluded, withdrawing backward to her perch atop the seat behind Walker's own.

Sque's indifference to his situation made her affirmation of his choice of action that much more heartening. Paradoxically, the fact that she could have cared less about how he felt showed how firmly she countenanced what they had done. He settled back into his seat, duly reassured in mind.

Now all he had to do was hope that primitive human and superior K'eremu were not equally misguided in their mutual decision.

In its perversely consistent fashion, it was comforting to discover in the course of the long voyage to Niyu that Viyv-pym was no more brusque of manner or grating of voice than any other representative of her kind. In fact, when confronted in close quarters with more than two or three Niyyuu conversing at once, Walker often had to manufacture an excuse to flee the location lest the pain from the sound of their overlapping voices lead to the kind of stabbing migraine he had not suffered since quitting football. He suspected that with time he would get used to the jarring, rasping, scratchy vocalizations. He would have to.

Their new hosts' irritating voices did not trouble the affable George nearly as much, barking being a less than mellifluous method of communication to begin with. As for Braouk, the massive Tuuqalian was not bothered by them at all, while Sque regarded all forms of non-K'eremu-modulated communication as unworthy of serious evaluation anyway.

So Walker was left to listen in solitary discomfort to the queries and musings of the crew and the other passengers, struggling as best he was able to avoid cringing every time he was subjected to a particularly screechy turn of Niyyuuan phrase. His Vilenjji implant did its usual excellent job of rendering otherwise unintelligible alien conversation comprehensible, but it could do nothing to mute the actual sound of their speech.

Weeks into the journey saw him gradually becoming inured to the effect, rather like someone who has been bitten numerous times by a poisonous snake and has consequently developed a certain immunity to the toxin. Or maybe, he decided, his outraged ears had been damaged to the point of being unable to discriminate between Niyyuuan vocalizations and any other kind.

Whether by accident or subconscious design, he found himself spending a lot of time in Viyv-pym's company. He did not worry about relaxing too much. For one thing, she never missed an opportunity to remind him that the only relationship they had was that between employer and employee—though she was not engaging him personally. She was only acting as an agent for her government. Additionally, while her appearance and attitude was that of a beauteous alien apparition, her behavior was more akin to that of a crude visitant from some backward region of civilized space. Not that she was in any way boorish or ignorant, he determined. A lot of it had to do with the unfortunate manner of Niyyuu speech.

While he learned much from her about the physical nature of her homeworld, she was oddly reticent to discuss social mores and attitudes. "Yous find out after arriving," she would always tell him. He got the impression she was being tentative rather than deliberately evasive.

George was less convinced. "She's keeping something from

us. Not necessarily concealing. Just skipping around certain subjects."

Sitting in the room they shared, dog and Walker exchanged a glance. The Niyyuuan sleeping platform on which he was lying was almost seven feet long but so narrow that he had to be careful not to fall onto the floor whenever he turned over during the chosen sleep period. George had no such difficulty with his platform. It could have easily accommodated a dozen Georges.

"Why would she want to hide anything?" Walker wondered how Braouk was handling the journey. While he could bend low enough to clear the ceilings within the Niyyuuan vessel, the Tuuqalian could only fit through a few exceptionally wide corridors, and then only by turning sideways. As a result, for the duration of the trip he was largely confined to the single storage area that had been converted for his use. While his comparative isolation was unavoidable, Sque's was voluntary. Unless it was obligatory, the K'eremu saw no reason to mix with lower lifeforms on a social basis. This was not a problem, as the more they learned about Sque and the more often she was encountered, the more her self-imposed isolation suited the Niyyuu as much as it did the K'eremu.

"If we knew that," the dog was saying in response to Walker's question, "we'd probably have some idea what she was hiding. Maybe I'm way off base here, Marc. I have to keep reminding myself that we're not captives on a Vilenjji collecting craft and that we're here of our own free will."

"It'll be better once we get there. You'll see." Rolling over, he leaned across the narrow divide that separated their respective sleeping platforms and began to scratch the dog's back.

George's eyes half closed, and an expression of pleasure crossed his bushy face. "Farther down. Farther." The dog's eyes shut completely. "That's it—both hip bones." Walker continued scratching until his friend settled down on his stomach. "Thanks. Every once in a while it's useful for me to be reminded why I keep you around."

Walker grinned. "Because if we happen to stumble across a

pile of dog food, you'll need somebody to operate the can opener?"

"Sque's right. You're learning." More seriously he added, "I may be paranoid, but paranoia's kept me alive more than once. You keep an eye on that Viyv-pym specimen. And not the kind of eye you've been using."

Walker feigned shock. "George, she's an *alien*. She's not even mammalian, in the scientific sense."

"It's not scientific sense that worries me here." The dog eyed him evenly, cocking his head to one side, ears flopping. "It's another one."

"Look, I won't deny that I find her attractive. But that's all. It's purely a matter of dispassionate aesthetics. The same's true for every Niyyuu. They're just a physically striking species, if verbally irritating." He was very earnest.

The dog nodded tersely. "Let's hope the irritation is confined to the verbal."

"If my spending time trying to learn about her world and her people is worrying you that much," Walker suggested, "why not ask Sque's opinion?"

George snorted softly. "I said I was concerned, not daft. I don't need to go looking for insults. I can find plenty without having to search for them." With that, he rolled over onto his back, thrust his legs into the air, and gave every indication of embarking on a quick nap.

Walker let the matter drop. He was bemused by Viyv-pym, perhaps even beguiled, but he was not worried. She was too direct to be duplicitous. If he hadn't felt that he could trust her, he would never have agreed to undertake the current journey.

Or would he? Had he been blinded by the chance to travel—hopefully—a little closer to home? Was there some aspect of her personality, of Niyyuuan nature, that his enthusiasm for the opportunity had caused him to overlook? He didn't think so. A part of him almost wished his friends had not agreed to come with him, though. Because they had, and because it was his idea, he felt responsible for them. Braouk would have shrugged off the notion with verse, while Sque would have considered it beneath debate. Only the ever-ready George would have dumped a dutiful dollop of guilt on his fellow Chicagoan.

That settled it, Walker decided with a small smile. In some earlier incarnation, George must have been a Jewish or Italian grandmother.

4

When word came down from ship command that arrival at Niyu was imminent, Walker's wonderfully durable cheap watch informed him it had been nearly a month since they had left Seremathenn. Knowing nothing of the particulars of transpatial travel except that it was all relative, Walker could not assess if the journey had been swift or slow, or if it would be considered long or short. It was left to Sque to enlighten him as they prepared themselves and their few personal belongings for incipient disembarkation.

"Everything depends on the comparative velocity a container achieves while traversing that singular portion of space-time that makes interstellar travel possible."

She elucidated while clinging to the crest of Braouk's upper body, her tendrils securely entwined in the yellow-green bristles that covered him. One Tuuqalian eyestalk curled up to monitor her position while the other remained level and drawn in, taking the measure of the path ahead of them. Though Braouk was only giving her a ride, the incongruous temporary coupling made it appear as if the Tuuqalian had unexpectedly grown a small, rubbery head while the K'eremu had developed a truly enormous lower body.

"I don't need a detailed explanation." Heading down a ramp, Walker was careful not to bump into George as the dog trotted alongside him.

"That is sensible, since you would not understand it anyway."

The K'eremu considered briefly. "Devoid of the necessary technical input and basing my remarks, you understand, on the most casual and infrequent observation of the stellar neighborhood through which we have recently passed, I should say that, unless for some unknown and unimaginable reason our hosts were compelled to take a circuitous route in returning to their homeworld, we have traveled a considerable distance."

Walker's tone would have done Sque herself proud. "Oh good—thanks so much for pinning it down for me." He and George turned a corner, following a male Niyyuuan's lead.

Tendrils fluttered as the K'eremu shifted her position slightly atop the Tuuqalian's crest. "Do not be impertinent. Do you expect one, even one such as myself, to be able to accurately estimate the distances involved in interstellar travel by simply eyeballing the view outside an optical port? It is not like pacing off the feluuls on a beach, you know. Besides, the direction we have traveled is far more important than the distance."

"What direction might that be?" George inquired, glancing back and up at her.

"The right one, we must hope." The K'eremu went silent. They were approaching an exit.

Viyv-pym was waiting for them there. The change in her demeanor was evident even to her non-Niyyuu charges. Her movements were more erratic, her manner of speaking even sharper than usual, while neck frill and multiple tails were in constant motion instead of rising and falling only when necessary to emphasize a point. Walker could not be sure of his friends' reaction, but to him their hostess looked decidedly nervous. So much so that as she shepherded them through customs checkpoints that were far less elaborate than those they had encountered on Seremathenn, Walker was moved to comment.

"Of course I edge-being," she snapped sharply in response to his query. "Do you not listen my talking on Seremathenn, on ship? This very important engaging I have made done with you all." As she spoke, her remarkable eyes were scanning the far end of the hallway.

Wondering as to its purpose, Walker was guided through an archway. Somewhere out of his range of vision, something beeped minutely. It must have been a favorable beep, because he was waved on. One by one, his friends followed—all except Braouk, who was too big to pass through. A trio of gray- and blue-clad Niyyuu armed with portable instruments promptly descended on him and proceeded to pass the business ends of the devices they carried over his body. The Tuuqalian tolerated the intimate inspection for as long as he could stand it. Then he lumbered forward to rejoin his companions. Apparently deciding that their inspection had been sufficient, none of the three Niyyuuan officials chose to challenge his departure, their collective inaction thereby reasserting their species' claim to higher intelligence.

"What's wrong?" Walker finally felt compelled to ask as they continued down the hallway. "Something's wrong, isn't it?" Whatever it was, he prayed it had nothing to do with their presence.

She turned on him so abruptly that he flinched. "Fool of a provisional decision! Is not clear you? I expend much in bringing yous to Niyu. Much more I invest in bringing yous onward to Kojn-umm." When he didn't reply she added, her exasperation unbounded, "Here, home, I am become just like you, paleskin Marc. I am employee too!"

So that was it, he realized as he strode along beside her. On Seremathenn she might have been dominant and in complete control of her fellow Niyyuu, but here she was subordinate to others. It made sense. In her defense, she had never claimed to be anything more than a posh procurer. But it was still strange to see the one on whom he had come to rely totally frill-flashing with unease at the thought she might have made a mistake.

It would be up to him, he realized, and his friends, to ensure that she did not suffer for making that choice. But mostly up to him.

The group that met them in the middle of an expansive, translucent-ceilinged rotunda was undeniably impressive, standing out from the bustle of other mostly, but not exclusively, Niyyuuan travelers. There were five of the greeters. Like Viyv-pym, each was clad in a variant of the familiar kilt-skirt and upper-body wrappings. Like her, each of the greeters flashed small bits and pieces of personal adornment to which the always-overdressed Sque paid particular attention.

Unlike the K'eremu, they carried forearm-length tubular devices that were strongly suggestive of weapons.

Why would a greeting party sent to welcome a cook and his friends find it necessary to come armed? Walker found himself wondering. Perhaps the devices served a more ceremonial than practical purpose, and were carried more for show than out of any fear of necessity. His thoughts were drawn in that direction because each of the spiral-holstered instruments flaunted one or more types of individual decoration, from engraving that had been performed on their plasticlike bodies to distinctive touches that utilized bright metal and polished gemstone.

None of the greeters drew his or her weapon in salute, however. The leader—a male, to judge by the color and shape of his frill—was almost stocky for a Niyyuu, though still markedly slimmer than Walker. Striding directly up to Viyv-pym, he briefly inspected each of the alien arrivals in turn before addressing their hostess. Walker's Vilenjji implant conveyed the meaning of the escort's speech with admirable clarity.

"Sayings tell you hire one. I see four."

She extended one long, sinuous arm in the attentive human's direction. "The one would not come without his friends."

"Friends?" The leader of the escort hesitated visibly. "No two is alike. All of different species."

"Yet friends they are," Viyv-pym insisted. "Was only matter of additional bringing. Was ample room on ship."

"Perhaps is a problem of adequate room in Kojn-umm." The escort leader made a gesture Walker did not recognize. He hoped it was more encouraging than the newcomers' words. "Not for me to say. Not for you to say." So not saying, he turned to face Walker and his friends directly.

"I am Abrid-lon, scion and accountant of Kinuvu-dih-vrojj, administrator of Kojn-umm."

An accountant. Definitely ceremonial, Walker decided on reviewing the weaponlike devices each member of their escort displayed.

"Nice to meet you." Walker thought about extending a hand,

but decided to hold off. While Viyv-pym was by now familiar with the human gesture, this Niyyuu was not, and it was too soon after their arrival to chance gestures that might be misinterpreted.

Though he wore the same type of external translator Viyv-pym employed, Abrid-lon ignored him. "This is the cook?"

"This indeed him," their hostess replied without hesitation.

Dominating yellow eyes peered down at the shorter but much bulkier arrival. "I welcome you—and you's friends. All has been made ready for you. Living quarters to match yous' standards on Seremathenn close as possible. Working site equipped with latest utensils and tools for nonsynthesized food preparation. Kinuvu-dih-vrojj and government officials look forward to you workings." His frill erected to maximum. "Kojn-umm renowned throughout Niyu for its respect for all arts."

Initially made uneasy by Viyv-pym's unexplained nervousness, Walker felt much better after Abrid-lon's brusque but heartfelt welcome. Behind him, he could sense his companions stirring impatiently.

"I look forward to beginning work," he informed the escort leader truthfully. "How far to our quarters? A time-part or so?"

Abrid-lon gestured apologetically. "Kojn-umm large realm. Some traveling time involved, I say regrettably. With best possible traveling, arrive there late tonight."

Oh, well, Walker mused. He would have the opportunity to view the approach to his new home another time.

He was left to chat with his friends as Abrid-lon engaged Viyv-pym in extended conversation. Distance rendered the Vilenjji implant inoperative, since it was dependent on his own hearing abilities to recover sufficient speech suitable for translation. As they were guided outside the port and toward a waiting transport vehicle, George inhaled deeply alongside Walker.

"Smell that! The air here is even fresher and more oxygen-rich than Seremathenn's. I know it's hopefully just a temporary state of affairs, but I think I'm going to like it here. The locals may be a bit gruff, but they're civilized and friendly enough."

In human and canine terms, anyway, the dog was half-right. The journey from the port to Kojn-umm's center of government was accomplished by means of small individual transports that traveled above open stretches of land. These cut through fields of waving, short-stemmed corkscrew growths that terminated in flowerlike cerulean and yellow bursts of color. They were more than fungi, less than flowers. A more visually appealing route would have been difficult to imagine. Walker's excitement at finding himself on yet another new world was muted somewhat by the knowledge that it was already late when they had touched down on the surface of Niyu, and that they would not be arriving at their new home until after dark.

Despite the earliness of the hour when they finally reached its outskirts, Ehbahr city was still sufficiently illuminated for the newcomers to be taken aback by its modest size. It would have barely qualified as a small suburb to one of Seremathenn's vast urban concentrations. Among the four fellow travelers, only Sque was not disappointed. The K'eremu preferred isolation and retreat to vast metropolitan concentrations, only joining together to form such when the needs of civilization and commerce demanded it. Walker, who had been expecting something like a smaller version of the great aesthetic conurbations that dominated highly developed Seremathenn, was openly disenchanted.

"Capital Ehbahr is larger than appears, especially at night. Much our industry built underground," Viyv-pym explained in response to their queries. "Better to preserve actual landscape for beauty, for living, for keeping of cultural history."

"Very admirable. We understand." Walker looked over at his closest companion. "Don't we, George. George?" Head on paws, the dog was sound asleep. The voyage and subsequent exhilaration attendant upon landing had thoroughly exhausted him.

"And for war, of course," their guide and hostess added.

Walker blinked. "Excuse me?"

"You heard her." From her position hanging upside down from the roof of the transport, Sque waved a couple of tendrils. "So much for trading one 'advanced' culture for another. A fine choice you have made for us, human."

"Wait, wait." One spoken word, assuming the Vilenjji translator had correctly conveyed its meaning, had banished all thoughts of sleep from his mind. "When I agreed to come here, Viyv-pym, you didn't say anything about your realm being at war. Who is Kojn-umm at war *with*?" His hopes, so neatly aligned and optimistic, had been shattered like orange juice futures by a frost in Brazil.

It was as if those vast, expressive, yellow and gold orbs had suddenly turned cold. "At moment, with realm of Toroud-eed. Next ten-day gathering, with somebody else. Then maybe Toroud-eed again, or possibly Sasajun-aaf. Who else would realm be at war with?" When he did not respond, she added unhelpfully, "Is nothing worry about. Is natural state of affairs."

A deep voice, the soul of glumness, rumbled from the back of the transport. "Here we sit, come all this way, conflict awaiting." Given his habitual melancholy it was often difficult to tell exactly how Braouk was feeling. Not now. The Tuuqalian was as disheartened by the unexpected turn of affairs as Sque was scornful. As for George, Walker was grateful the often-acerbic George was still asleep.

Helplessly, as they slowed and entered the city, he asked, "How can you be at war with anybody and say it's 'nothing worry about'? Much less say 'is natural state of affairs'?"

"You not have ongoing or at least periodic war between individual realms where you's home is?"

He looked away briefly. "Yes, we have such wars, I'm sorry to say. I have been told that Braouk's people do as well. Not Sque's, I believe."

"Only occasionally on a personal level," the K'eremu amended him helpfully. "When two individuals disagree excessively on a point of Melachian philosophy, for example, or concerning the worth of a new piece of siibalon vibrato. On such occasions, fighting usually commences with a vicious exchange of harsh language. On rare instances, blows may be thrown, perhaps even accompanied by a flung rock or two."

"That's not war," Walker muttered crossly. "That's a domestic dispute." He turned back to their hostess. "How long has this kind of episodic fighting been going on?" He trusted his implant to handle the translation of the relevant time frame.

It did. Whatever else one thought about the Vilenjji, their technology was admirably reliable. "About nine thousand years," Viyv-pym informed him without missing a beat. "Ever since Niyyuu become civilized."

"Not a contradiction, in war to engage, called civilization?" Braouk wondered aloud from the back of the transport.

She turned and strained to meet his raised eyes. "On contrary, Niyyuu thoughtfully observe other sentient species and wonder how they maintain civilization *without* occasional internal warring."

Walker's head began to throb as he tried to make sense of what he was being told. The Niyyuuan's warped logic was occasioning him more pain than the occasional jolt in their ride. "You say sporadic warfare helps you to maintain your civilization, but that it's nothing to worry about. There's a clash of reasoning there I just don't understand. I don't understand it at all."

"You will," she assured him confidently. "You not only do performancing for Administrator Kinuvu-dih-vrojj and government, you also prepare food for Saluu-hir-lek and his staff."

He frowned. The first name he recognized, but this was the first time that the second one had been made known to him. "I signed on to cook for whomever you wish, but who is Saluu-hir-lek?"

"Commanding general," Abrid-lon called back to him from the front of the transport, "and lord high protector of the conjoined territories of Kojn-umm. Very pleasant person. You will like him."

Curioser and curioser. He was drowning in incomprehension. "I thought Kinuvu-dih-vrojj was the leader of Kojn-umm?"

Viyv-pym exhaled softly in his direction. Her breath washed over him like essence of roses. "Kinuvu-dih-vrojj, she head of government. Saluu-hir-lek, he head of traditional military. One not superior to another. Just different work taxonomy. I procurer. You exotic food preparation demonstrator. You's friends—they receive appropriate classifications in due time." A long, willowy arm reached out toward him.

"You tired, Marc. Long journeying from Seremathenn. Relax, not worry. Kojn-umm pleasant place. Ehbahr city and citizens enlightened, congenial. You will like it here."

Apprehensive and anxious, he slumped back in his seat. "I'm sure I will—unless you lose this war and are overrun by your enemies."

Her painted circlet of a mouth expanded in amusement as she coughed twice. "Perhaps lose. Have lost before. Is no realm that has not. Could not manage world society otherwise. But Kojnumm not be 'overrun,' in sense you suggest. Cannot happen."

"Why not?" he asked straightforwardly, without wondering if the question might be viewed by his hosts as tactless.

"Because would not be civilized thing to do. You think Niyyuu barbarians? Not as advanced as Sessrimathe, maybe, but plenty civilized and refined are my kind. You will see. Maybe even," she finished considerately, "you like try you's hand at fighting, too, someday."

Walker was quietly aghast. "I agreed to come here to create cuisine, not to kill!"

She gestured placatingly. "Is your choice. Did not mean upset you. Is not necessary participate. Very much competition for spaces in traditional military, anyway."

He sat stunned and silent, unable to believe what he was hearing. It was so at odds with everything he had come to believe about the Niyyuu. Or, he asked himself, was it only what he had *wanted* to believe about the Niyyuu? Had he settled hopes and expectations on Viyv-pym and her people that were grounded only in wishful thinking?

"Have *you* fought in this war, in the military?" he finally heard himself asking.

"Oh, most for sure." The eagerness in her voice could not be denied. "Was fortunate enough be awarded two whole full enlistment periods."

"And . . . you killed?"

"Of course." Golden eyes glittered with recollection as her voice quivered with suggestions of thrills remembered. "Not real war without killing."

How could he argue with that? he told himself. For the first time since he had met her, the beauteous and exotic Viyv-pym receded once again into the realm of the utterly alien.

As was often the case, it was left to Sque to emotionlessly

evaluate what they had been told. "There are ramifications here we do not understand," she declared quietly from her hanging place in the center of the swaying transport's ceiling. "We must work to acquire the obligatory cultural referents before we can pronounce judgment. Operating in ignorance, we cannot hope to properly assess composite indigenous conditions."

Walker latched onto her uncertainty like an overextended client to a fresh line of credit. What the K'eremu was saying was that there was more here than met the eye, or the ear. Though for the life of him he could not fathom what that might be, he was willing to give it time in the hope that a sensible explanation would present itself.

Traversing parsecs to swap their situation on peaceful, accommodating Seremathenn for a millennia-old ongoing war was not what he'd had in mind when he had signed on hoping to improve their chances of getting home.

Often dimly illuminated, the buildings they passed differed in design, shape, and size from those on Seremathenn. Such was to be expected, since Viyv-pym had informed them that much of Niyu's commerce took place belowground. There was certainly enough nocturnal illumination, however, to guide incoming hostile aircraft, much less anything more sophisticated. Therefore it was abundantly clear the people of Ehbahr city did not fear an assault from the air. That suggested several possibilities, none of which made any more sense to him than what he had already been told. He gave up trying to figure out what was going on and determined to wait for an explanation that did. Hopefully, one would be provided to them.

There was certainly nothing wrong with or Spartan about their quarters. Prepared in advance according to specifications supplied by Viyv-pym, they bordered on the luxurious. Having been provided with particulars by its new employees, the government of Kojn-umm had gone out of its way to make them feel at home.

Walker's personal space on Seremathenn had been accommodating. His quarters in a luxurious section of Ehbahr city consisted of separate, spacious rooms for sitting, sleeping, receiving guests, and performing personal ablutions. Instead of

a view of other transformed buildings such as he'd had on Seremathenn, he had transparent barriers that opaqued or vanished
at the wave of a hand to allow egress to a porch that overlooked
a small stream running through carefully maintained Niyyuan
forest.

Flashing multihued phosphorescent scales, small creatures of
the night scampered to and fro between foliage and stream.
Since the connected rooms did not boast the responsive, all-
pervasive synthesized voice-response system of an advanced
Seremathenn dwelling, he was shown how to request service
from a live Niyyuuan attendant. George would share quarters
with Walker, they were informed, while on casual inspection
the easygoing Braouk found his private accommodations to be
more than satisfactory. Upon being shown her own lodgings,
which included a section of the nearby creek to provide constant moisture, even Sque had less than the normal number of
complaints.

Promising to meet with them again in the morning, both
Viyv-pym and Abrid-lon left the newest employees of the government of Kojn-umm to their own devices. Toying with the receiving room's entertainment/information system, Walker
found it to be as highly developed as anything he had used on
Seremathenn. Neither it, nor the peacefully sleeping city, nor
the attitude of the individual Niyyuu he had encountered since
arriving squared with the reality of continual, ongoing combat.
For about five minutes, he worried about being killed in his
sleep on the special resting platform that had been provided for
him. Then another kind of reality took over, and he fell into a
deep and untroubled sleep.

5

Walker sat up sharply in the approximation of a bed, awakened by something that sounded like forty chickens being simultaneously strangled. Looking around wildly for the source of the horrible screeching, he searched the entire room twice before he realized it was only the Niyyuuan equivalent of a gentle, mellifluous, preprogrammed wake-up song.

Have to have that recording changed, he told himself shakily as he descended from the sleeping platform to manually cancel the persistent wail. No doubt more than a few of the provisions that had been made for his life here would require comparable modifications.

Passing by one of the darkened view-walls, he directed it to vanish. The energizing tingle of fresh air filled the room, accompanied by a flush of bright sunshine. Walking out onto the small porch, he found himself gazing across the nearby stream that had been only a dark sliver muttering to itself during the night. A quintet of humming furballs he did not yet have a name for bobbed past, seeking surcease, shade, and nectar. Rustlings in the underbrush on the other side of the brook hinted at the presence within of alien ground dwellers. The noises did not concern him. If any danger existed from native animals, he was certain he would have been informed.

Above and beyond the undulating crest of the carefully maintained riparian habitat he could see tall buildings rising from the center of the capital city. The Niyyuu were fond of domes and other bulbous architectural oddities; a partiality that contrasted sharply and perhaps intentionally with their own svelte forms. Beyond the glistening, well-scrubbed towers of the city, which were modest in size compared to the structures he had seen on Seremathenn, a line of mountains stretched across the horizon. No snow capped the visible peaks, an absence that might have been due to latitude, season, altitude, or a combination thereof.

"See anything?"

Turning, he saw that George had come up behind him. The dog yawned mightily, shook from nose to tail, and stretched, his forelegs extending as far forward as possible.

"Urban structures," Walker informed his height-challenged companion. "Parklike stream and vegetation just below us. In the distance, mountains—not too high, I think."

"No sign of fighting, uninhibited internecine bloodletting, or rampaging cadres of naturally anorexic soldiers?"

Walker returned his attention to the babbling brook and outlying buildings. "There's something in the creek that looks agitated, but that's about it."

"Good. I'm hungry. Let's find something to eat."

Walker waved a windowlike transparency back into place before turning away from the gap. Where was evidence of the ongoing war of which Viyv-pym had spoken? "Wait. I have to get dressed."

"I don't." The dog trotted energetically through a portal that opened obediently in response to his curt bark. "Meet you in the common room, or dining room, or however the appropriate place for taking meals is designated here."

It made no sense, Walker deliberated as he fumbled with his shirt while doing his best to follow his companion. If the countryside existed in a state of perpetual war, where were the signs of concern, the hints of resistance? The city had been well lit during their arrival the previous night. Was it possible to imagine a civilization that possessed starships but not aircraft? For that matter, bombs could be dropped from balloons, but there was nothing to indicate that the people of Kojn-umm feared any attack from the air. Could the confusion he was experiencing be due to a simple misunderstanding over what he had been told?

But Viyv-pym had said clearly that it was "not real war without killing." He decided to try to set his bemusement aside. Surely clarification would be forthcoming.

George was right about one thing. He was hungry, too. Maybe food would help to alleviate the headache he was beginning to develop. And he hadn't even started work yet. Would he need to acquire defensive attire in addition to the appropriate utensils?

The dog located a common room that fronted on a small indoor garden. None of the plants were known to either of them. Within the garden, yellow vied with green as the dominant color. One particularly distinctive growth put forth a single flower that was as long as Walker's arm. It smelled abominable.

The synthesizer that responded to their requests had been programmed to fulfill their needs, but the equipment, while far in advance of anything that had been developed on Earth, was no match for the sophisticated instrumentalities of the Sessrimathe. Biting into a disc of pale pink something, Walker's face screwed into an expression that was a perfect visual representation of the taste.

"If this is an example of the local cuisine," he observed when he had choked down enough of the substance to be able to talk again, "I can see why my services are so eagerly awaited here."

"You're too picky, Marc. You always are." George dug with unreserved gusto into the plate of proteins as colorful as they were unidentifiable that the synthesizer had set before him.

That left Walker to contemplate an unpalatable choice between looming starvation and distasteful consumption. As he picked at his food, Sque arrived to join them. Scuttling into the room on half a dozen of her ten tendrils, bits of polished metal and colorful plastic jangling around her body, the dripping wet K'eremu left a trail of water behind her. Preferring to remain as damp as possible for as long as possible, she had not bothered to dry herself following her most recent immersion.

Though barely four feet tall when erect on all ten tendrils, she had no difficulty pulling herself up into the chair that was intended for much taller Niyyuu. In fact, she was arguably more comfortable on the alien piece of furniture than her human companion was. Designed to accommodate the far narrower

Niyyuuan posterior, Walker's chair would have made an uncomfortable perch for any human. Constant shifting in search of a more restful position failed to find one.

"Fortunately, I have already eaten. Thank you for asking," she snapped brusquely before anyone could venture so much as a "Good morning." As a sign of further disapproval, several bubbles emerged from the flexible pink tube that was her mouth and rose halfway to the ceiling before bursting.

By now completely used to her moods, Walker ignored her scorn as he picked unhappily at his own food. "I assumed that you had, Sque, or you would have been demanding it as you came in." Slipping a slice of something like slivered eggplant into his mouth, he chewed slowly and experimentally. His palate was less than impressed, but his stomach did not rebel.

I would kill, he mused dejectedly, *for a Polish dog. With mustard, and onions, and relish, and sauerkraut.* At the thought, his mouth manufactured saliva in quantity sufficient to impress even Sque. As for barbeque, he dared not even visualize the concept. Instead, he made himself eat another slice of alien eggplant.

To take his mind off historical impossibilities like kielbasa, he engaged the K'eremu in conversation. "How did you sleep? While they're not as stylish as those we had on Seremathenn, I thought my quarters were pretty comfortable."

"I did not ask your opinion," she replied tersely. Two tendrils pulled a conical container toward her and deftly upended a sample of the liquid contents into a smaller container from which she sipped daintily before continuing. "As you observe, these Niyyuu are not as advanced as our former hosts. Neither are they especially primitive. My rooms occupy a level lower than yours. This was done intentionally, I am told, so that I might have regular and unimpeded access to the nearby stream and its refreshing, cooling flow. Such forethought expended on the comfort of a higher being is to be commended. I rested adequately, thank you."

"And how did you find breakfast, Snake-arms?"

As always, she ignored the dog's insult as being beneath her. "Nourishment, though synthesized as expected, was tolerated by my system. It could not compare, of course, to victuals properly prepared." Several slender limbs gestured in Walker's direction. "As they might have been by the primitive but gastronomically talented amateur in our company, to give but one example."

Walker nearly choked on his next mouthful. "Are you paying me a compliment, Sque?"

Silvery eyes looked away, toward the nearest transparency that provided an external view. "Truth compels. You may proffer appropriate obeisance at a later time. I do not wish to interrupt your intake of the dreadful molecular combinations you consider worthy of ingestion."

Walker beamed. A compliment. Sque never gave compliments. The closest the K'eremu came to praising another being was to refrain from insulting it on a regular basis. Walker hardly knew how to respond.

Defying any sense of propriety, local or imported, George hopped up onto the table and began sniffing some of the other offerings. Walker managed to look pained.

"Come on, George. Really."

"Really what?" The dog eyed him impassively. "Really get off the table, or really relax because if I had arms and hands I wouldn't have to do this?" Settling on a chunk of something that smelled like meat even if it looked like cantaloupe, he picked it up in his teeth and returned to his chosen spot on the floor.

They remained like that, in mutual silence, for several minutes—man and dog eating, K'eremu contemplating their primitive activity—when a sudden thought occurred to Walker. Looking up and around, he took in their immediate surroundings before venturing aloud to no one in particular, "Anyone seen Braouk this morning?"

"Not me." George returned to his meat melon.

"I have not yet encountered the ungainly giant." Pulling herself up onto the table, Sque took on the appearance of a kaleidoscopic calamari. Another place, another time, another set of onlookers, Walker knew, and she would be deemed dinner rather than diner. "Maybe he's still resting in whatever warehouse-sized room our lanky hosts have made available for his use."

As breakfast wore on without any sign of the melancholy Tu-uqalian, however, Walker found himself beginning to worry. "We'd better go find him, make sure he's okay." He pushed back from the table and stood, glad to be free of the narrow, uncomfortable Niyyuuan chair.

"Worry about that wandering mountain?" George hopped up onto an empty chair to bring himself closer to eye level with his friend. "He worries everybody else, not the other way around."

"I'd feel better knowing for sure that he's okay."

The dog snorted, considered relieving himself on one of the table supports, decided to hold off. Unlike another dog, their hosts would probably frown on such a response. "Might as well, I guess. Nothing else to do here yet anyway."

They found the giant on the roof. In addition to a series of small domes whose function was not immediately apparent, there was a broad deck that had been landscaped with fully grown trees and shrubbery to blend perfectly with the preserved natural environment below. Though it rose to a height of only four or five stories above the ground, the edifice that had become their new home still loomed above the majority of government structures surrounding it. The deck offered a sweeping panorama of the city and the surrounding mountains.

Braouk was standing on the northwest side, careful not to put any weight against the delicate swirl of railing that in addition to being too low for him could never have supported his mass. In contrast, it was almost too high for Walker. Picking up George, he cradled the dog in his arms so his friend could also see clearly. As for Sque, her multiplicity of limbs allowed her to easily scamper up the nearest dome.

"Nice view," George commented approvingly. "Handsome mountains. No mountains where you and I come from."

"Is not mountains, that I stand studying, this direction." The Tuuqalian raised a pair of powerful tentacles and pointed. "There. That outcropping or promontory, that rises just to the left of the main pass. Do you see?"

Walker strained. With his huge oculars mounted on the ends

of flexible stalks, Braouk had the best distance vision of any of them. "I do see something. Some kind of building?"

"More than that." This time the Tuuqalian pointed with all four tentacles, the tips touching to form a conical indicator. "Look again, harder."

With a familiarity she would never have dared attempt back aboard the prison ship of the Vilenjji, Sque clambered up Braouk's back, climbing him like a tree, until she stood atop the furry crest with one bulbous Tuuqalian eye raised on either side of her.

"I cannot see anything except these mountains. My eyesight has evolved for precision viewing, not for far-seeing."

George had better luck. "I see smoke, and moving figures. Lots of moving figures. The structure itself is different from anything down here. Looks to be pretty big, and all sharp angles. No tapering towers, no graceful domes."

"I believe it, to be a primitive fortress, without question." As they drew closer together, the better to sharpen the Tuuqalian's view, the muscular eyestalks threatened to squeeze Sque between them. "A castle, or redoubt, of primitive design. Even as we stand here watching, a battle is taking place before its gate and on its ramparts."

"The war!" Now that Braouk had described the scene, Walker found that he was better able to discern individual elements of the distant vista. "Strange. You say that fighting is going on. But I don't see any flashes of light, any explosions."

"Me neither," George added. As an indication of how seriously he took the situation, his tail was virtually motionless.

"That is because there are none," the Tuuqalian informed them. "In keeping with the design and materials of the primitive structure that is under assault, the methods of combat being employed appear to be equally archaic. While it is difficult to tell for certain at such a distance, I think I perceive much tentacle-to-tentacle—excuse me, hand-to-hand—fighting."

Sque gestured with several tendrils. "There is both absurdity and contradiction in what you say. Yet being unable to see clearly for myself, I am unable either to deny or confirm the validity of your observations. I declared upon our arrival here yesterday that there are ramifications to this Niyyuuan war that we do not understand. I confess I am now even more puzzled than I was originally."

Turning, George nodded toward the far portal. "It's time to get unpuzzled. Let's ask her."

Viyv-pym was striding toward them, her slender limbs seeming to float across the floor. She had exchanged her previous attire for a dual casing of gauzy material: half turquoise blue, the other shimmering gold. Here and there, fragments of what looked like frozen methane gave off small wisps of condensation. Twisted tightly around her, the fabric gave her the appearance of someone bound in an oversized strand of DNA. With her high, pointed ears, switching tails, and wide, luminous eyes, she was perfectly breathtaking, Walker decided.

"Yous rested well?" she inquired cheerfully in her familiar grating burr.

Never one to waste words, George raised a paw in the direction of the distant mountain pass. "There's fighting going on up there, just outside your city, right now."

The sparkling Niyyuuan gaze rose briefly. "Yes, at the fortress of Jalar-aad-biidh. Combined forces of Toroud-eed have invested it almost two ten-days now. Under strategy devised by gallant General Saluu-hir-lek our defenders continue hold them off. Is very exciting."

"Exciting?" Once again, Walker found Viyv-pym's reactions in sharp contrast to her appearance. "Aren't your people, citizens of Kojn-umm, dying up there?"

"No doubt are some, yes."

"Well, what is going to be done about it?"

"Take you meet you's staff," she informed him happily. "Begin plan first meal-skill demonstration for government personnel. Important yous make good impression. Very important for you and for me." She eyed his companions. "Must make appearance all of one part. All participate, somehow. Sure you understand necessary justify bringing four not one all way to Niyu."

"Showtime," declared the ever-adaptable George.

"Amateur theatrics, no doubt." Though clearly not pleased,

having anticipated something of the sort, Sque kept the bulk of her objections to herself. "Hopefully there will be astronomers in attendance and we can make some contacts useful toward commencing the necessary preliminary studies for continuing on our homeward journey."

Fortunately, their hostess had not overheard the K'eremu's characteristically soft speech. Leaning down, Walker whispered urgently to Sque.

"We just got here. Try to be a little diplomatic, will you? Since we're undoubtedly going to have to ask these people for help, it would be better not to start off by insulting their hospitality."

"What hospitality? We are employees, not guests." Steel-gray eyes looked away from him. "Nevertheless, I shall endeavor to comply. You speak sense."

"Who, me?" Walker responded blithely.

"The universe is ever full of surprises." The K'eremu scuttled off to one side, away from Viyv-pym.

Walker turned back to their patient hostess. "How can anyone be interested in aesthetic food preparation when there's a war going on?"

"Most always a war going on," she told him. "Has nothing to do with living normal life."

"Has nothing to do with . . . ?" Sque was right, he thought. There was much here they did not understand, and it was growing more confusing by the moment.

Viyv-pym turned and beckoned. "Come now, please. Meet staff, explain needs. Have some time prepare properly, but not excessive amount. You interested in course of the fighting, yes?" Both Walker and George nodded. The human wondered if she could perceive the confusion in his expression.

Whether their Niyyuu hostess was that perceptive or not, she removed from within the folds of her garb a rolled-up square of plastic. Unfurled, it sprang to light and to life. Running her fingers over one side, she brought forth image after image until the flexible screen finally settled on one. Satisfied, she passed it toward Walker.

He accepted it without hesitation. It weighed very little, and he was able to examine it without breaking stride. Next to him, George was bouncing up and down curiously, straining to see.

"Let me have a look too, Marc. What is it? Not cartoons, I bet."

"No," Walker responded soberly. Bending over, he lowered the viewer until it was level with his friend's eyes. "See for yourself."

The dog found himself gazing at a scene of relentless and deceptively ruthless Niyyuuan carnage. Clad in armor of varying thickness and elegant but alien design, dozens of Niyyuu were engaged in a brutal clash outside what appeared to be the gate of an ancient stone fortress. While the design differed significantly from its nearest human analog of medieval castles, certain similarities were perhaps inevitable. Projectiles were slung from battlements, though there was no evidence of bows and arrows being put to use. A spear was a spear, though the blueprint might be slightly different.

Edged weapons differed from those that might be wielded by a human in a similar situation. They tended more to the saber than the broadsword—understandable, given the slenderer build of the Niyyuuan. Shields reflected similarly lighter construction. Man and dog saw more than a few that appeared to be composed almost entirely of metal filigree. Or plastic. Despite the clarity and variety of available images, there was still a lot of picture-distorting movement. Speaking of pictures . . .

"I'm afraid I don't get any of this." At once fascinated and horrified, Walker spoke without taking his eyes from the roll-up screen. "How are these images being broadcast?"

"I not technically educated myself in physics of broadcast apparatus," Viyv-pym told him. "Can obtain for you if you like expert in such matters to—"

"No, no," he said, hastily interrupting her. "I mean, some of these images are being sent from right in the middle of the fighting. Isn't that dangerous for the broadcast operator?"

" 'Operator'?" She eyed him quizzically. "Images are relayed by advanced instrumentation that operate under all conditions." As she grasped the deeper implications of his question, her ears quivered. "Operators on battlefield are clearly identified. No soldier of any realm dare harm media representative! Accidentally might happen, but that only possible way."

Her sincere shock at the possibility that a live image relayer might be injured in the course of reporting on the conflict did not square with the very real carnage he and George were witnessing on the screen. It appeared that the skirmish was dying down. Fighters on both sides were retreating—the soldiers of Kojn-umm falling back to the fortress, their attackers withdrawing to some unseen bivouac. Both sides took their wounded with them. The rocky slope they abandoned was littered with bodies. Clearly visible were many body parts that had been forcefully divorced from their owners, and a copious amount of blood.

Peering around Walker, Viyv-pym stole a glance at the flexible screen. "Today's fight most substantial. I believe is standoff. For nows, anyway. If fortress can hold several days longer, I think Toroudians will go home. Kojn-umm will move up in preferential trade rankings."

Walker gaped at her. "Trade rankings?" He shook the screen, which flexed easily but did not sacrifice its image. "This hack-and-slash mayhem is about trade rankings?" While he was not exactly sure as to the significance of a Niyyuuan trade ranking, it did not sound like the sort of thing people ought to be dying over.

She indicated in the affirmative, her golden pupils expanding and contracting. "Saluu-hir-lek is fine leader. Sure he pursue dispute to conclusion that favors Kojn-umm."

"Just suppose the military situation is a stalemate, for now," Walker hypothesized. "But what if this enemy, these Toroud-eed, try a flanking movement or something? What if they attack the city itself?"

She inhaled so sharply and drew away from him so abruptly that for a moment he thought she had tripped over some unseen crevice. The Vilenjji implant conveyed her disgust at his words in no uncertain, and highly unflattering, terms. When she realized that his bewilderment, as well as that of his three companions, was genuine, she did her best to try to explain.

"Yous know still so little of Niyyuu society. So I try quick explain yous. Toroud-eed soldiers not never attack anything but Kojn-umm soldiers and recognized, long-established, traditional military targets. What you suggest is not conceivable."

"Just for the sake of argument," George put in, "what if they did?"

As she peered down at him, her tails were entwining in a clear sign of agitation. "Aside from fact such action unthinkable and unprecedented, every other realm on Niyu would gang up on them and raze entire territory of Toroud-eed to bare soil. Committing violence against a nonmilitary target would violate every law of civilized Niyyuuan behavior. General population, civilian population, is never involved in traditional fightings." A soft sighing escaped her round mouth as she resumed walking. Today that orifice was edged in paint the color of sliced limes and granite.

"Was different in primitive times, of course. As Niyyuu become civilized, organize into many thousands small warring states. Resultant general chaos retards development of progressive society. Each state ruled by warlord, military chieftain. People gradually come to recognize problem. Even warlords recognize problem—but not want give up individual privileges, respect, power.

"Decision made between Sixth and Seventh Interregnums to divide functions of state. Civilian peoples form administrations, governments, to deal with everyday livings. Warlords retain small armies to settle differences. But civilian governments never interfere in fightings, and warlord armies never touch civilians. So civilization grows and prospers, but many disputings still settled by combat. Today's armies entirely whole composed of honored volunteers." She straightened proudly. "I tell you before, I earlier participate in such myself."

Walker tried to picture the poised, lissome Viyv-pym tricked out in full body armor, slim bloody sword dangling from one two-fingered hand, jewel-like lightweight helmet steady upon her head. Somewhat to his surprise, it was not difficult to make the imaginary leap. He hurriedly pushed the image out of his mind.

Sque was less forbearing. "This local tradition of constrained violence is nothing more than another take on typical primitive means of avoiding the use of reason."

George was more openly forgiving as he addressed himself to Viyv-pym. "So what you're saying is that the general population isn't involved in these recurring fights at all. That these traditional warlord groups act as proxies for societal disputes while the general population goes merrily about its everyday business, blissfully free of any need to participate in actual combat." The dog eyed her intently. "But what happens when one side's army wins? What happens if you lose?"

"Then dispute that provoke it is considered settled," she told him, as if explaining the obvious to a child.

George still wasn't satisfied. "The victorious army doesn't come marching in? There's no sacking and pillaging and burning?"

Having dealt with previous outrageous statements, this time she was better prepared to respond to more of the same. "I tell you second time: warriors not think of attack civilians, and civilians not think of not supporting warriors. Besides being inviolable custom, is civic and moral duty of all concerned."

Sort of the antipode of Tibetan Buddhism, Walker found himself supposing. In that distant mountain land, people believed themselves obligated to provide food and drink for wandering priests so that the latter could properly perform their duties. Meanwhile, the priests prayed for the people. The lamas didn't try to tell the local electric company how to supply power, and the officials of the local utilities stayed out of the lamaseries. It was all very civilized.

Except that in the Niyyuuan version people died.

"Everyone respect results, of traditional ongoing killing, without argument?" Instead of bending to clear a low archway, Braouk contracted his four treelike walking tentacles and lowered himself by a foot.

"Argument is settled by winning of fight," Viyv-pym told him. "After fighting over, no argument left. Anyone with personal feelings about subject matter of dispute is always given place in army. Ample room then for letting deep feelings be known."

A wonderful way for society's disgruntled to blow off steam, Walker realized. Pick up a sword or spear and hack away at your frustrations.

As they entered one of the building's internal transports and were conveyed swiftly and silently to another linked structure, the juxtaposition of the advanced method of getting from one part of the government complex to another with what he continued to see on the roll-up visual prompted a question of a different sort. He hoped Viyv-pym's translator was capable of handling the same terms and referents as his own.

"I saw plenty of swords and spears, knives and slings, and in the background a few larger devices that looked like catapults and other primitive war machines." He indicated the high-speed, climate-controlled, virtually vibrationless capsule that was presently carrying all of them, including Braouk, in comparative comfort. "Your people have vessels capable of interstellar travel, complex translation devices that function even between species, machines that can synthesize many varieties of food from basic nutritional components, and communications equipment like this." He held up the flexible receiver. "But I didn't see one gun of any size, shape, or style in use during that battle. No explosives of any kind, nothing."

Behind him, Sque commented on his query with a rude bubbling noise. He ignored the K'eremu's snide remark, a typical reference to his manifest stupidity. Maybe the explanation *was* obvious—but it wasn't to him. At least George had nothing to say. The dog's attentiveness showed that he was as interested in the answer as was his bipedal companion.

"When original concord forged by all warring realms," Viyv-pym explained patiently, "it decided then and there to freeze means of disputation at technological level existing at time of final accord. Has not changed ever since. Permissible weaponry still same as that used during mid Seventh Interregnum."

Walker persisted. "But what's to keep someone on the verge

of having their head cut off from pulling out a pistol, just that one time, and blowing their assailant away?"

"Same steadfast compact that keep military from attacking noncombatants." Viyv-pym put a gentle arm around his shoulders. "Must try to see state of affairs from Niyyuu point of view, Marcus." He wasn't sure which was more unsettling: the arm resting on his shoulders and neck, or her use of his first name. "Ancient accord sustains harmony of all Niyu. If one realm breaks tradition, all other realms combine to punish it. If individual breaks with custom, own comrades would provide punishment. Accord has lasted thus for thousands of forty-days." Inclining toward him, she brought her face close to his own. He had to fight not to lose himself in the flaxen depths of her eyes.

"Is not same with you's culture?"

"Not exactly." He swallowed. "We have wars—we do fight—but we're not as . . . polite about it as the Niyyuu."

A soft barking nearby caused him to glance sharply downward. George was visibly amused. "I can see trying something like this on Earth. Might work with higher beings, like dogs. But humans? You can't even keep from using advanced weapons between mates. There's civilized behavior, and then there's human civilized behavior. Seems like out here there's different degrees and definitions of war, too."

As the transport capsule began to slow, Walker felt moved to defend his species. "At least we're different when it comes to broadcasting the horrors of actual warfare." He handed the roll-up screen back to Viyv-pym. "When it comes to that, the Niyyuu apparently aren't nearly as appalled by it as we are."

"Give me a break, man. You're not appalled at all. I've spent plenty of time on the street. Watched humans at fights. Street gangs versus bikers. Cops against lawbreakers. Always draws a crowd. Maybe their speech is full of horror, but their expressions tell it all. You want to know how your own kind really reacts to combat and violence, study their respiration and pulse and sweat glands, not their language."

"Appalled?" As the transport's door slid aside, Viyv-pym looked from human to canine. "Niyyuu not appalled by fight-

ing. Wars keep the peaces. Combat sustains the concordance."
She held up the screen. "Everyone follow each conflict with
much interest. War is politics. Is Niyyuu culture, commerce,
entertainment."

"Entertainment?" Walker was aghast.

She confirmed his dismay. "Anyone can quote yous history
of famous battles, involving many realms. Names of famous
soldiers, officers and common. You spend more time on Niyu,
you see. Battles broadcast all times. Pick favorite realm, favorite soldiers, favorite fightings. Much to see, much to learn.
Much to admire."

Like the gladiators who became media stars in ancient Rome,
Walker told himself unhappily. Watch them slice and dice each
other, have a few laughs, then go home to the wife and kids.
That is, if you didn't bring the wife and kids to the show with
you. Today's special: murder and slaughter. Family packages
available. All in the name of righteous service and maintaining
a widespread, functional peace between competing territories.
All without having to resort to the risk of general devastation
and the imposition of impoverishing military budgets on a dis-
inclined populace.

Probably the system also worked wonders for the racial psy-
che. Those who wanted to fight could do so without suffering
any social opprobrium. In the absence of advanced weaponry,
each individual was guaranteed some chance of surviving combat based purely on the development of individual skills. Those
who wanted nothing to do with such old-fashioned violence
could not only avoid it, they could participate vicariously
through the actions of volunteer armies: others as well as their
own. Sure, Walker rooted for the Bears and the Bulls, but back
home he and his friends watched other games as well, where
they also chose sides. Superficially, the only difference between
the sociopolitical situation on Niyu and the National Football
League was that the latter involved the spilling of less blood
while the former doubtless resulted in more far-reaching eventual consequences than a Super Bowl championship.

Though initially revolted, he had to admit the system had its
attractions. Too bad it would never work on or be imported to

Earth. For one thing, the necessary cultural background and referents were as different as the two species. War, even limited war, was not a game to be played out on a grassy field. At least not among loutish humans.

As George had so indecorously pointed out, humans were not sufficiently polite.

Eager to initiate the visitors into the intricacies of Niyyuuan society, Viyv-pym kept up a running commentary on the battle as soon as it resumed, pointing out eminent individual warriors and officers, commenting on tactics, remarking knowledgeably on battlefield conditions. Watching and listening to her, a disconcerted Walker found himself wondering if rain would be considered grounds for a bad-weather postponement of the battle. Thus far there had been nothing on the flexible screen to indicate the presence of referees. In their absence, it had to be assumed that the combatants policed themselves. A kind of "call your own fouls" conflict, where intentional tripping was supplanted by maiming, and unnecessary roughness was a contradiction in terms. He wondered if there was a Niyyuuan battlefield equivalent of illegal use of the hands, and doubted it.

Then she was rolling up the screen and slipping it back inside her double-wrapped costume. They had arrived at the food preparation area.

The half dozen or so Niyyuu lined up to greet them eyed him eagerly. His reputation having preceded him, Walker did not need to identify himself. More problematic was the matter of what role to assign to his companions. He was disappointed when Viyv-pym drew them off to one side to consult with an elderly local, leaving him to deal with the nutrition technicians alone.

They were enthusiastic enough. His requests for specific equipment were met with a chorus of ready responses, the combined harshness of half a dozen Niyyuuan voices all attempting to answer at once leaving him wishing that his first ingredient was a hearty dose of acetylsalicylic acid. Occasionally putting his hands over his ears he persevered, however, and soon the basic outlines of his demonstration began to take shape. This first performance should be a defining one, he knew. The last thing he wanted to do was disappoint, lest he and his companions find themselves unceremoniously shipped back to Seremathenn. They had come too far to waste time and effort in backtracking.

"This hot-air spinner," one of the younger assistants inquired, "what it be use for?"

"Carelth," Walker informed her. Among the many gourmet Niyyuuan dishes whose constituents he had memorized during the journey from Seremathenn to Niyu, carelth was one basic foodstuff that seemed to offer excellent opportunities for customization.

"But carelth is baked, not hot spun," remarked an older male.

"Not *my* carelth," Walker told him firmly.

After that surprise, he had them firmly in the grasp of his gastronomic vision. They were not quite sure what he was going to do, but every one of them looked forward keenly to seeing him do it.

6

"Where you come from?" the tall, slender, razor-voiced official inquired.

The silvery metallic eyes of the K'eremu gazed out at the assembled, seated governmental elite of Kojn-umm. Like most uncivilized beings, they chose to gather together to eat. Well, she could do nothing about that. Any more than she could do anything about the mortifying circumstances in which she presently found herself. Thrown together with a primitive if well-meaning biped, his smaller and slightly more developed shaggy companion, and a monstrous contradiction of a representative of another unknown world who was given to speaking in morose poeticisms, she was forced to rely on them for help in getting home. There being some doubt that even someone as gifted as herself would be able to accomplish that feat on her own, she had resigned herself to an inescapable sequence of successive demeanings—such as the one she was being compelled to suffer presently.

As the simple but earnest human Walker had warned her, "Please, please, try and be polite to these people tonight, Sque. We've got to have their help if we're going to get any closer to home than Niyu."

So she adjusted her own flashy accoutrements, eyed the lean, exceedingly lavishly dressed male Niyyuu, and replied, "My world, whose comforting clouds and dampness and isolation I long for more and more each day, is called K'erem." Two tendrils rose. "It lies some distance farther out in the swarm of stars that is, hopefully, this galactic arm. My companions and I have come to Niyu in the hope that it has brought us nearer K'erem and their own homeworlds. Whether that is the case we do not yet know. In the meantime, we are reliant upon your good nature and hospitality, twin traits that are the hallmark of the most basic civilization."

It was a longer reply than the questioner had expected, but it appeared to satisfy him. The other eminent Niyyuu in the room seemed equally content with the K'eremu's response, though one or two bridled slightly at the implication their civilization might somehow be classified as "basic."

Still, Walker decided as he and his Niyyuuan assistants continued to prepare the equipment and ingredients for his effort, for Sque the reply could be counted as exceedingly diplomatic. He tensed slightly when he heard someone among the assembled follow the first question with, "I was told you supposedly very smart species. Do something to impress us with you intelligence."

A silence followed. George muttered, "Uh-oh—I'd better get out there and start charming the locals," and rushed out to mix with the crowd of Niyyuuan notables. Off to one side, Braouk prepared to lumber forward and launch into his chosen recitation for the evening, a personally abridged version of *The Heroic Narrative of Darak-Dun the Third* and how he crossed the Jaquarianak Range alone in the dead of winter, over which the Tuuqalian had been laboring for the past several days.

But despite his efforts, he wasn't fast enough to override Sque's reply.

"Certainly." The K'eremu shifted her tendrils. "I will now discourse to you upon the relative differences in cognitive aptitude between your species and mine."

Omigod, Walker shouted silently. He was preparing to instruct Braouk to physically remove Sque from her location in front of the assembled when the K'eremu began to speak. Listening to her, some of the tension eased out of him.

"It should be clear to even the most casual observer that the tripartite conflation of neuronic axes relate oblately to the peripheral adjudication of hierarchical logic functions in any discussion. We may therefore be safe in assuming that . . ."

Walker had to assume that his implanted translator was functioning properly. If that was the case, then the K'eremu's rambling reply ought to be equally incomprehensible to the attendant Niyyuu. Glancing surreptitiously out at the assembled, he was able, despite his unfamiliarity with local expressions, to deduce that this was indeed the case. Initially mystified by the K'eremu's response, they quickly returned to more mundane pursuits such as chatting among themselves and sampling the gastronomic treats whose creation Walker had supervised earlier with his staff. While "hors d'oeuvres" had no direct counterpart in the Niyyuuan lexicon, the notion of eating small bits of some food before the rest was straightforward enough.

Sque did not so much conclude her tortuous response as find herself shunted aside by the massive Braouk. Incomprehensibility shaded into uncomplicated recitation as the Tuuqalian launched into his half-spoken, half-sung version of yet another ancient fable of his people. Whatever half-perceivable insults the K'eremu might have delivered were subsumed in the giant's performance.

Upon concluding her own impenetrable discourse, Sque turned to amble past the still-stressed Walker. "That ought to put them in their place," she murmured contentedly. "It is a mark of their own intelligence that no objection was raised to my extensive stating of the obvious." A bubble of satisfaction emerged from the end of her speaking tube.

"Yes, you sure showed them," Walker assured her, forbearing from pointing out that even with the aid of their own translators it was likely that not one Niyyuu on the receiving end of the K'eremu's intricate dissertation had been able to understand more than a word or two of what she had said.

Then it was time for him to go to work. Time to justify the faith Viyv-pym had placed in him and to cement the presence of himself and his friends on this first stepping-stone toward home. As his Niyyuuan assistants moved swiftly to fine-tune equipment, he took a deep breath and stepped out into public view. Wide, penetrating eyes turned to look at him as Braouk concluded the last of his entertaining but interminable recitation with a wave of all four upper tentacles. Surely, Walker mused, this audience could not be any more difficult to please than the many he had entertained on more sophisticated Seremathenn. The proof, as always, would be in how they responded to the products of his labor.

Cooking, he had already decided, was harder than brokering commodities futures, but ultimately far more satisfying.

He needn't have worried. From the time he activated and took control of the stabilizers and manipulators, the previously talkative and occasionally downright rude audience followed his every move with rapt attention.

Who would not? Who would have expected the mass of carefully prepped vegetative and protein components to align themselves not with the cooking apparatus, but in the form of an advancing army, larger ingredients in the rear, smaller scattered to front and sides like so many edible scouts? Who would have expected the various heating and toasting and mixing devices to stack themselves not in a neat, traditional horizontal line, but vertically in the shape of a toy fortress? And with cookery and menu constituents thus confronting one another, like a kid playing with a box of toy soldiers, Walker began to bring them together.

Soulless but determined vegetables assaulted waiting preparation bins, and were consumed. Protein components flung themselves through the air, to be captured by waiting cylinders. Responding only to Walker's directions, the persevering provisions found themselves diced, sliced, toasted, flash fried, waved, sautéed, puréed, and flambéed. Disdaining decorum several minutes into the presentation, someone among the spectators blurted aloud.

"It the fortress! The alien is replaying the battle of Jalar-aadbiidh—with food!"

The swelling tide of verbal appreciation rang in Walker's ears as he fought to concentrate on the work at hand. Initially at a loss as to how to make the presentation of his gastronomic creations properly entertaining, he had hit on the idea of arranging his mobile cooking equipment in the shape of the ancient fortress that guarded the traditional northern approaches to Kojn-umm, and then "attacking" it with the ingredients he had chosen for the evening's meal. At least he no longer had to worry if anyone present would realize what he was doing. Thanks to one enthusiastic spectator, everyone was now aware.

The dark tempest that swept over and brought the edible performance to a dramatic close was the capper, the punch line, to his presentation. The fact that it was composed of a swirling, raging, miniature storm of carefully selected local spices provoked an outbreak of hooting—the Niyyuuan equivalent, he supposed, of wild applause.

Following the conclusion of his presentation, portions of the finished dishes were distributed by live Niyyuu attendants operating under Walker's instructions. He relaxed only when it became clear that the guests appreciated the taste of his food as much as they had its highly visual and dramatic preparation. There were compliments all around. And when the meal began to draw to a close, he found himself swept up in a whirl of dignitaries, all eager to thank him by stroking his head and upper body. The Niyyuu, he already knew, were a very touchy-feely folk. Fortunately, their complimentary and curious caresses weighed considerably less on his person than, say, Braouk's did, so he did not mind.

Viyv-pym also came up to him to praise his effort. Her golden eyes were even more luminous than usual, he decided. The single piece of material she wore draped her like chiffon that had been used to strain flecks of gold from a running stream. Yet again he had to remind himself that, superficial aesthetics notwithstanding, it was an alien body that stood before him.

"Tonight yous all justify my decision bring you Niyu." Touching the side of his face, the tips of the two long fingers of her right hand slid down to his shoulder, then his chest, before retracing their route and withdrawing. "Already this night I am commended many times for making that choice. Result is very good for me. Also very good for you." Frilled head twisting around on its long, slender neck, she indicated the knot of figures that had surrounded Kinuvu-dih-vrojj, the premier of Kojn-umm. Saluu-hir-lek, the general officer who had been in charge of the defense of Jalar-aad-biidh, was there as well. Insofar as Walker could interpret Niyyuuan expressions from a distance, those of the two important officials appeared animated and content.

Then he saw that they were looking downward instead of at one another, much less at him. Searching, Walker located the object of their delighted attention. Between them, a small shaggy dog was standing on its hind legs, dancing in a circle while pawing the air, tongue lolling.

George didn't need complex equipment or special skills to amuse and entertain, a knowing Walker reflected. Not that he minded. There were ample laurels to share this night. Abruptly, a number of insistent dinner guests crowded close around him, anxious to meet and converse with this alien master of gastronomy, and he lost sight of his small friend completely.

Off to one side, Braouk lowered a single tentacle and effortlessly lifted the much smaller Sque up to a level where she could see over the heads of the milling after-dinner crowd. The K'eremu inspected the contented throng with typical condescension.

"Look at them all. A supposedly advanced species making all this fuss over something as simple as a meal."

Braouk leaped to Walker's defense. "It not simple, great skill was involved, in preparation."

"Of a basal physical sort, yes, I suppose. Still, in the final analysis, the result was only nourishment. Our mutual bipedal friend brought forth a meal, not a small sun. However, I do expect his performance will increase our standing among our hosts. That is a certainly good thing, to be desired. Contrarily, it will also increase our standing among our hosts. That is not necessarily a good thing."

Braouk's eyestalks inclined toward the K'eremu, so that one globular orb hovered on either side of her. She was indifferent to the stereo stare. "You say the same thing twice but assign a different conclusion each time. I do not understand."

"Of course you don't," the K'eremu agreed unhelpfully. "In the course of our enforced cohabitation, I have learned that sub-

tle reflection is not a trait characteristic of your species. You are
not to be blamed for this, naturally."

A deep rumble rose from the depths of the massive Tuuqalian. "Am I to be blamed if I throw you against the opposite
wall?"

"I would stick," she responded, waving several tendrils. "To
elaborate on what I said: it is good that friend Walker's skills are
appreciated by our hosts. But I worry that he is perhaps too accomplished. It might be better if subsequent explorations into the
realm of Niyyuuan food preparation are less awe-inspiring, lest
he be declared a national treasure or some similar foolishness,
and denied the opportunity to leave."

"Ah. I understand now." Braouk's eyes shifted, literally, away
from the K'eremu he was supporting. Peering over the top of
the crowd, the Tuuqalian found the human. Walker was still surrounded by admiring Niyyuu. Surely the K'eremu was only being her usual pessimistic self. Surely the Niyyuu would not
become so attached to the human Walker's work that they
would refuse to let him go.

Did that matter? he found himself wondering. Suppose he
and Sque and the quadruped George were given the chance to
move on, nearer their homeworlds, but Walker was forced to remain behind? In such circumstances, what would he do? He
knew what Sque would do. Of George he was not so certain. He
was even less sure of himself. The resulting potential moral
dilemma pained his thoughts.

No reason for that, he told himself, since it did not yet exist.
Worry about it if and when it presented itself. Meanwhile, best
to participate in the evening, share in the contentment of their
hosts, and leave pessimistic brooding to the small skeptic with
the many limbs.

Yet as the days stretched into ten-days, and the ten-days into not
one but several multiples, the Tuuqalian found himself reflect-
ing more and more on what the anxious Sque had told him that
night.

It was not as if their time passed in misery or boredom. Just as
there had been on Seremathenn, there was much to see, do, and

learn on Niyu, albeit on a less overawing level of sophistication. But the longer they remained, and the more familiar they became with the sometimes seemingly contradictory but rarely dull culture of the Niyyuu, the further into the galactic distances the dream of returning to the fields and forests and cities of Tuuqalia seemed to recede.

One morning when feeling particularly lonely, he confronted the human directly with his concerns.

Walker was alone at his console, verbally organizing and arranging the components of a custom presentation that had been ordered by a private group centered in Ehbahr. The fact that, largely through his skill and expertise, he and his friends were no longer in any way reliant on the charity of the government of Kojn-umm was a source of considerable pride to him. George was sleeping nearby, curled up on a cushion. While it was not animate in the manner of the custom-made Seremathenn rug the dog had brought with him, its semiorganic contents did rise and fall as well as change temperature automatically according to the needs of his body. Eying the small quadruped, Braouk envied it. George needed very little to satisfy him.

Perhaps, the Tuuqalian thought, *if only I did not have, as do so many of my kind, the soul of an artist.* He could not deny, nor did he ever try to, that like many of his people he was inclined to melancholic brooding.

Nevertheless, despite his characteristic glumness, he did his best not to inflict it on the human, who, as Sque frequently pointed out, was subject to wildly vacillating and unpredictable bouts of emotion. Having something of value to contribute to their efforts to return home, Braouk had observed, had noticeably improved the human's disposition.

"I offer greetings, on this fine midday, my friend."

Walker nearly jumped out of the narrow Niyyuuan chair, whose rail-thin support he had improved by adding a wide cushion of his own design. "Dammit, Braouk! Do you have to sneak up on people like that?" He eased himself back onto his seat. "I'm always amazed that someone your size can move around with so little noise. I'm afraid you're going to amaze me once too often."

"Apologies." Eyestalks inclining down and forward, one orb peered over each of the human's shoulders. "How go the preparations for your next culinary extravaganza?"

"Pretty good. There are some new fresh fruits just arrived from Dmeruu-eeb, the realm that borders Kojn-umm to the south, and I'm thinking of doing something tropical and sunshiny with them."

Braouk was not certain precisely what the human's explanation signified, but it did not matter. His interest of the moment was not on food. "Marc, I am no less beholden to you for the merit your skills have gained for us among our hosts the Niyyuu than are George or Sque."

"You're welcome." Walker murmured the response without turning away from his intent study of images of food and equipment that floated in the air before him.

"But we have been here for some goodly time now, and we are no closer to continuing on our way homeward than when we arrived."

That made Walker turn away from his work. Behind him, images of foodstuffs and cooking gear hovered patiently in the air, awaiting his attention.

"That's not really true, Braouk." In their time together Walker had learned to focus on one Tuuqalian eye and ignore the other when they were being held far apart, as now. "We've secured the goodwill of our hosts and have successfully established ourselves in their society."

"Our goal though, I must remind you, is leaving. Our aim is to move onward from this place, not to set up a home meadow or become infatuated with the local culture."

Walker glanced to his left. George had raised his head from his pillow. "The hulk is right, Marc. I've been thinking the same thing: that we're getting a little too comfortable here. Maybe that's just what our good friends the Niyyuu want." The dog's eyes narrowed. "Maybe you ought to spend a little more time looking for a way off this ball of dirt instead of drooling over the alien sylph you can't have anyway."

Walker stiffened. "I don't know what you're talking about, George."

The dog let his head flump back down on the cushion. "Uh-huh. And some of my best friends are cats that spray in my face."

Braouk's eyestalks moved uncertainly. "What is George talking about?"

"Nothing," Walker replied irritably. "He considers himself an expert on the behavior of everyone but himself."

"Speaking of butts—" the dog began. Walker cut him off.

"I'm doing all that I can, Braouk. Every time I meet with a government official I mention that we'd like to speak to some astronomics specialists. Appointments are being set up, but nothing's come of them yet. You know how the Niyyuu like their protocol."

"They like your cooking," George interjected curtly. "And they don't want to lose it."

Walker turned on his friend. "Come on, George. You're not implying that the government is deliberately keeping us from meeting with those people?"

The dog stood up on the cushion. His tail was not wagging. "You're right. I'm not implying it. I'm stating it. Think about it, Marc. We've been here how long? You and I and Braouk and Sque have initiated how many formal requests? What is there to keep local astronomics experts so busy? It's not like the stars and nebulae that form the basis of their usual study are going to take a hike any time soon."

Walker looked away, muttering, "I don't believe it. The Niyyuu aren't like that. They've been nothing if not helpful and courteous."

George's dog-logic was relentless. "Except when it comes to that one thing, that one particular request." He glanced up at the looming mass of the Tuuqalian. "What about you, Braouk? Don't you think it's funny that the one kind of Niyyuuan specialists we can't seem to make the acquaintance of are involved in astronomy?"

"It does seem odd." A massive tentacle gently nudged Walker, pushing him back only a step or two. "We are all reasoning beings here, Marcus Walker. Does this avoidance, of one scientific type, seem deliberate?"

"One way to find out." George growled softly at Walker. "Invite a whole slew of 'em to one of your special presentations. That'll put your alien she-lollipop and her friends on the spot. They can't claim *every* astronautics expert in this part of Niyu is swamped with work or out of the realm at the same time."

Walker considered. There was nothing wrong with the dog's idea. And it might settle the argument, one way or the other, once and for all.

"I'll do it." He sat back down at his console. "I'll put the request to Abrid-lon personally."

George was initially subdued when that official readily agreed to Walker's request to organize such a meal. The dog further had to eat his words when, one ten-day later, the event actually took place. Prepared for the main scientific society of all Kojnumm, the event was not overlooked by the avaricious local media, so there could be no claim that researchers and workers in specific specialties failed to be made aware of it.

Among the delighted attendees were more than a dozen specialists in the fields of general astronomy and astronautics. The latter included officers of Niyyuuan starships, prominent among whom were the commander and assistant commander of the very ship that had brought Walker and his friends to Niyu from Seremathenn. Certainly those in attendance were reflective of those Niyyuu with the most wide-ranging knowledge of this corner of the galaxy.

But as George wandered casually through the attentive, seated group of scientists and researchers—Sque being deemed too acerbic and Braouk too intimidating to assure suitably uninhibited responses—he was met by one denial or evasion after another.

"Nobody knows nothing—or will admit to it." The dog's disappointment as he reported to his companions following the conclusion of the performance and meal was plain to see.

"Are you certain you put forth the queries properly?" The continuous movement of Sque's tendrils revealed her agitation.

George eyed her sharply. "I asked them as we rehearsed them. 'Have you ever had contact with any of the following worlds?'

I'd say, and then name each of ours in turn. The response was always negative. 'Have you ever had contact with anyone else, of any intelligent species, that might possibly have had contact with any of the three worlds in question?' Same reaction. 'Prior to this evening, have any of you ever encountered *representatives* of any sentient species matching our descriptions, or encountered others who might have done so?' More of the same. None of them, or at least none of those present here tonight, have ever heard of humans and their Earth, Tuuqalians and their world, K'eremu and K'erem." He shifted his feet, his tail moving slowly.

"I asked if there might be other, more knowledgeable astronomers or galactic travelers elsewhere on Niyu who might be better informed on such matters. I was told that while the independent realms of Niyu engage in healthy intergovernmental conflict where matters of culture and commerce are concerned, when it comes to dealing with the rest of galactic civilization they act as one. Furthermore, science is as advanced here in Kojn-umm as anywhere on Niyu, as evidenced by the expedition to Seremathenn that brought us here."

"A reasonable assertion," the thoughtful Sque declared somberly, "that in lieu of further evidence I see no reason to dispute."

The dog moved closer to the K'eremu—close enough to reach out with a paw and touch the slightly swelling, slick maroon skin. "That's not what disturbs me, though. It was the lack of curiosity." Backing off, he eyed his three companions meaningfully. "You'd think that a bunch of supposedly inquisitive scientific types would be more than casually interested in four previously unencountered intelligences claiming to hail from three utterly unknown worlds. But whenever I found a chance to push the matter with an individual, every one of them without exception seemed more interested in changing the subject, or talking about Marc's food presentation, or the latest fighting at Jalar-aad-biidh, than in wondering about what part of the galactic arm we might have sprung from." He cocked his head slightly to one side. "Strikes me as mighty peculiar."

"Most assuredly unscientific in spirit," an intrigued Sque

readily agreed. "As if those to whom you spoke sought to deliberately avoid pursuing the subject."

Braouk was openly bewildered. "But why avoid, a subject of interest, to all?"

"Maybe," George suggested, squinting beneath shaggy brows, "because they were told to."

The Tuuqalian's bemusement only deepened. Both eyes, which together were nearly as large as George himself, inclined downward on their stalks to regard the dog. "Are you suggesting, that such avowed ignorance, was deliberate?"

"All I'm saying," George responded as he turned to leave, "is that for a bunch of sentients whose business it is to ask questions in the pursuit of the furtherance of knowledge, they were a mighty closemouthed bunch."

"Why wouldn't they be interested in trying to find out where we all come from?" Walker wondered aloud.

"Maybe," George added over a shoulder as he trotted away, "because someone is worried that if we find that out, we'll want to go back there."

The three companions were left to stare at the dog's metronomic tail until it vanished out of sight around a corner. It was silent for a long minute before Walker finally spoke up.

"Surely," he murmured uneasily, "I'm not *that* good a cook."

"Novelties," Sque muttered through her slender, weaving speaking tube. "We are all of us novelties." Steel-gray eyes regarded him expressively. "Possessed of no intrinsic value, such as precious metals or gems, a novelty's worth is determined solely by those for whom it has applied value. It may be that your small smelly friend demonstrates true insight. Certainly it cannot be denied that our constant requests have been met with apathy, if not outright unconcern. Tonight's continuance of that condition suggests nothing less than a deliberate policy."

Walker shook his head slowly. "I can't believe that the Niyyuu intend to keep us from leaving here."

"Nothing is preventing us from leaving here," Sque pointed out as she too turned to retire to her own quarters. "There is simply no help forthcoming in assisting us in determining which way to go when we do leave. And without direction, there is no point in going. One might as well spin on one's appendages until dizzy and scuttle off in any random direction. In deep space, that would be suicidal. The withholding of information is not the same as the withholding of a physicality, but the result is the same."

The departure of the K'eremu left Walker alone with Braouk. After a moment the Tuuqalian too moved to withdraw to his chamber. "It's worth thinking, about what's been said, here tonight. Indifference is not hostility—but not friendship, either."

"What can we do about it?" Walker wondered aloud as he watched the massive Tuuqalian shuffle off toward the exit.

Both eyes curled back on their stalks to look at him. "Why not ask your good friend Viyv-pym?"

Was there a hidden suggestiveness in the Tuuqalian's question? Nonsense, Walker told himself. It was a good idea. The only trouble was, he had on more than one occasion pressed Viyv-pym about the lack of response to their requests, only to receive evasive, noncommittal answers similar to those received by George tonight. That in itself was suggestive.

And not at all reassuring.

"A fraction of you evening-time, might I have?"

His companions having departed, Walker had remained behind to check and ensure that the last of the equipment that had been cleaned by his assistants had been properly deactivated for storage. Thinking himself alone in the empty Niyyuuan durbar hall, he was surprised to find himself confronting a single female.

She was notably shorter than the average Niyyuuan; no taller than himself, and for one of her kind, verging on stout. Her crest was fully erected and flaring a dark blue—taken together with the constant fluttering of her tails, a sure sign of anxiety. In attire she was, again by Niyyuuan standards, conservative, her body wrap consisting of a single yellow- and white-striped satiny material. But her eyes, like those of all Niyyuu, were large and luminous as those of any lemur, and her voice as raspy as that of a lathe shaping wrought iron.

"I am Sobj-oes. I am senior instructor in distant astronautics and vector navigation not only for Kojn-umm, but a consultant for four other realms as well." A two-fingered hand moved to touch his shoulder. By now wholly familiar with the intimate form of greeting, he did not flinch.

"You enjoyed the presentation, I take it?" he asked her, not knowing what else to say.

"Very much so's." She looked around, high, limber ears working. They were alone. "Yous wish go home."

Keeping his voice level, he tried not to look or sound anxious, even assuming she could recognize the meaning of such subtle changes in tone or personal appearance. "That would be a valid assumption, as my friend Sequi'aranaqua'na'senemu would say. But in order to continue our journey from here, from Niyu, we need the assistance of others. To help point the way. Others such as, perhaps, yourself."

Her free hand made a gesture he recognized as an encouraging response. "Yous sentient creatures, not all so very different from Niyyuu. Appearance means nothing." The two fingers of her left hand gently stroked the side of her elongated skull. "What is here is everything.

"I am one of those who was made aware of yous' request, to try locate your homeworlds. This is very difficult business. Even one arm of galaxy is immensity personified. Thousands upon thousands of star systems."

"Astronautics are developed on all of our worlds, so my friends and I are aware of that. All we have is hope, and that others might help. That's all we've been asking of the government of Kojn-umm, and the worldwide organizations that link the Niyyuu together on matters such as science. To date, we have had no response."

Once more his visitor glanced around. With her expansive oculars, it did not require her to turn her head very far to do so. "Yous' query *was* passed along. But with accompanying admonition."

Walker frowned. "What sort of admonition?"

"To conduct search for yous' homeworlds, in line with yous' request. But not to displace other work to do so, also not to make priority."

"I see." He considered carefully. From his years in the business of commodities trading, Walker was intimately familiar with the subtleties of bureaucratic obfuscation—with the ability to seem to say one thing while really meaning another. "Would you say that your 'admonition' might be interpreted to mean an order to go slow in the search for the homeworlds of my friends and I?"

Her right hand lightly touched his chest. "Many interpretations of meaning are possible. That could be one."

"But why?"

She looked away, embarrassed without having any reason to be. "Yous four all unique individuals. No others like you on Niyu, ever. No others like you on Seremathenn, or anywhere else scientific establishment can determine. Your presence here a special thing for Niyu. Extra special for Kojn-umm. Pride involved. Pride and logic frequently mutually exclusive occurrences. Besides, you extraordinary food preparator."

He nodded slowly, murmuring to himself, "So George was right. The authorities want to keep us here."

"Not necessarily prevent from leaving," she corrected him. "More akin to not be overly helpful in assisting departure. Difference is political."

"But the result is the same," he muttered. "If the government won't help us, then we're stuck here."

"Not government, no." Her voice softened from the intensely grating to the merely irritating. "Are one or two sympathetic individuals among my colleagues. Must be careful in such work. All afraid, if displease superiors, of losing official position. Few willing take such risking on behalf of strange aliens."

He lowered his own voice. "But you will," he guessed expectantly.

Another gesture he recognized—this one signifying accord. "Is also one other. Famous researcher, much revered by public as well as colleagues. But not untouchable. Must work clandestine, he and I. Have taken what information on yous has been made available by government. In free time, away from official projects, are searching the vastness for transmission samplings of all yous: visuals, language snippets, references by other species not yous but knowing of yous. Maybe, with much lucks, come across something." She eyed him questioningly. "You can suggest preference in area for searching?"

He mulled her query. His companions had long since departed for their own quarters. Alone with the astronomer, it would have been easy for him to instruct her and her distinguished colleague to limit their searching for signs of human life only, to look first for Earth. The sarcastic Sque and the lumbering Braouk could wait their turn.

But what if K'erem or Tuuqalia lay nearby, within easier detection range of Niyyuuan instruments? Could he deny that access, that chance, to people who had gone through the hell of Vilenjji capture and captivity with him? And they were his friends, even if one had a mouth that sometimes seemed bigger than her whole body and the other tended to bore to distraction when he wasn't threatening to accidentally crush anything and anyone who happened to come too close to him. As for George, he knew what the dog would say.

But it wasn't what he chose to say.

"No. No preferences. Whichever of our respective homeworlds whose position you can establish, that will be great. K'erem, Tuuqalia, Earth: locate one and we'll manage a way to get there. Then we'll worry about finding the others."

She indicated her understanding. "I hope we can help yous. Is not right be kept so long and so far from one's own kind when that gap can be spanned. Of course, certain is, the very good chance in attempting search such an immense area that we will not be able locate any of yous' homeworlds."

Extending a hand and keeping his touch as light as possible, he let it stroke her right shoulder in the accepted Niyyuuan manner. "It's enough that someone is trying to help. That you're looking."

She gestured one last time before turning to go. "Niyu not such a bad place. Maybe not Seremathenn, but good air, good food, good people. If search never find anything, yous always have respected life-positions here. Meantimes, keep cheerful." Lengthening her flowing stride, she left him standing among his equipment, watching her distinctive slight sway as she exited the room.

She was right. Despite the constant undercurrent of devious political and cultural machinations, Niyu offered him and his friends a comfortable life and lifestyle.

But no matter how one sliced it, it was a long, long way from Chicago.

7

He was not aware of any outward change in his mood or appearance subsequent to his clandestine meeting with the kindhearted astronomer, but evidently something about either or both struck Viyv-pym forcefully enough to comment on it. It was several ten-days after his surreptitious encounter. Viyv-pym was meeting with him in his quarters to discuss the final details of an elaborate banquet that was being prepared for an interrealm guild of computation engineers, at which his performance was to be the star attraction.

Bending her head slightly to avoid the assembling components that drifted in the air before them both, she tried to meet his gaze. "Something troubles you, friend Marc. It not new. I have been noticing for some time now. Will you not share with me?"

So preoccupied and depressed was he at the moment that her proximity failed to stir within him the usual basket of confused emotions he always felt in her presence. "It's nothing. Forget it." Sighing softly, he looked up at the integrants that patiently awaited his attention and did his best to feign interest in the proceedings. "Let's get back to work."

"No." Reaching out with a long, limber arm, she waved her hand through the hovering holos. They obediently dispersed.

Now he did turn to her. "What did you do that for? It's all saved, but now we'll have to reconstitute before we can finalize."

"Too much works you, maybe, I thinks. You need a change."

He could no longer look at her without wondering how deeply she was involved with or how much she was aware of her government's intention to keep him and his friends restricted to Niyu for as long as possible. He had become very adept at concealing such feelings.

"I'm open to a change," he replied indifferently. Work or a change, it was all the same to him. Both were relentlessly, inescapably Niyyuuan.

Ennui notwithstanding, the comment she offered in response did succeed in surprising him. "There many prominent Niyyuu who admire you work. Prominent among them is Saluu-hir-lek."

Walker shrugged carelessly. "Don't recognize the name." Other than those Niyyuu he worked with, such as Viyv-pym and his own performance assistants, he had not paid much attention to individuals among their hosts. He had met too many to remember them all.

"He attend you first important recital. Saluu-hir-lek is traditional military commander for Kojn-umm, defender of the realm, leader of conventional defense of Jalar-aad-biidh."

"Very nice for him. What has it to do with me?"

"He wants meet you." She was watching him closely, he saw.

"I'm happy to meet with any Niyyuu who appreciates my work," he replied expansively. "When would he like to get together?"

She didn't hesitate. "Tomorrow would work well. I am told is at that time likely to be lull in fighting."

"Tomorrow's fine. Mind if I invite my friends along?"

"They not specifically included in invitation, but should be not problem, I think. I will make certain beforehand. You have experience in combat?"

Whup. Evidently he had missed something. Something important. She now had his full attention. "What has that got to do with me meeting this guy?"

"Battle for fortress of Jalar-aad-biidh is ongoing. Saluu-hir-lek cannot relinquish command merely to facilitate friendly visit. Therefore meeting must take place in fortress. Reaching fortress means crossing line of technological demarcation. Once cross line, any normal Niyyuu is subsumed in rules of traditional combat. Can be captured or killed." Seeing his alarm, she hastened to reassure him.

"Line crossing will take place under proper escort, timed for least likelihood of combat. But when making crossing, must always go prepared. Settle you fears. I will watch over you."

He bridled instinctively at the offer. As an ex All Big Ten linebacker, no member of the opposite sex, alien or not, was going to "watch over him." At the same time, he was perfectly aware as the testosterone fizzed within him that he was being stupid, that his present circumstances hardly merited comparison with accomplishments on a football field back home. That did not render the implications inherent in her thoughtful offer any less potent.

"As a matter of fact," he shot back, "I do have some experience in hand-to-hand combat, though probably not the kind you're thinking of."

"I pleased hear this. You will be equipped with authorized weaponry." She studied his build, which was far stockier than that of the stoutest Niyyuu. "Armor may be a problem. Perhaps by linking several pieces together . . ." She broke off. "Not to worry. It will be managed."

"Won't matter," he told her, "with Braouk accompanying us."

But it developed that Braouk was not interested in accompanying them.

"I say firmly, no interest have I, in fighting," the Tuuqalian replied when Walker explained the situation to him that night.

"It's highly unlikely you'll have to." Pacing the dining area, unable to eat, Walker worked to cajole the big alien. "The sight of you in armor alone ought to be enough to send even the most intrepid Niyyuu fleeing. Hell, it even makes *me* quake a little, and you're my friend."

Avoiding Walker's gaze, both eyes hovered close together above the Tuuqalian's massive plate of food, their stalks nearly touching. "But if they did not flee, I would have to defend myself. You know what, my temper can be, once roused. I do not want to get involved in the interregional disputes of our hosts, and I most certainly do not want to hurt anybody. I'm not going with you, Marc."

"Fine. Stay here, then." He turned to Sque.

The K'eremu had swollen to half again her normal size, and her flexible, tubular mouth was emitting bubbles like crazy. This uncontrolled laughter was sufficient to prevent Walker from even asking her if she would be willing to accompany him. Thinking he already knew the answer to his final appeal but nonetheless feeling compelled to make it, he turned to George, only to be surprised yet again by another of the dog's unpredictable responses.

"Sure, I'll go up with you," his small friend declared around mouthfuls of food. "Be a chance to see something new. If there's an attack on the place while we're up there, it ought to be quite a show."

Walker hardly knew what to say. "I thought you, of all people, wouldn't want to get involved in any fighting."

The dog looked up from his meal. "Who said anything about getting involved in fighting? If your whippet of a girlfriend—"

"She's *not* my girlfriend," Walker snapped irritably.

"—says they're going to try their best to sneak us in, then I think it's worth a shot. Besides, we'll be crossing part of a battlefield." He smiled, showing small but sharp canines. "There's likely to be bones."

"The Niyyuu might not take kindly to the thought of an alien visitor nibbling on the remains of their kind."

Lips pulled back, the smile remained. "I hope I get the chance to find out." Sticking his face back into the server before him, he returned to his feeding.

Both Sque's laughter and body swelling having settled down, the K'eremu eyed her human companion shrewdly. "I know you too well by now, Marcus Walker. You have not accepted this invitation out of a desire simply to play tourist. Especially not with a chance of real danger, however minimized, involved. You have another rationale in mind."

He turned defensive. "Maybe."

She waved a pair of tendrils at him. "Would you care to share it with us poor unenlightened ones?"

"I'm still considering possibilities," he told her honestly. He took a deep breath. "It just occurred to me that since we're not

making any headway in our efforts to engage the Niyyuuan scientific community in our efforts to progress homeward, it might
prove useful to make a friend or two among the military."

"Planning to lead a revolt and take over the pound?" George
challenged him.

"I don't believe the Niyyuu think like that," Walker replied.

"How do they think about such things, then?" Sque inquired
thoughtfully.

Round brown eyes locked with silvery horizontal orbs. "That's
one of the things I'm going to try and find out," he told her.

The transport that conveyed them through the bustling, modern,
smoothly running city and up into the foothills of the surrounding mountain range stopped well short of the line of demarcation.

"From here we walk," Viyv-pym informed Walker and
George. "As you been informed, only minor contemporary
technology is allowed inside areas designated for traditional
combat. Not even communicators. Communication from within
is carried out by courier, in old-time manner."

What a polite method of killing one another these people
have devised, Walker reflected as he exited the transport. Em-
ploying strictly defined rules and limitations, slaughter and
slaying could be conducted enthusiastically, with every individual and government firmly bound by the results. Certainly it was
a better way than reducing entire territories to ruin and whole
populaces to penury. Pity it would never work for humankind.

As George trotted to and fro, sniffing hopefully at the
corkscrewing ground cover and bizarrely shaped bushes that
clung to the slight slope, Walker decided that their hostess
looked even better in sword and armor than she did in her usual
daily administrative attire. Tinted a dark golden hue, almost
bronze, the armor covered her in linked engraved piecework
from neck to feet. Her helmet sported holes to allow her tall ears
to protrude easily and a ruler-sized slab to protect the flattened,
narrow nasal crest while leaving the rest of her face and her
enormous eyes free to scan her surroundings in as many unob-
structed directions as possible.

For the ascent, they were accompanied by half a dozen similarly clad soldiers. Though all were well trained in the use of modern wave and projectile weapons, inside the restricted zone none carried anything more lethal than a rapier or throwing blade. A couple hefted loaded weapons that resembled small crossbows. In deference to the Niyyuuan's slender builds, none of the devices weighed very much.

Despite Viyv-pym's earlier assurances, it developed that none of the armor available could be made to fit Walker. He was three times as broad across the chest as the stoutest Niyyuu, and fifty pounds heavier. The "heavy broadsword" they gave him would have been hard-pressed to qualify back home as a saber in a fencing competition. Which did not matter, since what little he knew about swords, fencing, and armor was derived entirely from watching old movies on television. He could only hope that in the event of actual conflict, his natural athleticism would carry him through.

"Should not be any trouble," Viyv-pym reassured him as she adjusted her shoulder braces. "We make access from south. Toroud-eed prefer frontal attack on fortress, also careful to watch access road from west to prevent reinforcements from relieving Jalar-aad-biidh garrison. East and south are open. And forest here will provide cover."

Nodding, he followed her as the small contingent continued to climb.

He was not certain exactly when or where they crossed the line of demarcation. Only that while he struggled uphill, George was having entirely too good a time, dashing from each new growth to the next fresh smell. Walker had always done well in the sprints—but long runs defeated him. And he had never been required to run wind sprints uphill. In college, running the stadium seats was an activity that had thankfully been reserved for backs and receivers, safeties and corners.

Evening was settling in damply around them when the first soldier died. The bolt, or short arrow, caught him in the throat, in the vulnerable opening above the chest armor and below his helmet. Shouts erupted all around Walker as the air was filled with alien exclamations unimaginably harsh in tone. Giving loud and threatening lie to Viyv-pym's earlier assurances, armed Niyyuu burst from the cover of the stunted trees on both sides of the ascending party. The attackers wielded an amazing assortment of weapons, from blades that curled back upon themselves to almost form circles, to pikelike devices that terminated in barbed tips seemingly more suited to catching fish than hand-to-hand combat. They were designed, he realized quickly, for successfully striking at quarry that was nimble and fast but not especially muscular. Though tall, the ultraslim Niyyuu made difficult targets for thrusting spears and swords.

He had just enough time to also note that the attackers' armor was steel-gray instead of golden-bronze before he found himself wildly swinging his own sword in an attempt to ward off a pair of onrushing assailants.

His ferocious but histrionic swings did nothing to slow the attack, but his appearance certainly did. Expecting to confront only others of their kind, the two hard-charging Toroud-eed warriors pulled up short, clearly taken aback at the unexpectedly alien aspect of their intended target. Assailants and quarry stared at one another. One of the Toroud-eed finally took a hesitant step toward the unwieldy apparition, who after all was holding a Kojn-umm sword. A moment later his companion let out a startled yelp and turned to see a small furry alien quadruped hanging by its jaws onto his lower right leg.

A bewildering confrontation with one alien being was unsettling enough. Finding themselves attacked from the rear by a second completely different in size, shape, and appearance from the first, whose teeth for all they knew might contain enough poison to kill a dozen soldiers, the pair turned and fled as fast as their long, lean legs could carry them. Taking note of their retreat, George relaxed his grip, shook his head, spat, and trotted back to rejoin his friend. Sword dangling from one hand, a stunned Walker gaped down at him.

"I didn't know if those two were going to . . . Thanks, George. You made up their minds for them."

The dog looked around warily. Though they were standing off from where most of the fighting was taking place, he was not about to let down his guard. He'd been ambushed and attacked in too many alleys, on too many back city streets, to relax while combat raged around him.

"Too bad Braouk isn't here," he growled conversationally. "If those two were spooked by the sight of you, the appearance of our Tuuqalian friend would probably have dropped them in their tracks." He looked up, tail wagging. "You okay?" His breathing steadying, Walker nodded slowly.

"Good. Hate to lose my human." He indicated the small-scale but intense battle that was playing out nearby. "Our friends the Niyyuu don't look so civilized right now, do they?"

You'd think an individual on the verge of having their throat cut or their torso run through by a sword would break with tradition and pull out a gun, even a small gun, if only to save their own life, Walker mused as he watched the fighting. But nothing of the sort happened. Despite the ready presence of advanced weapons in the city and on the ship that had brought him and his companions from Seremathenn to Niyu, not one of the combatants raging through the forest produced so much as a canister of pepper spray in their own desperate defense.

The Kojn-umm did not kill all of the attackers, but they slew or disabled enough of them to compel the survivors to beat a frustrated retreat. A moment later Viyv-pym was at his side, the two fingers of her left hand wrapping around his arm, urging him upward.

"Quickly now, friend Marc! Those who took flight may have others station nearby. Surprise at yous' presence will not stop them kill or capture you if they come back."

Badly winded, he was immensely grateful to discover that they were not all that far from the top of the ridge. The forest had hidden the inward-sloping outer walls of Jalar-aad-biidh from the climbers' sight. Moments later, anxious Kojn-umm fighters from within the fortress were escorting the survivors of the ambush into the safety of the sturdy ramparts.

Though exhausted, Walker had suffered damage only to his pride. Stunned by the swiftness of the unexpected attack, after the first confusing moments he had pretty much stood by while Viyv-pym and her comrades had fought off the assault. Safe and secure now, he had time to reflect more systematically on the events that had taken place and on his reaction to them. Or rather, his nonreaction. Though Viyv-pym and her comrades had expected nothing of him, he peered inward and found himself wanting. Hell, even George had drawn blood.

When he offered apologies for his lack of assistance, neither Viyv-pym nor any of her fellow soldiers appeared upset at his lack of participation. "After all," she told him without a hint of insincerity, "it our job protect you, not other way around. You not trained in our ways of fighting." She caressed his arm. "You cook."

It was the most hurtful thing anyone had said to him since the day he had been abducted by the Vilenjji.

He determined then and there to rectify at the first opportunity his ignorance of swordsmanship and Niyyuuan military training. Such schooling would have to come later, he knew. He had not been escorted to Jalar-aad-biidh to learn swordplay. Also, his own private reason for agreeing to make the dangerous visit in the first place came back to him. He had not made the trip to learn better how to survive on Niyu, but to seek possible assistance in getting off it.

While Walker's escort exchanged excited banter with the defenders of the fortress who had swarmed out to greet them, Viyv-pym escorted him and George deeper into the complex. Though constructed of humble native stone and other simple, natural materials, the rock walls appeared solid and inviolate. As far as he could tell, they did not make use of steel rebars or any high-tech galactic-standard reinforcing materials. To have done so would have constituted a violation of accepted Niyyuu standards for traditional combat, which extended to the construction and maintenance of physical defenses as well as individual weaponry.

"A bit more excitement than I thought we would see." Striding fluidly alongside him, her armor scratched and dented by the blows of the enemy, it was hard for Walker to see Viyv-pym as the same graceful, sophisticated governmental delegate he had first encountered at the elegant reception on Seremathenn. "I glad yous both unharmed."

"We's both glad, too," declared George genially as he trotted along beside Walker. "I only like to play at being dead, thanks."

Negotiating the twists and turns of the inner fortress, it was hard to believe that just outside and beyond the ridgetop redoubt lay a sprawling modern city steeped in technology sufficiently advanced to make any place on Earth look like a mud-wattle village in comparison. The dissimilarity was startling, but not absolute. The inhabitants of the fortress did not stumble about in rags and primitive attire, and the prohibition against the use of modern technology apparently extended only to those elements that could be utilized in warfare. There was ample evidence that modern methods of dealing with hygiene were in use, while the media broadcasters who relayed scenes of the fighting around the planet did so with all the advanced gear that could be put at their disposal. Walker queried Viyv-pym on the latter seeming inconsistency.

"What's to prevent one of these reporters," he asked as a pair of them, draped in the electronic elements of their profession, strode past, "from relaying on-the-spot information to a local commander in the field?"

"Is true such temptation is great," Viyv-pym admitted. "Especially when one side losing badly. But detection not difficult. If what you say attempted and found out, penalties are very severe. Individuals involved sacrifice their position and never find such work again. Are banned for life from such work anywhere on all of Niyu. Also, big communications company responsible lose its right to broadcast all future conflicts. Ratings—" (yet again Walker found himself praising the efficacy of the Vilenjji implant, which could even convey the meaning of local colloquialisms) "—too important to big companies to risk breaking of regulations for temporary gain—even to save lives of soldiers. Everyone on Niyu follows and watches such conflicts. Much in politics is decided by these traditional battles, yet only volunteer military suffers injury. Rest of world goes about daily business in peace and security."

War as politics, and both as entertainment. Was it all so very dissimilar from home? he found himself wondering. Or were the basics the same and only the rules different? He envisioned an imaginary Niyyuuan newspaper, divided into the usual sections: World, Local, Business. The only question was, would you allot war its own section, or file it under Entertainment? Or, possibly, Sports? Perhaps the National Hockey League. Rome under the Caesars would have known how to handle and classify it.

He did not remember his previous meeting with General Saluu-hir-lek. During that first outrageous, frenetic night when he had performed for local luminaries, he had been introduced to a veritable blizzard of alien faces. George did not remember Kojn-umm's most prominent military personality either. The only faces the dog recalled were those he had been placed in close proximity to, during those moments when he had been picked up and cuddled by enchanted locals. Neither man nor dog knew what to expect.

As it turned out, neither the general nor the room into which they found themselves ushered matched their preconceptions. Despite the alienesque medieval surroundings, there was no throne, and certainly no throne room. Saluu-hir-lek operated out of an office that was quiet, unadorned, and businesslike. Charts and maps, all of them appropriately primitive and two-dimensional, filled the walls and covered several desks. None of the fortress commander's subordinates paused in their work when the trio was admitted, though a few did glance up to steal a quick look. Walker wondered if these were directed at him, George, or their striking female escort.

Rising from behind his desk, Saluu-hir-lek picked up the external translator he had ordered and made sure it was functioning. In response to Walker's question, Viyv-pym explained, "The device has no indigenous military application and is therefore permitted."

"Like flush toilets," George pointed out tactlessly.

Still fiddling with the device, though it was largely automatic, Saluu-hir-lek greeted them effusively, reserving particular acclaim for Walker.

"Ah, the famous small-ear food presenter!" The general glanced downward. "And his irrepressibly cuddly companion."

George made a rude noise that was not translatable. "It wonderful see you again. I am pleased to be yous guide and interpreter this aspect of Niyyuuan culture."

The general was much smaller than the average Niyyuu, Walker noted, though far from Napoleonic in stature. Alien and human regarded each other eye to eye. Other than being half a foot shorter than Viyv-pym or the other officers in the strategy room, and noticeably older, Saluu-hir-lek was little different in appearance from the majority of Niyyuu Walker and George had previously encountered. His uniform consisted of a simple brown tunic and the long, wide shoes favored by his kind. Only the three emblems heat-sealed to the center of his shirt indicated his rank. Whether this sartorial simplicity was a reflection of the individual himself or standard-issue attire for general officers Walker did not know.

"I great admirer of you work," the general was saying as Walker studied him. "Never seen such skill. But of course, you learn on Seremathenn." His voice took on the Niyyuuan equivalent of a bittersweet tone, the round mouth contracting. "Someday I like very much visit Seremathenn. But always duty to Kojn-umm calls. Whenever Toroud-eed or Faalaur-oor make trouble, responsible sources come deliver to me their insistence. 'Take command of forces, Saluu-hir-lek! Protect us from evil! Save us from attack!'" One twin-digited hand waved diffidently. "Protect commercial contracts, they mean. Traditional warring is for obtain business advantage, or water port, or favorable trade terms. I understand such local foolishnesses no longer apply on more advanced worlds."

"That's not always the case," Walker told him, thinking of Earth. "Sometimes a culture's technology far outpaces its social development." He indicated their surroundings. "I think the Niyyuu have made an interesting accommodation with their traditional way of settling disputes between neighbors."

"It is kind of you say so. Kind of you think such of Niyu, when you find yourself so far and so lost from your own world."

Sympathy from a general. Well, Walker would take it where he could get it. It boded well for his original rationale in agreeing to this visit. Idly, he wondered how much pull Saluu-hir-lek might wield in the same local corridors of power that wished to keep him and his friends resident on Niyu.

The general gestured toward the doorway through which they had just entered. "Would you like to see some more of fortress of Jalar-aad-biidh? It has served as gateway and protector of capital for many thousand-days."

Why not? Walker thought. "That would be very nice." Near his feet, George nodded assent. The dog was less interested in a tour of traditional alien military fortifications than he was in fresh air. The war room had no windows.

"Excellent!" Saluu-hir-lek moved to lead them. "There small battle for main gate going on right now. Hope is not inconveniencing for you."

Before Walker could raise question or objection, the general was showing them the way out the door, leaving neither time nor discreet opportunity for the human to object.

8

Bound together and launched by some unseen and unfamiliar alien mechanism, the three sharpened shafts spun around a central axis as they flew toward him—the spinning, barbed points clearly designed to do maximum damage to anyone they struck. Walker ducked behind shielding stone as they whizzed past to shatter themselves against the wall behind him in a spray of broken metal tips and splintered wooden shafts. All around him was shouting, screaming, and the "nails scraping on blackboards" Niyyuuan equivalent of bloodthirsty cries. Given the inherent raspiness of the native speaking voice, the latter made up in ear-grating harshness what they occasionally lacked in volume.

Huddled at the base of the stone rampart and Walker's feet, George glanced up sullenly. "So much for having a quiet meeting and making polite inquiries."

"Just stay down," Walker advised him. "You'll be fine."

"Sure. Unless the fortress is overrun. Then I'll be fine barbeque."

"What makes you think any local with any sense would try eating something as alien-looking as you?"

The dog turned his face to the wall. "I can't imagine why that thought doesn't make me feel completely secure. Incidentally, you might give it a tumble yourself."

It had not occurred to Walker that the assaulters of Jalar-aadbiidh might regard him as a fit subject for nibbling. As a newly skilled cook, he was not used to regarding himself as a potential cookee. While Saluu-hir-lek—displaying commendable, or foolish, disregard for his own personal safety—rallied his forces, Viyv-pym leaned against Walker to reassure him.

"That arthret that just miss you was an aberration, a lucky launching. See?" She tugged gently on his arm. Not wanting to appear fainthearted in her company, he allowed himself to be pulled forward for a better view.

The panorama spread out before him very much resembled paintings he had seen of ancient medieval battles. The participants were alien, their accoutrements foreign, and the design and layout of the fortress itself different in a number of aspects from what humans would have constructed, but hand-to-hand fighting was fairly similar regardless of body size, shape, and the number of digits on weapons-wielding hands.

He was struck once again by the slenderness of both the combatants and their weapons. The tall, slim Niyyuu swung or stabbed with spears, pikes, and narrow-bladed swords. There was nary a battle-axe or mace in sight. Absent the need to protect barrel-chested warriors, shields were similarly slim and lightweight. Unexpectedly, he almost laughed. In spite of the fact that blood was being spilled in copious quantity, assorted body parts were being carved from torsos, and individuals were dying, the crowded battlefield that spread out in front of the fortress's outer wall appeared populated by clashing armies of heavily armed, heavily armored, high-couture models. Despite the very real death and destruction, a part of him couldn't help thinking *Vogue/Cosmo* rather than *Soldier of Fortune*.

That somewhat risible image vanished instantly when a sling-boosted short spear went right through the neck of a bolt-firing Kojn-umm soldier standing atop an elevated platform off to Walker's left. Dropping her weapon, the female warrior grabbed reflexively at the protruding shaft of the lance as she toppled over and plunged into the swirling throng of fighters below. No more laughter bubbled up in Walker's throat.

Saluu-hir-lek remained in the thick of the fighting: ranging back and forth along the wall, urging on his soldiers, altering defensive strategy in response to shifts in the enemy's plan of attack, shouting commands, all the while doing serious damage with his own sword. Walker could see why the general was lionized by Kojn-umm society. Whether it was tactically wise for him to place himself in such danger was not a matter for visitors to question. Walker hoped the general would survive the battle. While other Niyyuu had been of little help to him and his friends in their quest to get home, dead ones would be of no use whatsoever.

Bobbing up and down in the midst of the ferocious skirmishing like so many electronic imps were representatives of the media from both Kojn-umm and Toroud-eed. They were easily recognizable by their bright orange attire and the fact that they wielded recording and broadcasting equipment, not armor and weapons. Amazingly, they moved with ease among the combatants, who largely ignored their presence.

Walker pointed out the nearest. "Surely the media must suffer the occasional casualty. A stray spear, or short bolt?"

Today painted half blue and half crimson, Viyv-pym's mouth expanded as if she was simultaneously shocked and amused by the notion. "Only rarely. At such times, they become news themselves. No soldier wants injure correspondent. Is bad for career. Soldiers want be interviewed. Good for career. Injured correspondents cannot conduct interviews."

Made sense, Walker knew. A warrior, or an entire army, would not want to be on the receiving end of the unfavorable press the maiming or killing of a correspondent would bring. Mindful of the ramifications, he pressed her further.

"The battlefield reporting—is it honest? I mean, is it straightforward? No picking and choosing of scenes for propaganda purposes?"

"Oh, no," she insisted. "Citizens want, citizens need, to see everything. Good and the bad." She indicated another pair of orange-clad figures moving effortlessly among the combatants. "Communications facilities of Kojn-umm and Toroud-eed share field pickups of both sides. Also others present, reporting back to realms not involved in fighting."

Once again, the sports analogy reared its bloody head. Was there a special global media feed for all of Niyu? The round-the-clock, "all war all the time" channel? Sadly, he realized such an innovation was also possible on Earth.

The fighting was beginning to wind down. "What happens if the Toroudians win? If they were to overrun and take the fortress?" Given what he had already learned about the conventions of Niyyuuan combat, somehow he did not think such a result would end in widespread rapine and looting.

He was right. "Since Jalar-aad-biidh defends capital city," she told him, "Kojn-umm would have to formally surrender to Toroud-eed. In such unlikely happenstances, Kojn-umm would probably pay compensation—indemnity—to victors. Possibly also trade concessions. In extreme case, loss of territory."

"What about a triumphant Toroud-eed taking over your realm completely?"

"It happens, but such a thing is rare in our history." Watching her watching the fighting, Walker could sense that she would rather have been down on the battlefield swinging a sword instead of watching from the comparative safety of the high battlements nursemaiding an alien chef and his small companion.

The latter looked up from where he had squeezed himself into as small and protected a place as possible. "What's to keep a few realms from taking over everybody else and controlling the whole planet?"

Viyv-pym peered down at the dog. "If one realm get too big, too powerful, is inevitably attacked by allied forces of many others and so reduced in size and strength." She spoke with considerable conviction, Walker noted. "That also happens—and is also rare in our history." One long, willowy arm rose to point over the wall. "Not happen here, this day. See!"

The campaign was beginning to slacken as the forces of Toroud-eed, fought to a stalemate if not actually defeated, began to retreat. Their siege engines having failed to breach Jalar-aad-biidh's massive outer stone wall and their swarms of attacking soldiers having been repeatedly forced from its ramparts, they started to pull back. Given the ferocity of the fighting he had witnessed, Walker was surprised as he surveyed the field of battle that it was not littered more profusely with dead bodies. Perhaps, he decided, the Niyyuu cultural dichotomy of war allowed for the application of modern medicine to the wounded. He made a mental note to ask Viyv-pym about it later. Meanwhile, he fought to compose suitable congratulations for the general who was now striding toward them.

Saluu-hir-lek's armor was dented as if he had been run over by a large vehicle, and it was actually cut clear through at one leg. But the general himself appeared to be physically uninjured. His round mouth was expanded to its maximum diameter, while his huge eyes shone with an inner glow. Quadruple tails switched sharply back and forth, and blood stained him from head to toe.

"That should slow them, those effing offspring of Eed!"

Persuaded that the fighting was done with, George rose from where he had been lying. "You mean, they won't attack again?"

Saluu-hir-lek turned to peer over the ramparts and follow the attackers' retreat. "Too soon say for certain. Have better idea tomorrow, when scouts make morning report on enemy disposition. Disposition of forces, disposition of mind!" The general was in a very good mood indeed.

An excellent time, Walker felt, to hit him up for support.

"Come!" Lightly dragging a bloodstained finger down Walker's chest in friendly Niyyuuan fashion, Saluu-hir-lek bade his visitor accompany him. "I must clean up for presentation tonight. Then we talk more." From within the lightweight but sturdy helmet, vast yellow-gold eyes regarded the human. "Maybe I can persuade you cook for me and my staff."

"Kind of short notice, but it might be arranged," a thoughtful Walker told him. "When someone is in a position to provide a special service to a friend, it's always nice to be able to help out."

Any secondary meaning inherent in Walker's response flashed right past the general. Perhaps their respective translators had mangled the verbalization. But from what he had seen of Saluu-hir-lek, Walker was sure the general would remember it.

There wasn't much to work with. While the great fortress of Jalar-aad-biidh was amply stocked for war and for the fulfillment of the basic needs of its defenders, there was a decided

dearth of advanced, nonessential material. Even its commanding officer had limited access to luxury goods. Walker was relieved to discover that the food preparation equipment, like the
medical facilities, was apparently exempt from the cultural restrictions that were placed on any modern technology related to
combat requirements.

In concise terms, what that meant was that he had the apparatus with which to exercise his gastronomic skills. Though raw
material was lacking, he took its absence as a challenge. The
eventual results showed off his innate creativity and talent in
ways that swapping raw rubber futures on the Chicago Exchange could not have come close to duplicating.

Certainly Saluu-hir-lek and his staff were more than pleased,
if not outright overwhelmed. Following the dramatic culinary
presentation and the expansive meal that was its outcome, the
general once again invited George and Walker outside. This
time they found themselves higher up than before. To the right,
the private balcony overlooked the distant, rambling metropolis
of Ehbahr, Kojn-umm's wholly contemporary capital city.
Straight ahead, a gradually descending slope glittered with
splotches of illumination that marked the location of the
bivouac of Toroud-eed's troops.

"Wonderful meal, simply wonderful!" the general declaimed
to the cool, indifferent night. His round mouth was contracted,
sphincterlike, around a transparent tube that dispensed measured quantities of tartly flavored alkaloids. While the slowly
dissolving powder produced a pleasant taste and mild rush in
the Niyyuu, it would have wreaked serious havoc on Walker's
more sensitive digestive system. He had long since learned
which local molecular combinations he and George could tolerate and which, harmless though they might be to the natives,
man and dog should at all costs avoid. These personal limitations did not hinder his practice of performance gastronomy.

"Glad you enjoyed it." Resting both arms on the high, solid-
metal barrier, he let his gaze wander over the ranked lights
below. At a distance, they reminded him of so many stars fallen
to Earth. Silent soldiers patrolled the walls of the fortress, alert
for any inimical nocturnal intrusion. Music, nearly as harsh as

Niyyuuan speech, scratched and clawed its way up from the ancient courtyard below. The smaller of Niyu's two moons, irregular of shape but bright of albedo, hung high in the night sky.

"I hope you don't mind my saying," he continued, "that while my friends and I have enjoyed the time we've spent here on your world, like anyone else cut off and long away from their home, we're anxious to be on our way." Nearby and unable to see over the railing, George sniffed meaningfully.

"That only natural," the general responded encouragingly.

"The problem is that we don't have any idea which way, out of an infinity of possible ways, to go from here, and the Kojnumm government and its allies won't send a ship outward on our behalf until we can choose a reasonable course."

"Also natural, I imagine." Saluu-hir-lek was studying the now-silent field of battle. Distant lights were reflected in his wide eyes.

"It would be helpful," Walker went on, "if someone, someone in a position of real power, could use their influence to persuade the government to initiate on our behalf a real, serious search of the surrounding starfield, with an eye toward locating our homeworlds. *We* certainly aren't in a position to do it. We've filed repeated requests, only to be told to be patient and that the appropriate resources are being employed on our behalf. But this has been going on for some time now, and so far we've heard nothing."

Saluu-hir-lek did not look at him. That was not encouraging. "I faintly aware of yous' situation. Such searches, I understand, can take long time. Sometimes very long time."

"We understand that." Walker tried not to sound impatient. "It's just that we've heard nothing at all. Possibly if someone like yourself looked into the matter, or used their influence, the relevant government agencies might be more ... forthcoming."

Their round, muscular mouths did not allow the Niyyuu to smile. Instead, Saluu-hir-lek tried to offer a sympathetic apologia by means of gestures. "Cannot do. Too much responsibility already, being charged with traditionally defend all of Kojnumm. I sorry, but can do nothing for you." His tone brightened. "I thank yous for staying night. Perhaps following sunbreak, can prepare small morning meal?"

With a heavy sigh, Walker turned away. "Yes, of course I'll conjure breakfast."

"A strange, untranslatable term. Understanding is clear, though. I thank you in advance." He started toward the open portal behind them. "Now is retire time. Soldier needs good sleep as much as sharp sword. Maybe cook as well."

"Whatever." The dog had his head down as he moved to follow the general. The private nocturnal meeting had not produced the results he and Walker had hoped for.

"Is okay yous share habitation? Not much free-spare space in fortress."

Walker glanced down at the dog and mustered a sliver of a smile. "We'll manage. George and I have shared a lot more than a room together."

Tonight they would also, he reflected as he followed their host, share their disappointment.

Their quarters were more comfortable than either had expected, equipped with many of the comforts of modern Niyyu-uan technology. As usual, though soft and long enough, the customary sleeping platform was too narrow for Walker to sleep easily on it lest he roll over in the middle of the night and tumble off. With a second full-size platform at his disposal, George had a much easier time of it—once Walker helped his small friend up onto the high bed.

"Well, when considered as a summit in search of local allies, that sucked big-time." Pacing out a circle atop the platform, George promptly flumped himself down in the middle of the aerogel padding.

Boosting himself up onto the edge of his own platform, Walker regarded his friend glumly. "The general was nice enough, maybe even understanding, but that was as far as it went."

George sniffed derisively. "Me, I don't even think it went that far. I think he was being disingenuous the whole time." Rising, the aggravated dog walked to the edge of the platform. "Look, this Saluu-hir-lek is the top military guy in all Kojn-umm. It's crazy to think that he's not in on top-level policy decisions. And I have to believe that the employment and disposition of four aliens at government expense counts as a top-level policy decision."

Walker deliberated. "Then you think he's in on this 'go slow in helping us to return home' policy?"

"Of course he is." George let out a short, sharp growl. "Just like all the other upper-level local Niyyuu. It's pretty clear to me from the way he reacted to your low-key request that he's not going to help us any more than any of the other government officials we've talked to over the past couple of months." The dog eyed his friend sagely. "You're too good at your new vocation, Marc. I've been paying attention, listening to conversations. That's one benefit to being my size. Bigger folk start to overlook your presence. Not only do the Niyyuu like your cooking presentations, they're basking in the envy of their neighbors. Nobody else has a human chef. Not to mention a chatty canine, a verse-spouting Tuuqalian, and an encyclopedic, if smart-mouthed, K'eremu. You can be sure of it: they're going to keep us marooned here as long as they can." Returning to the center of the platform, he repeated the careful "pacing in a circle" ritual before lying down once more.

"Right now, 'as long as they can' is looking more and more like forever."

A thoughtful Walker studied the communications ovoid that stood to the left of his sleeping platform. At a command, it could provide all manner of services and entertainment. But in accordance with Niyyuuan tradition, it did not permit reciprocal contact with the outside world. That had to be done by courier, or mirror signals, or some similar old-fashioned method that did not contravene the strict laws governing traditional Niyyuuan combat. Like the rest of the fortress, their sleeping quarters were an eclectic mix of the antiquated and the completely up-to-date.

While their long journey from Seremathenn to Niyu had hopefully brought them closer to home, their voyaging had subsequently stalled due to the lack of cooperation on the part of the Niyyuu of Kojn-umm. If George was right, and Walker saw little reason to dispute the dog's assertions, an official if unspoken policy of benign neglect had landed permanently on their repeated requests for help in locating their homeworlds, or even ascertaining in which direction they might lie. In some ways, outright opposition to their requests would have been simpler to deal with. But facile prevarication was a tougher opponent: slippery and hard to pin down.

Take the attitude of their current host. There were moments that suggested Saluu-hir-lek empathized with their situation. He simply wouldn't do anything to help them, would not go against governmental dictates. How could Walker and his friends demand action when individuals like the general and his civilian counterparts insisted they were doing their best?

There was the hope that Sobj-oes, the senior scientist who had confronted him late one evening, would eventually come forth with some useful information. But suppose she did? he told himself. Then what? Knowing where Earth—or Tuuqalia, or K'erem—might lie in relation to Niyu would bring the respective orphans of those three worlds closer to home only emotionally.

"We need to be more proactive in our cause."

"What?" Half-asleep, George looked up at his friend.

"We need to stop asking for help and do more to help ourselves."

"Uh-huh, sure." The dog's head slumped back down onto his paws. "When you're ready to hijack a Niyyuuan ship and its crew, let me know. Sometimes—sometimes I wish we'd recognized reality and stayed on Seremathenn. Or I wish I had."

Walker had been frustrated. Now he was angry. Slipping off the platform, he strode over to the other, grabbed the startled dog by his forepaws, and lifted him up until he was standing on his hind legs. It brought them nearer to eye level.

"Now you listen to me! We didn't fight our way out of Vilenjji captivity to end up stuck on Niyu or Seremathenn or any other alien world. Neither did Sque or Braouk. We're going to get home, all of us!"

"Let go of me, or I'll bite the crap out of your fingers," George warned him.

Walker let the dog drop back down onto all fours. "We need to stick together and to focus on one thing, George—and it's not making ourselves as comfortable as possible in an alien environment. We need to concentrate on ways of getting home."

"Swell." Unable to stay angry at anything for very long, the dog had lain back down and was licking his forepaws where the human had gripped them. "First we have to find it."

"We will. Somehow, someway, whether the Niyyuu help us or not, we will. And once we've done that, we'll damn sure figure out a way to get there!"

"A positive attitude," the dog mumbled sleepily. "That's useful. Since you find Saluu-hir-lek so sympathetic, maybe you can get him to conquer a few neighboring realms for us. Then you can *order* their scientific communities to do what we want."

"Wouldn't work even if we could," a more subdued Walker murmured. "Remember what we were told? That if any one realm becomes too powerful, the others gang up on it to put it back in its place?"

George yawned. "Very civilized. Nothing like trading commodities, I bet."

"No," Walker agreed. "This is nothing like that. Nothing at all."

He returned to his sleeping platform and directed the room to darken. But unlike the dog, he did not immediately fall asleep. In fact, he did not fall asleep for some time. His thoughts would not let him. Like the steaming, thick java brewed by his favorite coffee shop on the corner of the office tower back home where he used to work, they were percolating.

9

Morning dawned as so many had since their arrival on Niyu:
bright, sunny, cloudless, and depressing. A fine day for fighting,
according to the aide who woke them.

As he slipped mechanically into his clothes, Walker noticed
that George had not stirred. "Not coming." With a nod of his
head, the dog indicated their immediate surroundings.

"There's not much to do here," Walker pointed out. There
were entertainment recordings to peruse, but little else.

The dog lifted his head from his paws. "Not much to do until
we leave this place, either. We came looking for help. We didn't
find any." The furry head dropped back down. "At the risk of
appearing impolite, or impolitic, if anybody asks, tell 'em I'm
not feeling well. Which is true enough. I've no interest in
watching the natives ceremoniously slaughter each other."

"To tell you the truth, neither do I." Walker moved toward
the doorway. "But in spite of the general's diplomatic refusal of
assistance, you never know when he might let something useful slip."

"If he does, just make sure you don't fall on it."

Walker hesitated, thought to say something else, finally concluded with a familiar "See you later, then," and exited the
room. He didn't blame George for staying behind. While adding
to their knowledge of Niyyuuan culture, their visit to the
fortress had produced nothing in the way of concrete assistance.
Not that this was anything less than what they had expected.

Inquiring as to the whereabouts of their host, he was informed that the general was up on the central bulwark. And that was where he found Saluu-hir-lek, intently engaged in a study of the hills and central plain spread out in front of the fortress, organizing tactics for the day's battle. To Walker's disappointment, Viyv-pym was not there. There was no reason for her to be present, of course. Traditional combat was something she had seen before, had experienced on a far more personal level than he ever would.

He did his best to appear cheerful. For his part, Saluu-hir-lek greeted him effusively. The general had as much energy as any Niyyuuan Walker had yet encountered.

Looking past the much broader human, he inquired, "Where you small associate?"

"Not feeling well this morning," Walker told him.

"*Asghik.* I hope it not from eat you's cooking."

Walker blanched, then recognized that his host was making a joke. The general was full of surprises. "Expecting a rough day?" Turning, Walker contemplated the field of battle. All was quiet for now, with no sign of the besieging soldiers of Toroud-eed.

"I think they growing tired. Jalar-aad-biidh has not been breached, much less taken, in long time. This one valiant effort by them. All started because of some trade dispute. Is often the case. One more assault on outer wall fail, I think they go home."

"And what then?" Walker asked curiously. "Will you pursue and try to destroy them so they won't have the strength to attack you again?"

Morning light glinted from polished armor that had been forged in a modern factory and not by two-fingered hands working with hammer and tong. Saluu-hir-lek eyed him from the depths of wide, inquiring eyes. "You interested in military tactics, human?"

"Let's just say that for much of my early life I spent a lot of time dealing with battlefield strategy." He did not add that the object of that strategy had been to advance a small, oblong-shaped, inflated ball down a grassy field. Tactics were still tactics, whether the eventual objective was seven points or seven deaths.

"I am pleased by you interest. Besides cooking, you have perhaps in mind other goals?" Though Walker was mildly boggled by the Niyyuuan's unintentional pun, the general, of course, remained utterly unaware of it.

"I want to go home. My friends want to go home. You know that already, General."

The Niyyuuan gestured acknowledgment. "As I told you yesterday, not my area of influence. Can do nothing. Regrets only I can give you."

They were both silent for a long moment before Walker, simply with an eye toward making polite conversation, thought to ask a question of his own. "What about you, General? What are your goals? Besides the ones your government and your official position have charged you with? Every sentient has personal as well as professional aspirations. Myself, I never thought I would become a professional food preparator. Now I find myself not only cooking, but doing it on different worlds for different species with entirely differing dietary requirements and tastes." Moving a little closer, he lowered his voice conspiratorially. "Given a choice of anything, what would you do? What do you, Saluu-hir-lek, want most?"

A limber, pale hand reached out to him. Starting at Walker's shoulder, two long, flexible, unarmored fingers traced a pattern down his arm.

"Such a thing is not for general speaking." Perhaps this time, Walker mused, the pun was intentional. "But you not Niyyuu, not Kojn-umm. I tell you something, you keep secret. Tell no one. You eyes attest to this?"

Drawn to the alien's unmistakable intensity, Walker did not hesitate. What personal ambition was so dodgy that an individual as powerful and connected as Saluu-hir-lek had to secure assurances of confidentiality before revealing it to an alien visitor?

"Of course," he replied. Then he added formally, "I attest with my eyes that I will repeat to no one of this world what you are about to tell me."

Saluu-hir-lek gestured solemnly. Then, instead of responding immediately, he turned to gaze once more out across the still-peaceful field of battle.

"It an uncommon thing, I know. Other officers, of all ranks, content enough to do their job. To follow orders. But when one is put in position not to follow orders but to give them, sometimes perception of reality, of world itself, can change." He glanced over at Walker. "You have, maybe, some personal understanding of this phenomenon?"

"I'm not sure." Something told Walker to tread with extreme care on this new subject, lest his host drop the matter entirely.

The general gestured enigmatically. "I endeavor explain. I am commander all traditional military forces of realm Kojn-umm. Rise fast within hierarchy. Many promotions." All this was given as fact, Walker noted, for informational purposes only and insofar as he could tell, without boasting. Certainly the speaker did not wait for comment, genuflection, or other approval from his alien audience of one.

"I achieve much already. Defeat forces of Toroud-eed several times. Defeat forces of Biranju-oov twice. Could have taken both guardian fortresses of latter."

"Why didn't you?" Walker asked him.

Saluu-hir-lek's disgust was plain to see, even to a newcomer such as Walker. "Governments make agreements between selves. Civilian control always overrules military, except when actual integrity of realm at stake. Was ordered both times to break off fighting and pull all attacking forces back to Kojn-umm."

"You were disappointed." Walker had quickly lost interest in the silent battlefield beyond the high wall.

Dominating the lean visage, huge dark eyes peered back at him. "You understand—perhaps."

Walker dug in, persistent. "Last night you said that you sympathized with the situation my friends and I find ourselves in. I think I find myself sympathizing with you. You suffer from what my people would call thwarted ambition. Believe me, Saluu-hir-lek, from my previous profession I know many individuals who are afflicted with the same ailment."

The general gestured understandingly. "It good to meet someone who appreciate condition. Even if that someone a great clumsy awkward alien creature like youself."

"Thanks," Walker replied dryly. "I think that, like myself, you also suffer from frustration—though it arises from a different set of circumstances." He moved as close as he could without actually making contact. "You can tell me about it if you like, General—who would I pass the information on to? Given the opportunity, what would you most like to do with your life?"

Saluu-hir-lek paused, as if suddenly aware that he might already have said too much. But the strange, short-earred, lumbering creature was right. Who would it recite the telling to? There was no reason for it to do such a thing. Particularly since it was apparent that the government in power was doing its best to ignore the alien's own requests.

"I tell you something now, human Walker. Confession before morning meal, you may think it. I come this close"—he pressed both fingers of his right hand lightly together—"to taking both traditional defending fortresses of Biranju-oov. Capture both fortresses, means realm suffering the defeat must make major concessions to vanquisher. In commerce, taxation, tariffs, residency matters—everything." His other arm swept forward to encompass the still-tranquil battlefield.

"When finally defeat these attacking forces of Toroud-eed here, I could subsequently muster greater army and chase them back to borders of their own realm. Defeat them also there, I am certain of it! First Toroud-eed, then Biranju-oov. Would become greatest traditional military commander in entire history of modern Kojn-umm." He waited with obvious interest for Walker's reaction.

The human merely replied softly, "And then?"

A great sigh eased out of the general, leaving him for an instant as thin as a reed. "You *do* understand. You have same feeling, I think maybe."

"No," Walker told him firmly. "I'm not interested in what you're interested in, though I would someday like to be head of the company I used to work for. If that can be called all-conquering, then I'm all for it. What I *am* interested in is getting home. Every day that my friends and I are restricted to Niyu is one day more we haven't moved any closer to getting home. It's becoming abundantly clear that in order to get the kind of assistance we need from official Kojn-umm sources, we need more powerful allies among its governing elite." He eyed the general meaningfully. "The greatest military commander in the history of modern Kojn-umm would certainly be one candidate for that list."

Saluu-hir-lek's mouth expanded. "Strategy and tactics. If I were the individual of whom you theorize, is true I might be able to help yous with yous' wishes. But I not that. Cannot be that." He looked away. "You been on Niyu long enough know that one realm grow too powerful, others combine to put it in its place."

"If its power is readily apparent, yes," Walker agreed. "But there are many ways to camouflage intent. To disguise one's true objective. That's something I used to be very good at."

Saluu-hir-lek turned sharply back to face the human. "You have idea? One, or many?"

"One that is many," Walker told him, intentionally cryptic. "Interested?"

The Niyyuuan general remained wary. "This very chancy subject for open discussion. You make morning meal first. Bring you friend along if he feeling better, please. I interested also in his opinion."

"The gist of my idea does not fall within his area of expertise," Walker replied.

"I understand that. But I interested in his opinion all the same. You not object to presence during discussions of you's own friend, do you?"

"No, of course not." Walker had no choice but to concede the point. To have argued it further, he sensed, would have killed the general's interest in such a touchy subject completely.

As it was, Saluu-hir-lek was clearly pleased. "Always better eat first. Not good discuss sedition and duplicity on empty stomach." Putting a long, limber arm around the human, the general escorted him off the rampart and back into the depths of the fortress.

                                *   *   *
"Well, what do you think?"

The waterfall at whose base they had gathered was not high, but it was noisy, which was what Walker was after. As always, their appearance garnered the usual stares from passing Niyyuu. None approached the foreign visitors to the nature park, however. Visiting aliens were accorded the same privileges as locals. That extended to privacy.

And if common courtesy was not sufficient to discourage infringement, Braouk's intimidating presence was sufficient to keep the otherwise intrigued at a distance.

Espying a shallow sandbar, Sque slid gratefully into the water. She remained there with only the upper half of her body breaking the surface, forcing her companions to settle themselves around her. No one minded the proximity to the manicured cataract that over the centuries had undergone a transformation from wild torrent to well-mannered cascade. Though carefully maintained native vegetation, lush and vibrant, flourished throughout the park, Walker would have traded every gaudy frond and twisted fiber of alien exoticism for one glimpse of a solitary daisy.

They had not come to enjoy the scenery, however, but to discuss their immediate future. One that Walker's proposal promised to perturb appreciably.

"Is taking a chance, that could seriously unsettle, existing relationship." Himself larger than many of the surrounding growths, Braouk's initial response to Walker's plan reflected his natural caution. "We have fashioned a comfortable arrangement with the Niyyuu. Involving ourselves in a scheme such as you propose, Marc, could damage that irreparably."

Walker had anticipated numerous possible objections to his proposal. Braouk's was one of them. "How? All decisions will be made by Saluu-hir-lek, all orders will be issued by him, and he'll be the one to execute and follow through on every action." He smiled knowingly. "That's so he can also claim all the credit. No problem there. We're not looking to get credit out of this. Our objective is to strengthen one important ally to the point where he'll be able to demand instead of request the kind of assistance we've been asking for."

As a relaxed George dog-paddled nearby, Sque focused her laserlike attention on the human. "It is apparent you have given this as much thought of which you are capable. I confess that I am more intrigued than I expected to be. But our moody Tuuqalian makes a point. Suppose that events do not proceed in the fashion desired. Our hosts are not so developed that their base desires have completely atrophied. This society still understands revenge, for example."

Ignoring the fact that he was soaking his pants, Walker waded into the water and crouched down close to her. There was a time when such proximity to a four-foot-high tentacled nightmare like the K'eremu would have sent him screaming. Time and close acquaintance had long since altered both his view and his reaction.

"In that case, what's the worst that could happen? The Niyyuu know we still have friends among the Sessrimathe. They'd probably just expel us, send us back to Seremathenn. In that case, we'd be no worse off than we were before we made the decision to come here."

Half a dozen slender tendrils stirred the water lazily. Half in, half out of the cool stream, Sque was at her most physically comfortable. Mentally, she was still skeptical.

"It is true that if we do not do something, we condemn ourselves to remain forever poised on the cusp of inertia: a poor motivator of proaction." Silver-gray eyes peered intently at him while her pink speaking trunk weaved back and forth close to his face. Used to its utterly alien presence, he ignored its fluttering.

"In order to have a chance of bringing this off successfully, I'll need your knowledge and your help, Sque."

"Of course you will," she agreed tellingly. "You would have no chance whatsoever of succeeding without my active involvement. If nothing else, you will need the participation of a higher intelligence merely to keep track of all the possible ramifications of your proposed machinations. Which, I must admit, show a level of sophisticated multithinking I had not previously associated with you."

"Believe me, I'm just as taken aback as you to find that certain requirements for success in my former profession fit the present situation unexpectedly well. How they'll play out remains to be seen." His legs were beginning to cramp from crouching in the sitting position, and he straightened up, water dripping from his pants. "Saluu-hir-lek is certainly fascinated by the proposal I laid out for him." Turning to his left, he raised his voice to the giant, who remained back in the shade of the trees and well clear of the fast-moving watercourse.

"What about you, Braouk? Will you go along with this? As long as it doesn't violate any accepted tenets of traditional Niyyuuan warfare, I'm sure the general would be delighted to see you in a suit of custom-made Kojn-umm armor."

"More fighting is, not to my liking, right now."

Walker did not try to force the issue. Given time and sufficient motivation, he felt he could inveigle the Tuuqalian into fighting. If not necessarily on behalf of their hosts, then in support of the broader effort to get all of them home. Convinced that was the real goal, Braouk might be willing to set his temperamental recitations aside and pick up a specially forged heavy sword. Four of them. The appearance of an armored Tuuqalian on the battlefield ought to be worth at least a company of regular soldiers to Saluu-hir-lek. The more invaluable they could make themselves to the general, Walker knew, the less likely he was to abandon the visitors' goal once they achieved some measure of success.

That was Walker's ultimate objective: to create an enterprise with a momentum of its own. One that not even Saluu-hir-lek, should he have a change of mind or heart, could halt. All would find themselves swept up in the same risky, mutual challenge.

Could he bring it off? Despite the assurances he had given the general, Walker's confidence wavered. What he had proposed was something rather more demanding than selling pineapple juice futures short. Among his companions, George was a reluctant participant at best, Braouk still remained to be fully convinced, and one could never tell for certain when Sque might change her mind completely about something.

Then he remembered his own argument, and voiced it aloud to his companions. "We'll do this because we can make it work. Because it will ultimately help us in our essential goal, which is to find our way home. But most of all we'll do it because it's the only thing any of us has thought of to get things moving here, since official policy apparently is to politely but firmly ignore our pleas for meaningful help."

"And I shall also participate," Sque added with unexpected passion, "because I am bored—*bored*!" Following this confession, she took on a startled appearance. Limbs flailing fervently, splashing water in all directions, she whirled in the stream to see what had assaulted her from behind. Grinning, George paddled rapidly away.

"I hate to see anyone bored," the retreating dog shouted back as Walker wiped water from his face. "Especially someone with so many loose limbs hanging around just begging to be yanked."

With the perpetrator of the outrage thus self-confessed, an irate Sque went after him. Faster in the water and much bigger than the mutt, it seemed an unequal contest. However, George managed to keep the infuriated K'eremu at bay with the one weapon she did not possess: teeth.

Watching them, Walker marveled at how far he and his friend had come. Not only from Earth, but *of* Earth. He was as comfortable now with K'eremu and Tuuqalian, Niyyuu and Sessrimathe, as he had been with friends and coworkers and girlfriends back home. If it was true what they said, that travel broadens the mind, then his had been broadened beyond the wildest dreams of all but the most mind-expanded travel writers. It had certainly all been fascinating, and enlightening, and awe-inspiring.

But even taken in toto, it was no substitute for a good concert or a night out with friends.

*   *   *

Though a bold and forthright fighter, Saluu-hir-lek was capable of subtlety when it was required. Preparations were begun quietly, without shouting or the usual kind of loud, patriotic exhortations to the populace that normally accompanied a significant military buildup. It helped that a major assault on the integrity of Kojn-umm had just been repulsed. The citizenry, not only in the capital but elsewhere throughout the realm, had experienced their fill of local combat. Enthusiasts had turned elsewhere, most notably to the war currently in progress on the other side of Niyu between the powerful realms of Gwalia-uun and Tigrada-eeb.

Largely ignored by the media as well as by the government, Saluu-hir-lek was able to slowly but steadily marshal his forces, increasing the size and strength of his brigades, most importantly those responsible for logistics and support. The latter, Walker knew, would be crucial to the success of his proposal, since if events transpired as hoped the expeditionary army of Kojn-umm would be in the field far longer than was customary.

It took a significant number of ten-days for the army to make ready. As the public became aware that a military campaign of unusual dimensions was being planned, questions about its propriety were raised in the media throughout the realm. Some were doubtful; some were supportive. Used to the respectful excesses of conventional Niyyuuan warfare, the great majority of citizens simply ignored the maneuvers while getting on with their daily lives. Unable to influence the outcomes of battles that nevertheless affected them deeply, they had grown used to trusting the strategic decisions of their military leaders. If it was determined that a punishing invasion of belligerent Toroud-eed was needed as a follow-up to that nation's attack on Ehbahr's traditional fortifications, then so be it. They would provide their support, as always.

And besides, if the assault was to be commanded by Saluu-hir-lek, their finest officer, there was always the chance of achieving a notable triumph, if not a spectacular victory. Commercial advantages could accrue. There was no lack of financial backing for the proposed expedition.

The media duly reported on the extensive planning, which

could not be concealed. These reports made for solid, if somewhat monotonous, coverage and were always good for a fill if the day's other news inclined toward the passive. As regular visitors to the main bivouac, Walker and his friends were fascinated by the contrasting combination of high tech and low reality that comprised the preparations.

Advanced air-repulsion vehicles banned from any field of battle delivered supplies that were laboriously transferred to selgeth wagons. The selgeth were hippo-sized bipeds with long trunks and comically floppy ears whose stout bodies ran to an excess of fat. Harnessed to large-wheeled wooden wagons in groups of three, they munched contentedly on whatever plucked vines and cut grasses were laid before them. Blessed with an inherent patience—and a complaisant stupidity—that verged on the somnolent, a troika of selgeth could pull a fully loaded wagon all day long without tiring or complaint. Others were yoked to mobile siege engines whose designs were thousands of ten-days ancient.

Custom allowed barrels and crates, but not their contents, to be made of plastics and other modern materials. Swords and spears and slingbolts could be fashioned by machines in automated factories, but once delivered to the army could only be sharpened and maintained by hand. More out of a desire to be able to defend himself in possible unforeseen circumstances than from any yearning to participate in actual fighting, at his request Walker was given instruction in their use. His senior Niyyuuan trainer was fascinated by the profusion of fingers on each of the human's hands. Though shorter than the two digits that terminated in a Niyyuuan hand, and less flexible, human fingers were strong and had the advantage of numbers.

As for the other potential combatant in the group, Braouk needed no martial instruction. Utilizing all four powerful upper tentacles, all he had to do was grip whatever weapon was at hand and swing. Whether wielding sword, club, or stray wagon, the Tuuqalian was bound to do considerable damage. Especially if, as had happened several times when they were captives aboard the Vilenjji ship, he lost control of himself. At such moments, Walker would not want to be a member of a rival army.

Surprisingly—though a rare event—there was nothing in the extensive official canon of traditional Niyyuuan warfare that prohibited the participation of an alien in local conflict, provided only that it utilized nothing more lethal than traditional forms of weaponry.

As for George, having nothing to grip a weapon with, he pointedly removed himself from instruction in their use, while Sque refused absolutely any martial schooling whatsoever. Primal physical hostilities, she remarked without having to be prompted, were beneath her and her kind. They had advanced beyond such foolishness. But she was quite willing to offer her often unsolicited opinion on tactics and strategy. Just because her kind did not make war among themselves did not mean they had not studied its format and consequences among other species.

The day chosen for the departure of the army dawned overcast and clammy. Walker and George would have preferred more sunshine, Braouk had expected nothing less, while Sque was delighted with both the darkness and the damp. As for the soldiers of Kojn-umm themselves, they were so keyed up by many successive ten-days of preparation that they had to be held back by their officers. It had been a long, long time since the forces of Kojn-umm had made a sortie against those of Toroud-eed. For years they had been restricted by their cautious commanders to the defense of ancient fortresses such as Jalar-aad-biidh. Now they were to be offered a chance to give the Toroudians a taste of their own medicine.

And then the politicians arrived.

There were four in the delegation who had come up from the capital. They were well dressed, well informed, and well meaning. As they addressed Saluu-hir-lek and his officers within the somewhat-claustrophobic confines of the staff wagon, they cast occasional glances in the direction of the three aliens who were also present.

"What are they do here?" one of the important visitors asked almost immediately.

The general gestured casually in the direction of his guests, as if the presence of outré aliens on a traditional Niyyuuan military exercise were an everyday occurrence. "They bring fresh views and a different perspective on tactics to the grand expedition. I value their advice, though of course I make my own decisions." Saluu-hir-lek leaned toward the leader of the visiting delegation. "What do it matter? Does the government value gastronomic talents of biped so highly it would seek to restrain him from accompanying?"

The inquisitive official was immediately on the defensive. "Nothings, no, General. Was only curious to see them here. Is unexpected."

If they think our presence is unexpected, Walker mused, *wait until they see Braouk in full armor.* The Tuuqalian was not present at the gathering for one simple reason: even shorn of armor and weapons, if he were to squeeze into the staff wagon there would be no room left for anyone else. No doubt he was even now off somewhere ingratiating himself to the Kojn-umm soldiery with lengthy recitations of venerable Tuuqalian sagas.

"The government has concerns," another of the officials declared doggedly. She was unusually tall and slim, even for a Niyyuu, though the appropriately high-ceilinged interior of the staff wagon meant she did not have to bend to fit within. "It not that they troubled by thought of attacking Toroud-eed. Has been trade and other disagreements between our two realms for many long-times. But to attack an enemy just defeated seems to some an ill-mannered adventure."

Truly, Walker reflected, the Niyyuuan way of war was more than a little different from the brand waged by his own kind.

"You fight force from Toroud-eed at wall of Jalar-aad-biidh for several ten-days," the third member of the visiting party observed. "Beat them back each time. Most commendable victorying." He made a gesture that Walker recognized as a praise flourish. "Why suddenly now the need, at considerable expense to the treasury, to follow so soon to attack that already-defeated force?"

Saluu-hir-lek glanced ever so briefly in Sque's direction. The K'eremu did not react. The attendant politicians would probably not have noticed if she had.

"Toroud-eed expeditionary force seriously weakened by their losses sustained before Jalar-aad-biidh. They barely back in barracks. If attack them now, good chance they not strong enough to assist much in protection of Toroud-eed traditional fortifications. Exists for us excellent possibility of overwhelming defenses of the realm. Could bring momentous, if not necessarily total, defeat on traditional level of Toroud-eed itself."

The tall female looked at the associate on her left before returning her attention to the general. "That quite a claim to make, General. Is also possible by committing so much of military resources of Kojn-umm to this offensive that we could be as weakened in turn. Assault will be widely broadcast across all of Niyu. If attack falters, other traditional adversaries of the realm might be tempted attack Kojn-umm while its main army occupied in front of fortresses of Toroud-eed."

For a civilian politician, Walker decided, the tall representative had a respectable grasp of military tactics.

Saluu-hir-lek was ready with a response. "Integrity of Jalar-aad-biidh not seriously compromised by Toroudian assault. Other traditional walls and citadels not impacted at all. Sufficient forces remain in Kojn-umm to successfully defend time-honored interests of the realm. If I not believe this with all my self, I would not propose or plan this expedition against Toroud-eed." His gruff, grating voice ascended until it filled the interior of the staff wagon with a sound like gravel being crushed.

"Is long overdue time we teach lesson to Toroud-eed once and for all. Who here not wish to see such a triumph?"

While impressed by his vision and his commitment, the visitors were not overawed. "All patriotic citizens would desire to see such an eventuation, General," the first speaker declared. "What we not wish see is same thing happen to Kojn-umm while main army of the realm is occupied with ill-conceived escapade elsewhere."

"We not here to stop you, General," the tall female added. "You have approval of Council already. We here to inform you that we aware of all possible consequences." Her wide eyes met his. "For sake you's excellent career as well as future of realm, we wish you good fortune, good speed, and caution."

"Yous' constructive tidings welcome and accepted," Saluu-hir-lek assured them expansively. With a flourish of his own, he escorted them from the wagon. Once outside, the eldest of the visitors glanced at the sky.

"No one believe anymore in omens. We a mature species—except in certain aspects of our culture." He turned to face his host, his eyes flicking occasionally to the peculiar aliens who always seemed to be hovering in the background. "I hope you make this happen, General. I have seen many concessions made to Toroud-eed, Biranju-oov, and other adjacent realms. Is time surely for proud people of Kojn-umm to assert themselves more forcefully." He stared at Walker, who remained standing near the rear of the staff wagon. "I hope the strange friends you have acquired help you to victory, and not to ruin."

"Regardless shape or size or origin, I listen open to any who have good advice," Saluu-hir-lek reassured the venerable delegate, "and then I make the decisions that best for Kojn-umm."

Whether this response was sufficient to satisfy the elder, Walker could not tell, but neither the questioner nor any of his companions raised any further objections. They boarded the gleaming, nearly silent vehicle that would whisk them back to the capital in comfort and speed and were out of sight in seconds. But before they departed, one member of the delegation, who had heretofore stayed aboard the now-departed craft and out of sight, emerged to remain behind.

In late evening there was no sunlight to glint off Viyv-pym's traveling armor as she approached the staff wagon, but Walker thought she looked splendid anyway. Next to him, George snorted in disgust, shook his head, and wandered off in search of something to eat.

Halting before him, she stroked his right shoulder and upper arm in greeting. He responded with a light touch of his own. As always, he risked losing himself in those eyes: sunshine and gold.

"Hello, Viyv-pym. Come to wish us good luck?"

"Come to join in great expedition." Her eyes flashed. "Having already served two tour of military duty, had to request special dispensation to participate. Final permission from relevant department received only this morning." She searched his soft, rounded, alien face. "You have objection?"

"Who, me? No, no," he told her, perhaps too quickly. It was a good thing George had already left, Walker realized. Listening to his human friend's near stammer, the disgusted dog might have piddled on his leg. "Glad to have you along. Someone else to talk to."

"I am happy my presence please you." One limber hand dropped to the hilt of her sword. "Opportunity also for small personal glory, and to kill a few rival of Kojn-umm." Together, they started toward the dwelling wagon he had been assigned. "This very bold decision by Saluu-hir-lek. Destination is no secret, of course. Almost impossible conduct any military activity on Niyu in secret. Media are everywhere."

Walker knew that in addition to the expected sizable contingent of media observers from Kojn-umm, broadcast units were also arriving to cover the undertaking from other realms— including Toroud-eed. The presence of enemy media representatives among them did not faze the soldiers of Saluu-hir-lek's army. It was the way traditional warfare had been conducted on Niyu since the beginning of civilized times. "Well-mannered," as one of the departed cautioning politicians had put it. There were ratings to be had, products to be sold, philosophies to be disseminated. A nice, steady, prolonged battle at the ancient gates of Toroud-eed would be good for everyone. Except for the soldiers who died, of course. There was only one glitch in that expected scenario.

Saluu-hir-lek had no intention of engaging in a prolonged conflict.

Unlike troop movements, it *was* possible to keep battlefield tactics reasonably hidden from the enemy. The defenders of Toroud-eed, hopefully still worn out from their failed investiture of Jalar-aad-biidh, would know that the forces of Kojn-umm were coming, but not what they intended to do once they arrived. No military strategist himself, Walker's basic understanding of tactics stemmed from his days on the football field. From what Saluu-hir-lek and Sque had confided in him, he thought the overall plan had a chance of working. How good a chance he did not know.

Like everyone else, he would find out soon enough.

As for Viyv-pym, she was more than a little excited by the chance to go into battle again. Her arrival, at the last minute prior to the army's departure, did arouse a question or two in his mind. He was not quite as smitten as George believed or Sque felt. Was she here for the reason stated, simply because she wanted to participate in the coming fighting? Or had she been sent to keep an eye on him and his fellow aliens, to see if they were engaged in some unsuspected activity inimical to the interests of Kojn-umm? Was she friend, or spy? Or had she been paid to watch over him and ensure that the premier imported culinary attraction of the capital came to no harm and was returned safely to work his gastronomic magic?

All were possibilities, by themselves and in combination. Time, he imagined, would reveal the truth. And if not time, possibly George, who could be positively prescient at times.

Meanwhile, they had a hostile regime to conquer. Walking toward his transportation, Walker found himself and his new companion assaulted, not by swords or pikes, but by media representatives anxious for material. The presence of the famous alien food preparator among the expeditionary force was a useful angle for questions. As Viyv-pym looked on in amusement, he answered all that he could, truthfully and without hesitation. They asked him about cooking, about food, about life on Niyu, about his opinions on the forthcoming campaign. Thankfully, they never asked him about tactics. That was natural enough. Such matters would not be regarded as something with which he would be involved.

Had they asked, he could have told them quite a bit, including some things that would have genuinely surprised, and perhaps even shocked them. Needless to say, he did not volunteer the data.

Because via the planetary media, the military as well as the citizens of Toroud-eed would be watching.

10

Walker had seen a number of movies in his life that depicted or dealt with medieval warfare. Slight variations notwithstanding, it seemed very straightforward. You assaulted the fortress with arrows and rocks and fire. Then troops carrying defensive shields and scaling ladders attempted to surmount and take control of the walls while other siege engines and rams sought to force a way through. Meanwhile, the defenders rained variations of liquid and solid lethality down on the attackers in coordinated attempts to alternately discourage, kill, or drive them off.

There were two notable differences between what he remembered seeing on the large and small screen and the assault on the Toroudian fortress of Herun-uud-taath. First, the combatants had access to destructive technology that far exceeded anything existing on Earth—but were forbidden by custom and ritual from making use of so much as a single-shot pistol. Second, and more importantly, he was not watching a fictionalized representation of some ancient battle: he was part of it.

Or more accurately, he was an active witness. Concerned with the safety of his strategic ally (and superlative chef), Saluu-hir-lek made certain that three of his four alien visitors remained safely away from any fighting. This was not a problem as far as Walker was concerned, since he felt exactly the same way about the carnage that was taking place at the walls of the fortress. The fourth member of their group, however, waded into the fighting with reluctant determination, causing havoc wherever he stomped. The panic generated by Braouk's efforts was more devastating to the opposition than the number of them that he actually slew. It was one thing for a Niyyuu to encounter an alien in the media or even on the street; quite something else to have to deal with it in person, in a battlefield environment. Especially when that alien was a fully armored, four-limbed, one-ton mass of verse-spouting Tuuqalian.

Sque, of course, remained above it all, though not uninterested. After all, she and her friends were participating because they had a personal interest in the eventual outcome, not out of any sense of altruism or deep love for their Kojnian hosts.

"Ruination as entertainment. Devastation as politics. If I do not find my way back to dear K'erem soon, I fear I shall go mad." Tendrils writhed in agitation, visual evidence of her frustration.

"You won't go mad." As they surveyed the distant field of battle, Walker spoke from the other side of the wagon's lookout tower. "You'd end up analyzing the descent into psychosis, and in the process retain your sanity."

Clinging easily to one side of the tower with seven of her ten limbs, she swung silvery eyes toward her human companion. "Do not think that only simple creatures such as your kind can go insane, Marcus. Complexity can also lead to confusion, confusion to angst, and angst to withdrawal. There are many kinds of madness." With a free tendril she gestured at the ongoing battle. "This is only one."

"Madness we can use to our advantage," he countered. In the distance, a gobbet of jellied hydrocarbon exploded in flame somewhere inside the fortress. Exempt from battlefield restrictions and clearly marked as such, a pair of small vehicles hovered low overhead, the shielded advanced recording devices they carried relaying the retrograde mayhem to enthralled viewers on all five continents.

"Time will tell. When surrounded by and dealing only with primitive sentients, I must take care to remain hopeful, if not overtly optimistic." Another free tendril curled up and back to scratch at an ear socket.

Viyv-pym was out there too, somewhere, Walker knew. He hoped she would be careful, and would return unharmed. Knowing her now as well as he did, he knew it would have been futile to ask her to refrain from placing herself in harm's way. Slender and light of weight she was, but so was a stick of dynamite.

At that moment, in fact, Viyv-pym was nowhere near the ferocious free-for-all that was washing up against the frontal defenses of Herun-uud-taath in waves of fire and blood. Having joined a select contingent of carefully picked troops, they had been transferred on tibadun mounts at high speed to a position in dense woods near the southwest rear of the Toroudian defensive complex. The greatest threat to the success of such a maneuver lay not in being surprised by defensive forces, but in being discovered by representatives of the media, who would attack the fast-moving troops with relentless requests for interviews and their unending search for personal-interest stories.

Having managed to avoid the attentions of both a counterattack and avid civilian interrogators, and having sent their loping tibaduns back to the front lines, the would-be infiltrators from Kojn-umm assembled for a final preassault briefing from their officers. Viyv-pym wondered how the visitors would react in such a potentially perilous situation. The giant Braouk would simply have listened in silence, absorbing all that had to be said. The Tuuqalian was even now occupying much attention at the forefront of the battle. As for the small, many-armed dose of ambulating sarcasm, Viyv-pym knew that she would remain as far from the scene of combat as she was aloof. The human Walker...

Walker was more problematic. Charged with assisting all the aliens in their interactions with her kind, she found him a continuous bundle of contradictions. That he could fight she had seen for herself, when he had been undergoing instruction in the use of hand weaponry. That he chose not to do so she attributed to a mix of personal and cultural convictions. Yet observing him studying combat, those times when he was unaware that he was being watched, she thought she detected hints of a repressed desire to throw himself recklessly into the ongoing fight.

Analyzing the motivations of one or more visiting aliens could wait. At the moment, she and her fellow fighters found themselves about to embark on a perilous maneuver that would succeed only through the boldest of actions. Such had been the intent of the risky stratagem from its inception.

Having received their final instructions, the members of the assault force silently spread out and hid themselves among the trees as best they could, waiting for darkness. An hour after the sun fell, following a hasty uncooked meal that made her yearn for Walker's superb cuisine, they began gathering in twos and threes and moving forward. The southwest rear corner of the great fortress of Herun-uud-taath, which guarded the traditional approach through the mountains into Toroud-eed proper, loomed above them. Forbidden from making use of modern sources of illumination, its defenders had lined the multiple ramparts with torches and glow spheres.

The infiltrators from Kojn-umm made no attempt to conceal themselves. They did not approach the complex slowly, by stealth and in shadow. Instead, as they emerged from the forest they formed up neatly into four columns and stepped out smartly onto the paved road that led to the fortress. Pavement soon gave way to the traditionally acceptable dirt and gravel.

Along with many of her comrades, Viyv-pym's mouth shrank to an almost invisible "O" as an inquisitive media scanner passed overhead. It dropped so low she could see the pilot and commentator inside. Marching along, eyes forward, she could almost feel the relay unit's pickup brush the tips of her ears. The uncomfortable sensation made her frill fibrillate and her tails twitch uncontrollably.

Satisfied, the scanner gained altitude without its integrated commentator voicing any queries. Moments later, the first challenge to the contingent's steady approach came from the fortress. A specially trained officer marching in the forefront of the columns replied. As they had been instructed to do, expressions among the approaching troops varied from studiously neutral to intentionally bored.

An enormous metal gate, forged and formed in the ancient manner, groaned inward. Uncontested and unchallenged, the soldiers of Kojn-umm marched in. Viyv-pym smiled inwardly as she passed beneath the gate's arched opening. The ruse, devised by a group that included not only Saluu-hir-lek and his senior officers but the human Walker and the K'eremu Sque, depended on fitting out all of the specially chosen Kojn-umm troops in uniforms not of their home realm, but in those of Toroud-eed. They were real uniforms, too. Originals that had been scavenged from the dead left behind by those Toroudians who had many ten-days earlier attacked the fortress of Jalaraad-biidh. The special troops had even been instructed in particular Toroudian mannerisms.

While marvelously executed, the ruse was not perfect. A few questions were asked. One Toroudian officer, descending a stone stairway, saw something that did not match his knowledge of What Ought to Be. Harsh Niyyuuan voices split the night, swiftly giving way to shouts first of uncertainty, then of alarm.

An officer in the front of the column rasped an order. Weapons were pulled from scabbards and concealment. Screeching defiance, the columns broke apart as the soldiers of Kojn-umm, Viyv-pym among them, clashed with the now-alerted defenders of the fortress.

The attackers had the advantage not only of surprise but also, initially at least, of greater numbers. By the time the alarm had traveled through the citadel, the invading contingent from Kojn-umm controlled the gate and its immediate vicinity. Despite prodigious efforts by the fortress's defenders to regain control of the occupied sector, the invading soldiers had solidified their position by taking control of several guard towers. Unwilling to risk additional casualties in what had clearly become an internal war of attrition, the commanders of Herun-uud-taath's defense decided to hold back and wait for dawn. For one thing, they badly needed to see what, if any, other surprises the invaders from Kojn-umm might be keeping in reserve.

By the time runners could convey news of the infiltrators' success to Saluu-hir-lek's headquarters, the general already knew of it from media reports. It caused quite a sensation. Such successful duplicity was something of a novelty in military campaigns. Like anything new on the news, news of it triggered burgeoning interest among millions of viewers.

Though without reinforcements and heavy equipment the infiltrators could not make further progress, neither could the defenders of Herun-uud-taath dislodge them from the positions the Kojnians had taken up inside the rear of the fortress complex. With the strategic situation thus stalemated, but with the forces of Kojn-umm now holding a definite, quantifiable advantage, Saluu-hir-lek rocked his opponents further off balance with his next action.

Instead of seeking immediately to press his tactical advantage, he requested a conference with his opposite numbers.

Understandably, the general staff of Toroud-eed was at first suspicious. When it was made clear that the request was sincere and contained no hidden provisions, they found themselves genuinely bemused. Dissecting but finding no harm in the proposal, they eventually, if a bit sullenly, agreed.

Preparations were made to meet not far from the base of the fortress's main western gate. The location chosen was just within range of Herun-uud-taath's heavy fire throwers but sufficiently distant so that any contemplated treachery was likely to fail. Since both sides had agreed on the terms of the summit, they were allowed to substitute a modern, portable, prefabricated structure for the more traditional fabric tent. This allowed for a meeting where, among other things, the interior climate could be controlled—a welcome development, since the weather had been unseasonably hot.

To its great regret and vociferous objection, the media that eagerly anticipated covering the elite meeting was banned from attending it. The commanders of both forces had to concur in order for such a ban to be enforced. This they readily did. Neither Saluu-hir-lek nor his Toroudian counterparts wanted flashing scanners recording and transmitting their every mood and word.

No one was more grateful for the declaration that the meeting was to take place than the soldiers on both sides, since all combat would be suspended while talks were ongoing.

The vetted participants arrived early. If the talks went nowhere fast, neither side wanted to lose a day's fighting, lest the other use the time to better position or provision their troops.

Saluu-hir-lek arrived clad in a freshly disinfected and cleaned uniform. Like the members of his staff, he displayed little in the way of adornment. No medals, no ribbons, no intricate epaulets, no serpentine gold braid. On Niyu, members of the military were considered professionals no different from healers or technicians, agronomists or astronomers. Modest insignia identifying their specialties were sufficient to proclaim their status.

His Toroudian counterparts were no different, save that their uniform wrappings were gray and purple in contrast to the Kojn-umm blend of yellow, brown, and silver. They were also an equal mix of male and female. There were no tables—only a sufficiency of the usual narrow-backed, narrow-seated Niyyuuan chairs, arranged in two crescents facing one another. In the absence of modern recording instrumentation, scribes stood ready on both sides to take down everything that was said, so that there could be no chance of confusion later. Though the method was ancient, the materials were not, and could be unceremoniously dumped into any reader and rapidly transmuted into electronic form.

The official Toroudian contingent was impressive. Toroudeed had fought and defeated several, often larger realms in the perpetual Niyyuuan search for commercial or political advantage. Its fighters were tough and determined, its government resolute, its traditional defenses well laid-out and maintained. All the more reason Saluu-hir-lek and his soldiers had gained so much acclaim for recently driving them away from Jalar-aadbiidh. It was safe to say that they had been surprised by the Kojnian's decision to counterattack so soon after their recently terminated siege.

That did not mean, the general knew, that they were so weakened that their realm could be easily overcome. Hence the need for this conference—and for elucidation. Formalities were held to a minimum. There were battles to be fought.

Once the obligatory introductions and stiff pleasantries had been exchanged, Fadye-mur-gos, the commander of Herun-uud-taath's defenses, unfolded herself and rose. She was of average height, average breadth, average everything except intelligence and resolve.

"I congratulate yous on deception yous devised to get yous' troops inside the southeastern gate. Unfortunately for yous, they now trapped there, unable to advance any farther into ours defensive complex or to retreat without being cut down both within and outside the walls."

Saluu-hir-lek rose and advanced to meet her. As was usually the case, he was notably shorter than his opposite number. As was also usually the case, he did not seem so.

"It all matter of interpretation. Is Wegenabb half-full or half-declining? I would say instead my troops now control southeastern section of Herun-uud-taath. Use of it is denied yous for any purpose. From present firmly secured position, soldiers of Kojn-umm can harry yous' forces from the rear, cut off any resupply of yous from that main route, and if necessary can fall back in good order with minimal casualties."

No outcries of disagreement rose from her staff, and her eyes did not dilate; but here and there the general saw the occasional half flexing of a frill, the tight contraction of a mouth, the stiffening of several tails. The tactical truth, he knew, probably lay somewhere between her assertion and his rebuttal, though he felt confident of his own position. Like any good officer, in conceding her contention a modicum of truth, he was simply being strategically conservative.

Despite their best efforts to conceal it, however, her staff knew who held the plausible advantage.

"In fact," he added for good measure, "we actually do have the means for reinforcing our position inside Herun-uud-taath." He was not certain if they believed that one, but the claim visibly unsettled some of the Toroudian senior staff even more than had his confident rebuttal.

Fadye-mur-gos was not about to let him spew claims unchallenged. "I disagree with everything you assert," she rasped back, shifting her stance so that her upper body and long neck inclined belligerently toward him.

Saluu-hir-lek was not fazed in the least, either by her words or her posture. "I speaking the truth. You may not know it, yous' staff may not know it, but yous' junior officers and soldiers on station know it." After letting that sink in and enjoying their discomfort during the pause, he let loose with something that for the first time genuinely did shock them.

"However, it not matter, because forces of realm of greater Kojn-umm ready to stop fighting right now."

At least two of the assembled officers seated behind their commander emitted exhalations of disbelief. She turned on them sharply, silencing any further outbursts of surprise with a warning stare, before returning her attention to her opposite number. She also resumed a fully upright stance.

"I not sure you listened to correctly. You presenting offer of surrender?" Despite her admirable self-control, she could not keep a hint of incredulity from her voice.

"That would be absurd, would it not be? With us holding the strategic advantage?"

"Yous hold no such advantage," she corrected him without hesitation.

He made a coordinated sinuous gesture with both arms. "I not call this meeting for argue merits of current battlefield situation. I making offer to stop fighting, not to surrender. Are very different callings."

"Surely," she responded, recovering some of her momentarily lost poise, "you not asking for ours?"

"No, I not." Head tilted back, huge eyes fully open, he met her gaze evenly.

Clearly, even someone as experienced and knowledgeable as Fadye-mur-gos had never dealt with such a situation before, and certainly not on an active battlefield. Despite her partisan bluster, Saluu-hir-lek was confident someone of her martial erudition was well aware that the successful infiltration of a portion of Herun-uud-taath had shifted the balance of power on the battlefield in favor of the invaders. Not decisively, perhaps, but meaningfully. So his offer to call a halt to the fighting, when the forces of Kojn-umm held the advantage, had thrown her and her staff badly off balance. As she tried to figure out what he was doing and what he was really after, she was doing her best to stall for time.

He had no intention of letting her.

"Then I confess I not understand what you really offering, Saluu-hir-lek."

He allowed his gaze to occasionally travel beyond her so that he could make eye contact with each and every member of her senior staff. Some of them were older than she was, he noted, and would find what he was about to say even more bewildering than what had already transpired.

"What I offering, on behalf of myself, my troops, and the government of greater Kojn-umm, is opportunity for both sides to win."

Fadye-mur-gos thought she had prepared well for this meeting, this significant confrontation. Even when the conversation with her renowned counterpart had begun to disintegrate into uncertainty, she was convinced she remained on top of and aware of all its possible ramifications, even to the seemingly outrageous. But now, for the first time in her long and distinguished military career, she found herself at a loss. It made her very uncomfortable. In the short term, her unease translated into outrage.

"You trying joke with me, Saluu-hir-lek. I have never hear of such a thing. This not a game we play in here today. Lives balance on the blade of our responses."

"All the reason more to listen close, all yous, to what I have to say."

Though still confused, she gestured strongly. "Oh, we all will listen well. I myself am most very curious hear you attempt clarification of the blatantly preposterous. Is no war, no battle, where both sides can win. Always one side win, one lose. Always one side advance to take control of field of battle, other side retreat."

"Not," Saluu-hir-lek told her, "if both sides advance together." Turning, he gestured tersely.

Two figures new to the talks entered the meeting area. While one was only slightly shorter than the typical Niyyuu, the other

was a squat, hirsute quadruped with small bright eyes, a wet
nose, and a tongue that lolled indifferently from the left side of
its open jaws. It flumped down next to the seat of one of Saluu-
hir-lek's senior officers as its somewhat less hairy bipedal companion advanced to stand beside the general.

Along with her own subordinates, Fadye-mur-gos stared at
first one new arrival then the other before returning her attention
to her counterpart. "These are two of four aliens arrived Kojn-
umm some many ten-days ago. I know of them from sightings
on general broadcastings. One is entertaining personage; other
is celebrated for skill in culinary arts. Neither is soldier. Why
they here, at this summiting? What have they to do with action
of and on battlefield? You perhaps think to bombard us with expensive food?"

Expecting to encounter no aliens, she wore no translator, but
in the long months since they had been on Niyu, both man and
dog had managed to acquire a working knowledge of the principal language. Like the Niyyuu themselves, their speech was discordant but straightforward. If his appearance at the conference
was something of a shock, his growling knowledge of their language was even more so. Meanwhile, Saluu-hir-lek stood back
slightly, hugely enjoying himself.

There was a time not so very long ago when Walker would
have been completely intimidated by the kind of audience he
now faced. No longer. Thanks to the time he had spent in the
company of a diversity of aliens while in Vilenjji captivity and
encounters subsequent with many more, he had reached the
point where he no longer thought of any alien as particularly
"alien." They were simply other beings, with elaborate makeup
and often impossible forms but with personalities and cultural
affectations no stranger than some he had encountered on the
streets of downtown Chicago. He faced the bemused, hostile
representatives of the defiant military establishment of the
realm of Toroud-eed squarely.

"I am called Marcus Walker. I come from a world that is not a
part of what passes for galactic civilization. As such, I am a
neutral party to the current conflict." As always when he spoke
Niyyuuan, his throat hurt. The nearest earthly analog, he knew

from once having seen a documentary on it, was Mongolian throat-singing. But he persevered, and each time he did it, the lining of his throat protested a little less.

"You travel with and support aims and objectives of realm of Kojn-umm," one of the Toroudian officers countered sharply.

Walker met huge, accusing eyes to which he was no longer a stranger. "I travel with the army of Kojn-umm, yes. I can fight but do not. Sometimes I cook for them. That is different from fighting. I would be happy to cook for the valiant soldiers of Toroud-eed as well."

Both his offer and his manner were designed to be disarming. They had the intended effect. The hostility directed toward him lessened perceptibly.

"How could that be?" inquired another senior officer. "Saluu-hir-lek speaks of advancing together. Advancing where, and to what end? You have some knowledge of this or you would not have been brought between the crescents."

"I am beginning think both the general and the alien speak obliquely of possible alliance." As she spoke, Fadye-mur-gos was studying Walker closely. "This is impossible thinking. Firsting, were Kojn-umm and Toroud-eed to ally, would create combined traditional military force powerful enough to alarm other neighboring realms, who would join against us. Seconding, who would we ally against, and why?"

"I'm aware of your traditions," Walker told her. "Probably more than I really want to be. However, that's the reality. I know that your two realms can't cement a formal alliance against a third party without incurring the attention of other realms. So the new kind of relationship that Saluu-hir-lek and the government of Kojn-umm is proposing would not be structured as an alliance, as such a joining together is generally understood. It would simply be your two governments acting in concert for a mutually agreed-upon end."

"Semantics," declared a grizzled veteran of Fadye-mur-gos's staff. "An alliance is an alliance. It is the action that is important, not the naming."

"Not," Saluu-hir-lek put in with satisfaction, "if we appear to act independently of each other."

The veteran was not convinced. His frill, Walker noted, was ragged with age and the scars of many battles. "This talk make my head hurt. A sword is more direct."

"If you break off this fight," Walker continued, "without striking a formal peace agreement, then technically the forces of Kojn-umm and Toroud-eed are still at war, right?"

Fadye-mur-gos turned to her staff, two of whom gestured strongly and without hesitation. "That is so," she hacked at Walker, her tone guarded.

"And if each of you independently and without apparent co-ordination attack a third entity while still formally at war with each other, perhaps even while continuing to engage in skirmishes against one another at the same time, wouldn't it be very difficult for anyone else to prove you were acting together against that third party? As an alliance?"

"I suppose it might so appear," she conceded. Her gaze shifted to the smug-looking Saluu-hir-lek standing nearby. "Of course, even with attempts to control such skirmishes they could easily develop into larger battles. If that happened, and inexplicable fast stopping was put to them, then deception would be exposed."

"Not," the general of Kojn-umm told her, "if they were adjudicated by a third, uninterested party. In such case, would be impossible prove one side colluding with the other."

"What third party could reasonably be expected judge such unprecedented kind of confrontations?" she shot back.

"Your annoying, nosy, ever-present media."

All eyes went to the latest arrival to the conference. Scuttling in on all ten limbs, Sque scrambled onto the back of an empty chair, a position that elevated her to eye level with the others.

"I am called Sequi'aranaqua'na'senemu. I am smarter than anyone in this cheerless fold-up of a building, and I can prove it. I can also prove it to anyone on this benighted world."

Walker winced, but held out hope that as she continued, his companion would moderate her usual contempt.

"If others of your world, including your omnipresent world-wide media, can see that the continuously argumentative forces of Kojn-umm and Toroud-eed continue to battle one another across an ever-widening field of combat, it should make it apparent to all that you are not functioning as true allies. Allies do not go on fighting and killing one another. Seeing this, it is unlikely a devastating coalition of multiple realms will be arrayed against you. At the very least, from my studies of your traditions, it will greatly confuse the matter. Debate will take the form of extended discussion, by which time your objective will be achieved."

"Objective?" Yet again Fadye-mur-gos found herself at a loss. It was not a condition she enjoyed. "What objective?"

"The subjugation of Biranju-oov," Walker told her.

There was a stir among the general staff of the army of Toroud-eed. None of them had any love for that powerful maritime realm. But strong as they were, Toroud-eed had never been powerful enough to contemplate mounting a traditional attack against their larger neighbor. Impossible as the relevant arrangements seemed on the face of it, the offer that was being put forward was too appealing to simply ignore.

Fadye-mur-gos remained doubtful. "This is a ruse, a subterfuge. No matter what ongoing skirmishing between our two armies the media may show, other realms will detect the ghost of an alliance if not the reality of one."

"But they will be uncertain as to its ultimate objective," Walker told her. "And being uncertain, they will delay. By the time they decide to join and move against you—if they even reach that point of agreement—Biranju-oov's traditional forces will be defeated and its government forced to make the concessions Kojn-umm and Toroud-eed have long sought from it."

They were tempted, he saw. It was a new idea. Continue fighting one another while surreptitiously striving toward a common goal. Like Saluu-hir-lek, they were wondering if it was workable, and if so, if it violated the strict traditions of Niyyuuan combat. To Walker the process was intimately familiar. It was exactly the kind of ploy traders used on the floor of the exchange when two or more parties wished to try to manipulate the market for a particular commodity. They would agree to bid against one another to drive a price up or down. It was illegal, of course, and if the respective parties were found out, people could, and did, get sent to jail.

But this was not Chicago, and the issue at stake was not the price of cocoa beans.

Fadye-mur-gos and her staff were wavering, he saw. It was time to push them over the edge. With a nod in Sque's direction and her acquiescent wave of one tendril, he spoke into the pregnant silence.

"There is one more thing." The enemy commander turned to him. "It is recognized that even with ongoing skirmishes between the forces of Kojn-umm and Toroud-eed, the appearance of collusion may persist. Therefore, Saluu-hir-lek has agreed to turn over 'official' command of the army of Kojn-umm to me and my friends. That would make the appearance of some kind of covert alliance between Kojn-umm and Toroud-eed appear even less likely."

This time even Fadye-mur-gos could not repress an exhalation of surprise. She looked immediately at Saluu-hir-lek. When that worthy responded positively, the burst of energetic discussion among her staff could not be suppressed. Once the import of Walker's statement sank in, however, she found herself gesturing knowingly.

"Very clever. Perhaps too clever. If little-known aliens appear have taken control of army of Kojn-umm, outside observers will be distracted by issues that have nothing do with matters of possible alliance. They be so busy trying analyze ramifications, war may be over before any kind understanding is reached." Her gaze returned to Walker. "This only adroit fiction, of course. Kojn-umm would never surrender real power to off-worlders. No Niyyuuan realm would do so."

"How you know?" Saluu-hir-lek challenged her. "When was last time such situation transpired?"

It was dead silent in the meeting room. She stared at him for a long moment—and then burst out in the coughing equivalent of robust Niyyuuan laughter, in which she was soon joined by both her staff and that of Saluu-hir-lek. Walker and George both winced. The collective noise sounded like a hundred metal files simultaneously working on one giant piece of rough iron.

When the coughing had died down, she approached her opposite number and drew the two fingers of one hand down the center of Saluu-hir-lek's chest. "On a battlefield, shrewdness sometimes worth more than extra battalions. I readily confess I myself find this distinctive proposal appealing. But not for me decide alone. Proposal must be put to Council of Toroud-eed."

The general indicated his understanding. "Naturally must be. Would be same for me if situation reversed. Meanwhile, fighting between us must continue. But perhaps not unrestrained. Is normal time for customary reassessment of strategic positionings. Troops shift here, catapults and arbalests move there. Now is time for repairing and reprovisioning. Latter is most necessary." Restraining his amusement, he gestured in Walker's direction. "New 'commanders' agree with this assessment." Approaching closer to her, he drew his own hand across her shoulder.

"Best for forces of both Kojn-umm and Toroud-eed to rest and take stock." He performed what Walker now recognized as the Niyyuuan equivalent of a meaningful wink. "Both armies needs be prepared for whatever significant confrontation is to be coming. Not to be suggesting anything, but only by way of illustration, is worth mentioning as example that is goodly marching distance from border of Toroud-eed to ancient walls of Biranju-oov."

11

"It is agreed!"

Viyv-pym entered the big dwelling wagon that had been reserved for the use of the aliens. Half of it was occupied by
Walker, George, and Sque. The other half was reserved for the
use of Braouk. Even so, the Tuuqalian was crowded. Typically,
he did not complain—though given his general melancholy it
would have been hard to tell the difference from his usual state
of mind even had he chosen to do so.

After the excited Viyv-pym had finished delivering her news
and withdrawn, George hopped up onto the side sleeping platform that had been added to accommodate him. "Great. Now no
matter what happens, we're stuck with it." He turned a jaun-
diced eye on Walker. "I was a member of a pack once. It's
great—unless things don't go well, food runs short, and they decide to turn on and eat the weakest member of the group."

Walker nodded somberly. "Then we'd better keep working to
ensure that there's plenty of 'food' to keep the armies of dear
old Kojn-umm and Toroud-eed busy."

"Speaking of consumption," Sque ventured, "I presume you
have given thought as to how eventually to deal with Biranju-
oov, assuming that our initial plans proceed as well as we
hope?"

"I'm working on it," Walker assured her touchily. "Let's not
get ahead of ourselves."

"I am always ahead of myself." She curled her tendrils

around her, forming a platform of tentacles at her base, and blew a contemptuous bubble in his direction. "It is the K'eremu way. It is one reason why we are always ahead of everyone else."

At least he wasn't alone in this, Walker reflected. If things got difficult, he could always turn to Sque and George for advice. For obvious reasons, he hoped he would not have to do that.

At the moment, Viyv-pym's celebratory announcement was a clear indication things were going well. Very soon, word should come that the armies of both Kojn-umm and Toroud-eed had begun moving. Not toward one another, but southwestward, and fighting with one another all the while. From what he had learned about Biranju-oov, it would not be easy to assault, even by the more-or-less combined forces of Kojn-umm and Toroud-eed. If resistance proved as stalwart as expected, the real difficulty would involve keeping the attacking armies of two traditional enemies focused on their new target instead of on each other, while maintaining the fiction of the latter.

Such uncertainty and confusion proved advantageous when the time came to march. Expecting the forces of Kojn-umm to retreat or those of Toroud-eed to surrender, the civilian populations of both realms as well as observing media were flabbergasted when both began marching away from Herun-uud-taath—parallel to one another, and not back toward Kojn-umm. If worldwide media coverage had been extensive before, now it seemed as if every mobile scanner and famous commentator on the planet materialized around, behind, or above the skirmishing columns. As the marching forces continued fighting among themselves, disputing the changing territory that separated them, neutral military analysts found themselves at a loss as to how to describe what was happening.

If the two armies continued to challenge one another, then they could not be prohibited allies. But if they were marching together toward a single, as-yet-undefined goal, then they could be nothing else but. Troops on the ground knew only what they had been told, which was very little and not especially informative. Continue to advance as instructed in good order, and attack and defend against a perfidious nearby enemy that was doing exactly the same. As for the general staffs of both armies, who presumably had some grasp of the mysterious overall strategic picture that must lie behind such unprecedented maneuvers, when they were interviewed, each and every senior officer was conspicuously closemouthed.

Something rare and uncommon was happening. Of that, the mystified commentators were certain. When basic geography and some simple extrapolation suggested that both massed forces were stumbling in the general direction of the realm of Biranju-oov, pointed questions as to intentions were put to officers on both sides. All such inquiries were directed up the line of command, at whose terminus the increasingly frustrated inquirers received nothing more informative than pleasant greetings and expressions of regret at the lack of information that was available for general dissemination.

Certainly, it was a march like no other. As soldiers repeatedly attacked and fell back on both sides, their actions were covered in unprecedented depth by the brigade of media observers. Passing to either side of both parallel columns, or above it, casual travelers and commercial transporters added observations of their own. Media and public not only wondered what was going on, but what the ultimate objective was of the unprecedented clash.

By the time the two battling armies swerved away from Biranju-oov's modern capital—with its flexformed buildings, extensive sprawl, and busy spaceports—and headed for the old walled city, savvy observers thought they had finally divined the intent of the unprecedented exercise. There was to be an attack on the maritime realm's traditional defenses, in the traditional manner, by wholly nontraditional elements. For while the forces of Kojn-umm and Toroud-eed began to establish proper bivouacs and bring forward their siege engines, they continued to brawl actively with one another. If the latter was some sort of ruse, the commentators hovering above the incipient battlefield observed, it was being perpetrated with a vengeance: soldiers from both sides continued to die in the seemingly endless series of ongoing clashes.

As if this battlefield situation were not unconventional

enough, the military command of Biranju-oov that had settled
into the old city found itself presented with not one but two entirely separate sets of articles requesting its surrender: one from
each of the attacking armies. Though essentially identical in
content, they were put forward by two different delegations.
The response of the old city's defenders to this confusion was
straightforward.

"Kill them all," Commander in Chief Afyet-din-cil instructed
his subordinates, "and we sort out internal arrangements later."

Unlike Kojn-umm and Toroud-eed, whose traditional approaches were defended by fortresses built to control mountain
passes, the capital of Biranju-oov was a seaport of notable lin-
eage. While fighting commenced around and before the old
walled city and its two fortresses that backed onto a deep cove,
the massive modern capital itself had been built up around the
greater harbor off to the south. Only tradition preserved the old
city's importance. To make war on the capital proper would require modern weapons and tactics whose use was of course forbidden among the Niyyuu. So the defense of the realm was
focused on the old city's ramparts. These were stronger facing
the sea, from whence assaults had traditionally come in ancient
times. For Biranju-oov to be attacked from the land was unusual, but not unprecedented.

Every day, units from the army of Kojn-umm or Toroud-eed
would test the strength of the old city's walls and the resolve of
their defenders. These attacks were never made in tandem. The
two armies made no effort to coordinate their assaults. On a
couple of occasions, in fact, these first probes ended in complete confusion when the soldiers involved ignored the city
walls and their baffled defenders to turn viciously on each other.
At such times the guardians of traditional Biranju-oov would be
left gaping in amazement at the fighting taking place on the ancient floodplain below them and wonder what in the name of
the Ten Travails of Telek-mun-zad was going on.

No one had ever heard of, nor were there any records of in the
long history of Niyu, a three-way war.

Commentators from other realms and other continents exhausted themselves trying to find explanations for what was tak-

ing place. Whenever it appeared that the besieging armies were beginning to act in concert, they would fall to fighting among themselves. Just when the defenders of Biranju-oov believed the offensive against their integrity was about to fall apart, the forces of one army or the other would launch a furious individual assault against them. Or a battalion of Toroud-eed would attack and fall back only to have the assault taken up by the opportunistic forces of Kojn-umm.

Scrutinizing all this were powerful realms who had initially worried that a formal alliance had been forged between Kojn-umm and Toroud-eed. Concerned at first, these interested onlookers now found themselves adrift in a sea of bemusement. What kind of allies consistently attacked one another, even as they were assailing a third party? Was there a real danger to other lands here, a genuine threat, or would the assault on well-defended Biranju-oov collapse under the weight of its own disorientation? Being uncertain of what they were seeing, these outside observers were understandably unsure how to react.

There was some talk of several realms uniting to move against the attacking forces. But which ones? Those of Kojn-umm, of Toroud-eed, or both? No apparent rationale for such a mobilization existed. With confusion deepening among the onlookers, it stood to reason that it might also be deepening among the participants. Accusation of a formal alliance being a serious matter, it was decided to wait, and continue to watch, and see what happened. Besides, intervention in such disputes was always expensive, in terms of both soldiers and public treasure.

Of those involved, happiest of all were the media, who while covering the unprecedented and inexplicable tripartite conflict found themselves enjoying viewer attention that bordered on the historic. His individual impact on the battlefield being unprecedented, Braouk was a particular focus of attention. He submitted to a steady succession of interviews with a mixture of patience and resignation. At least these did not last long. All it took was for some commentator to inquire about the Tuuqalian's passion for recitation, whereupon an obliging Braouk would respond with an example. Ten or fifteen minutes of listening to unbroken moody Tuuqalian saga was invariably sufficient to cause even the most dedicated interviewer to insist that he or she was suddenly needed elsewhere.

The interest in Braouk also served to deflect attention from his less-imposing companions. Sque spent much of her time in solitary moist meditation in the specially hydrated wagon compartment that had been fabricated for her. Though devoid of forbidden modern technology, it was sufficient to keep her happily humid. Though known to food preparation specialists, Walker's fame had not spread quite as far and wide as Biranjuoov, a realm that was sophisticated but not intimate with Kojnumm. As for George, he was regarded as little more than a talkative novelty, a designation that suited him fine. The time they had spent in Kojn-umm had given him his fill of inane interviews.

So it was that with the military preoccupied with the conduct of the assault and the media focused on its ongoing action and details, no one noticed when a ten-day following the commencement of the siege, one thick-bodied biped and one short quadruped riding a borrowed tibadun slipped out of the Kojn-umm camp in the middle of the night. They headed not for the front lines, or for the parallel encampment of the forces of Toroud-eed, but back along the winding route the advancing armies had taken. After riding a modest distance back the way they had come, they abruptly changed their course and angled sharply to the south.

Reaching their first objective, they abandoned the tibadun. The animal promptly whirled and headed back in the direction of its distant stable mates. Standing on the ground cover of a minor shipping corridor, it was not long before the modern communicator Walker carried was able to hail an empty, automated public transporter. Ascertaining that their interrealm credit was good and notwithstanding their outrageous appearance, the vacant on-duty vehicle descended so that they could board. Having spent time researching their intended destination prior to their arrival outside the old city of Biranju-oov, human and dog relaxed in climate-conditioned comfort as the nearly silent transporter obediently accelerated toward the capital city of the realm.

The *modern* city.

Far, far from home, the unlikely pair of travelers commented on the size and extent of the Niyyuuan metropolis with a self-confidence that would have amazed their old friends. Their composure had a basis in experience: after all, they had seen Seremathenn. Traveling at high speed between ceramic-clad towers and forests of brilliantly lit residential complexes, the modern, efficient transport zipped them through the outskirts and deep into the central conurbation proper in less than an hour.

It slowed only when nearing their chosen destination: the seat of Biranju-oov's honored and much-admired government. There, local security took over the transport's internal guidance system. It did not bring them to a stop, nor did it deliver them unwillingly to a waiting station packed with armed guards. Instead, as covertly prearranged, they were efficiently channeled past monumental marbleized office complexes dating from the realm's venerable past, across meticulously maintained parkland speckled with pastel-hued lights and effervescent horizontal fountains, to finally slow as they neared an unspectacular but recently erected structure located on the far side of the complex's center.

Guards did meet them there immediately upon their disembarkation, but the slender, highly trained soldiers were present to serve as the visitors' escort, not as their apprehenders. After many, many ten-days exposed to hand-to-hand combat that utilized only traditional primitive armaments, it was something of a shock for both Walker and George to find themselves paralleled and guided by Niyyuu armed with sleek, compact energy weapons.

It being the middle of the night and the Niyyuu no less diurnal than the pair of alien visitors, the building was largely deserted. What work was being done was being carried out by individuals in isolated offices. Perhaps the busiest place was the Media Relations Section, but it was located in a different structure entirely. As was customary, all strategic military planning occurred in the delegated war rooms scattered along the length of the old city's walls. As both visitors well knew, the use of advanced computational devices or communications systems was by Niyyuuan convention not permitted.

That did not mean that every defender of Biranju-oov was at that moment posted somewhere within the old city or atop its solid stone walls. Four of the most powerful members of its general staff were at that moment awaiting the arrival of the two aliens. Tired and irritable, frustrated by the lack of progress of the ongoing struggle but unable to significantly alter its evolution, they waited for their visitors in a general state of mind best described as bothered and bewildered, if not actually bewitched.

Predictably, the emotions they felt were largely repressed as Tavel-bir-dom, three-term premier of Biranju-oov, focused his attention on the nocturnal arrivals. The biped was bigger than he had been led to expect: not particularly tall, but very, very broad. In contrast, its companion was smaller than the premier had anticipated.

I could break its neck with one swift kick, he mused silently. It was hard to imagine such an oddly matched pair, and from the same planet at that, as the source of so much confusion.

"It late, sleep necessary, and I for one not desire this meeting." Responsible for the command of half the realm's armed forces but finding himself largely sidelined by the current land-based assault, Admiral Jolebb-yun-det had arrived in a fouler mood than any of his contemporaries. His greeting showed it. "Better to have something of worth to say, or I personally tempted disregard articles of agreement sealed by government agency responsible and have you put in national zoo for younglings to throw food bits at."

Taking a couple of steps forward, George hopped up uninvited onto a low, empty cabinet and made himself comfortable. "We'll do our best to make sure you haven't lost sleep for nothing." He glanced at his companion. "Offer them the bone, Marc." The dog winked at the admiral, whose small round mouth, painted in war colors of alternating yellow and blue, contracted in bemusement. "It's a really big bone. Big and tasty."

Shadim-hur-lud, representative of the Citizen's Parliament of Biranju-oov, gazed down at the impertinent hairy creature. "I not put off a sound rest to be taunted by alien riddles." Her wide-eyed attention shifted to the patient Walker. "If you have something say, sentient, speak it now."

Taking a step toward them, Walker drew something from a pouch fastened to his belt. No one in the room flinched. The visitors had already been triple-scanned for weapons, sharp objects, and explosive chemical combinations. Had they carried any on or within their persons, it would have been detected by the relevant security equipment that swathed the small meeting room in an aura of complete protection.

Though no bigger than Walker's middle finger, the projection unit generated between himself and the sleepy representatives of the government of Biranju-oov a detailed three-dimensional image of the field of battle. A few flickers of interest showed among the assembled. Not at the use of a technology that was familiar to them all, but at the fact that so strange and unique an alien was making effortless use of it. As Walker spoke, tiny images shifted and moved within the roughly rectangular field.

"Already a ten-day has passed without any of the three sides having gained anything like a strategic advantage over the other."

"That will change soon," declared the fourth member of the group, who was representing the army at the meeting. "We gathering the means push back all attacking forces from old city vicinity and destroy them on open floodplains."

George raised his head briefly from where it was resting on his crossed paws. "Might succeed, might not. Try that kind of massive counterattack and you risk overreaching yourself. Not much chance to second-guess yourselves, if the effort turns out to come up short." The dog showed bright, sharp teeth.

The oversized, dark yellow eyes of Jolebb-yun-det glared down at him. "You very small being to be talking so big."

George shrugged, his fur rippling. "It's got nothing to do with me. My friend and I are just along for the experience."

The premier stared hard at Walker. "How can this be true?

You travel with army of Kojn-umm, reports claim you even in command, but now you say you not on their side?"

Official disavowal of modern intelligence-gathering apparatus or no, Walker reflected, it was clear the forces of Biranju-oov were not operating in a vacuum. They knew that he and George hailed from Kojn-umm and not Toroud-eed. But then, such information would have been readily available from public media reports.

"We travel with that army, yes," Walker told him. "Some say we command it, others that our supposed active participation is a front designed to confuse opponents. Regardless of which is true, it does not mean we necessarily share in all of its goals."

The premier reacted thoughtfully. "So if you not here to betray Kojn-umm, or tell us what its military really want, you must be here to tell us what it is that *you* want."

Sharp old polliwog, Walker thought. *Have to be careful here.*

"All my friends and I want, for ourselves, is to return to our homes. Since we are unable to do that, we've busied ourselves trying to help those Niyyuu we encounter get what *they* want."

Two fingers splayed, the army's representative slapped a hand hard against a nearby seat back. The sharp *bang* echoed through the room. "It plain to see what Kojn-umm and Toroud-eed want. The capitulation, in traditional terms, of Biranju-oov!"

Walker responded immediately. "Not necessarily. Although it's not widely known," he added as he lowered his voice conspiratorially, "the real quarrel of their respective governments is not with Biranju-oov, but with Charuchal-uul."

Jaws would have dropped had the Niyyuu in the room possessed such facial features. The premier's poise gave way to open bewilderment. "But if Kojn-umm and Toroud-eed not interested in subduing Biranju-oov, then why attack us? If dispute with Charuchal-uul, why not attack them?"

Walker adjusted the tiny handheld projector so that the field of battle was replaced by a detailed portion of Niyu's globe. This focused on that portion of the world everyone in the room was presently occupying.

"By themselves, and especially while continuing to fight each other, Kojn-umm and Toroud-eed could not hope to defeat Charuchal-uul in traditional combat."

"That for a certainty." The army representative made the assertion without hesitation.

Walker took no umbrage at the comment. He had no patriotic capital to gain in rebuttal, and the officer was only stating what everyone in the room knew to be a fact.

"It is too big and too powerful, in the modern as well as the traditional Niyyuuan sense. Furthermore, it has no particular ongoing dispute with either of the realms that are presently attacking you. But," he added softly, "it does with you."

Shadim-hur-lud pressed the tips of all four long, limber fingers together. "You know much about Niyyuuan society, visitor."

George yawned. "We've had plenty of time for study."

"The last formal clash between Biranju-oov and Charuchal-uul was never settled to your satisfaction," Walker continued. "Subsequently, your respective governments have tried their best to paper over the lingering differences. But resentment still simmers on both sides. Especially among certain influential elements of Biranjuan society."

"What, exactly, are you proposing, alien?" The parliamental representative had one tall ear pointed directly at him, the other at George. "Is it possible we may assume that you can claim speak for forces of Toroud-eed as well as Kojn-umm?"

"You may," Walker lied. Time for elaboration and clarification could come later. Right now it was crucial to secure a commitment from *this* government. "Despite what information to the contrary you may have acquired from the media, as an entirely neutral party with no personal interest in the outcome of your traditional fighting, my friend and I are authorized to broker an amendment to hostilities between your forces and theirs—provided that all can come to a mutual understanding how certain events should proceed in the immediate future."

The premier, for one, was taken aback by the scope of what was being implied. "Are we to understand that Kojn-umm and Toroud-eed offering to ally with Biranju-oov in battle against the corrupt and fraudulent government of Charuchal-uul?"

"Not exactly," George murmured, further muddying the political waters.

"*Ahskh,*" rasped the admiral. "Now truth will appear."

Walker turned to him. "You know that any such formal alliance would be strong enough to alarm every other realm on Niyu. They would immediately combine against it. But if it can be shown that the fighting between yourselves and the forces of Kojn-umm and Toroud-eed are continuing, such a marshaling of planetary forces might well be constrained. Besides which, the forces of Toroud-eed and Kojn-umm would continue to battle among themselves. Everyone would find it perfectly natural that you, of Biranju-oov, would try to make use of that continuing clash and turn it to your tactical advantage."

"A four-way war." By now even the initially mistrustful Jolebb-yun-det was intrigued. More than intrigued, he was becoming excited at the possibilities presented by the alien. "No one has ever heard of such a thing. The Charuchalans will be smothered by their own confusion."

"More than smothered," Walker told him. "Because while Biranju-oov continues to battle in the field with the armies of Kojn-umm and Toroud-eed, your traditional fleet of historic craft, Admiral, will strike the old fortresses of Charuchal-uul from the sea." He went silent—and waited. Nearby, George was unconcernedly chewing his toenails.

"What do yous think?" Tavel-bir-dom regarded his principal advisors. They were all fully awake now and oblivious to the lateness of the hour.

"The traditional navy has not had opportunity to show what it can do for many years," the suddenly energized admiral observed.

"This offers fine chance," the army's representative declared, "to settle historical wrongs of Charuchalans once and for all."

The premier turned to the one member of the group who had not yet spoken. "Shadim-hur, what say you? Will the parliament support, and underwrite, such an unprecedented venture?"

"For a chance to inflict a serious defeat on our old enemy Charuchal-uul, a willingness and a budget can always be found."

She turned to regard the pair of expectant aliens waiting in their midst. "I do find myself wonder about one thing, though."

Walker met her stare. "My friend and I are here to respond to your concerns."

"I wonder," she murmured in the archetypal Niyyuuan rasp, "if Charuchal-uul is the end?"

"Not until they are soundly defeated, which occurrence I did not think to see in my lifetime," Tavel-bir-dom remarked before Walker could reply. "Much less during my term of office." Grateful for having been spared the need to respond to the parliamentary representative, Walker smiled at the premier. Like every Niyyuuan, he was fascinated by the degree to which the human's mouth seemed to split his face in half.

"I am sure you comprehend," Tavel-bir-dom went on, "that a decision of such import for all citizens of Biranju-oov must be considered and voted on by full government." A willowy gesture encompassed his colleagues. "We here are only the focus of power, not the power itself."

Walker nodded. "My friend and I won't be missed for a while. With your permission, we'll wait here in Biranju-oov for your decision."

"Should not be long in coming," Tavel-bir-dom assured him. The premier's excitement was now palpable as he contemplated a future that included the defeat of his realm's most persistent and powerful adversary. "Meanwhile, you two will be treated as honored representatives. I ask of you only a little patience. Small enough to request in expectation of very big thing."

As they were ushered out, Walker glanced back to see Shadim-hur-lud following him with her eyes. Was she only typically curious about the strange alien who had addressed the gathering, or was her intensity reflective of the preternaturally perspicacious query she had so transiently posed? Walker did not know.

What he did know was that it would be best to take no chances, and for him and his friends to avoid the dangerously perceptive principal representative of the parliament of Biranju-oov as much as possible.

12

Tavel-bir-dom was as good as his ear-grating word. Three days had passed since the aliens' arrival when the eccentric pair was informed that the government of Biranju-oov had agreed to their unparalleled plan to move against Charuchal-uul. Despite this welcome news, Walker and George knew that their work was not done.

Now they had to convince the forces of Kojn-umm and Toroud-eed.

Because despite what man and dog had implied to the leaders of Biranju-oov, neither of those two commands had agreed to, or indeed had even been consulted about, such a plan. Neither had any hereditary dispute with the government or people of distant Charuchal-uul. Their quarrel was with Biranju-oov. Which was why Walker and George had been forced to seek the cooperation of that maritime realm at night, and in secret.

But the Biranjuans didn't know that. If events transpired as Marcus Walker the trader had planned, they never would.

Should the true nature of his Machiavellian machinations be found out, however, there was a good chance all three governments would each vie with one another for the chance to deal with the double-dealing, hypocritical, treacherous aliens in their own way.

Slipping unseen out of modern Biranju-oov, Walker and George went separate ways: Walker to talk to the Kojnians, the dog to inform and persuade the Toroudians. All this taking

place, of course, unbeknownst to the eager and already inveigled Biranju-oov. Meanwhile, the three-way hostilities continued on the battlefield before the walls of that maritime realm's
old city, with all sides seeking an advantage over the other. As
fighting went on, it became apparent this was a strategic impos-
sibility. If the Kojnians appeared to be gaining an advantage,
the Biranju-oov would step up their attacks on them. If the re-
verse was the case, they would concentrate more forces against
the Toroudians. And all the while, both Kojnians and Toroudians kept up their assault on the defensive walls of old Biranju-
oov while continuing to skirmish among themselves.

Under such circumstances, it was no wonder no one in any
camp thought to ponder the same question that so far had
occurred only to a certain wary leader of the Biranjuan parliament.

Walker pressed his case to his original Niyyuuan acquain-
tances with verve. Having already been convinced, Viyv-pym
was there in her limited capacity as alien handler to back him up.

"There's really no choice," he was saying as he addressed
Saluu-hir-lek's staff. As for the general himself, he struggled to
maintain an air of measured solemnity. Of all those gathered in
the prefabricated room, he was the only one Walker did not have
to convince, having been let in on the plan of action from the
beginning. Saluu-hir-lek watched his advisors and officers
squirm as the alien laid out what was for them an uncomfortable
reality.

"You *have* to assent to this agreement," Walker told them. "If
you decline, the Biranjuans will make a formal agreement with
the Toroudians against you. Since Biranju-oov will be seen as
defending itself from attack, and not as an aggressor, no objections to such an agreement will be raised in the media or elsewhere. Your army will be soundly defeated, if not wiped out, by
the combined forces that will be arrayed against you.

"But if you agree, then this much greater concerted attack
against arrogant Charuchal-uul will proceed, to the glory of
all."

One of the officers waved a finger in Walker's direction. "You
seem much captivated by this possibility, human Walker. What

attraction does triumph over distant Charuchal-uul hold for you?"

"None," Walker informed her unhesitatingly. "As it has been from the beginning of this campaign, my only concern is for the welfare of Kojn-umm. Just as it has always been ever since my friends and I first arrived on your world."

"Speaking of yous' friends . . . ," the officer began.

"They are presently occupied with other personal activities," Walker hastened to tell her. "The Tuuqalian in spinning his tales and seeing to his weapons, the K'eremu with her meditating, and the dog George with his usual unpredictable wanderings. Let's not lose sight of why your commander has called this meeting."

A senior advisor spoke up. He looked and sounded unhappy. "I, for one, not like this choice that is presented us. Charuchal-uul is far from Kojn-umm, and we have no historic differences with that vast and powerful realm. If we consent participate in this offensive, and it should fail, we risk incurring their enmity." He looked around at his colleagues. "Charuchal-uul more dangerous to have as long-term adversary than Toroud-eed or even Biranju-oov."

"But if they are defeated," another advisor remarked with barely suppressed excitement clouding his grinding tone, "that will not matter. Could be much to lose, is true. But if expedition ends in triumph, very much to gain."

"I am still troubled," the older advisor husked. "Is no assurance even combined forces of all three armies capable of defeating traditional military of great Charuchal-uul."

"Five armies," Walker corrected him quietly.

There was a perceptible stirring among the assembled. Even Viyv-pym looked at him doubtfully. Only Saluu-hir-lek retained his poise, already aware of what the wily alien was about to say.

It was left to a junior advisor on the general's staff to voice the question that dominated the thoughts of everyone present. "I never good much at mathematics, but last time I check field of battle, only three armies involved in this increasingly untidy conflict." Deep, glistening Niyyuuan eyes locked on Walker.

"Would much appreciate it if alien tactician could explain what he is cooking."

Exhalations of amusement issued from her colleagues. As for Walker, no one appreciated the injection of a little levity into what had otherwise been an unremittingly tense situation more than the room's sole human.

Though much shorter than those of the Niyyuu, his fingers had become adept at manipulating their tools. Now he used them to adjust the image that drifted in the air between him and Saluu-hir-lek's staff.

"To the northeast of Charuchal-uul lies the small but energetic realm of Divintt-aap. Their government has already agreed to allow the traditional navy of Biranju-oov to utilize their excellent old harbor. Though modest in number and never a real threat to their far more powerful southern neighbor, their own traditional armed forces are well trained, well equipped, and intimately familiar with the local terrain." Under his direction, the image shifted again.

"Southwest of the Tkak peninsula and the Bay of Ghalaud-pir, the realm of Dereun-oon sprawls over mountains and deserts that flank fertile valleys. These valleys, which constitute the soul of the realm, rely for their lifeblood on the water of great rivers that originate in the even-higher mountains of the Yivinsab Range. Those of you familiar with planetary geography know that the peaks of the Yivinsab lie within the borders of Charuchal-uul." One of the senior advisors uttered a terse exclamation of appreciation. Walker was suitably encouraged.

"Successive governments of Dereun-oon have long coveted full, not just shared, control over the headwaters of these rivers that are so vital to not only the economy of their realm but to its culture. They see in our proposed combined assault on the dominance of Charuchal-uul an opportunity to gain something that has eluded them for a great many years."

Unable to restrain himself any longer, one of the junior officers rose and began probing the interior of the projection with a long finger. "Larger view now becomes clear. Divintt-aap commands northeast while navy of Biranju-oov lands troops and deploys against traditional coastal fortifications. Dereun-oon attacks from southwest." The finger moved: swirling, planning, tracing. "Combined forces of Kojn-umm and Toroud-eed, still fighting with each other, battle way across land bridge between continents of Saadh and Ruunkh to strike traditional Charuchal-uul fortresses from behind." Withdrawing his finger, he looked cynically from the alien to his commander in chief.

"This not all devised by clever food preparator from distant world."

The ground having been prepared for him, Saluu-hir-lek strode forward as Walker stepped back. "Because of profession practiced on his own world, the alien sees opportunities here we, steeped in our own culture, may have overlooked. I have take his conceptualizing and expand upon it." Like any good general, he tried to appear as if he were addressing each of his individual subordinates particularly, to the exclusion of everyone around them.

"For this strategy to work, must continue to maintain fiction of nonalliance. Must continue light fighting with forces of Toroud-eed. As we fall back, not toward home but toward land bridge to nearest coast of Saadh, some forces of Biranju-oov will pursue, supposedly to harry both retreating armies. Media will focus on this strange three-way battle. Cannot be prevented them also noting provisioning and departure of Biranju-oov traditional fleet. But with making skillful effort at dissemination, fleet's true purpose and destination can be suppressed until last minute.

"With luck, cooperative weather, and coordinated timing, all forces will be in position to attack Charuchal-uul simultaneously. Expect fierce resistance then from that dominating realm, and strong counterattacks. But this is traditional Niyyuuan warfare. Charuchalans bound by convention not to utilize modern means of transportation. Will be difficult for them to know where to send reinforcements first. Their internal command and control will be spread thin." He waved an arm fluidly. "We can do this! Will be enough triumph for all to share."

Viyv-pym was not completely convinced. "What if other realms, on other continents, perceive that this is true five-way alliance? Could generate twenty-third world war—using traditional means only, of course. Majority of world and population will be impacted by consequences only when watching media reports."

"There may be efforts at mediation, to keep conflict from spreading even farther," Saluu-hir-lek conceded. "But military intervention unlikely. This is conclusion reached by myself and other advisors. Greater widening of clash would mean great expense to powerful realms not otherwise directly impacted. Is calculated gamble, surely. But this is unprecedented opportunity to acquire significant commercial and political gains. Fortune favors the bold. And as visiting alien has pointed out, for us to refuse to participate means possible strong alliance of Toroudians and Biranjuans against Kojn-umm. Situation for us now is like running on mud. We continue to advance with speed, or we sink in circumstances of our own choosing." He eyed his staff unblinkingly. "Are you all with me?"

The grating exhalations of support that filled the room surpassed even those that had greeted Saluu-hir-lek following his defeat of the attacking Toroud-eed at the walls of Jalar-aadbiidh.

Meanwhile, not all that very far to the south, a small furry quadruped from the same unknown world as the verbally and physically expansive human was outlining the exact same plan to a tentative audience of officers of Toroud-eed, warning them that if they did not agree to participate in the grand adventure, their treacherous quasi-allies from Kojn-umm would surely unite with the defenders of Biranju-oov to destroy them. While some among his listeners questioned the dog's motivation, none could find fault with his logic. Those who were reluctant were swept up in the general enthusiasm for the opportunity to get the better of the traditional defenses of a realm historically too powerful for far-smaller Toroud-eed to ever contemplate attacking.

If anything, the general confusion and conflicting rumors that resulted from the multiple agreements and half assurances usefully served to confuse not only the potential target of so much deliberation, but the mystified media that was struggling to sort it out as well.

*   *   *

Among those seeking to make sense of it all, only the government of the ancient and admired realm of Fiearek-iib managed to gain a real inkling of what was happening on the other side of the planet from its peaceful fields and upscale manufacturing communities. As powerful as distant Charuchal-uul, the overseers of that wealthy dominion observed via relayed media and their own operatives the gradual development of the grand strategy put forth by Saluu-hir-lek of Kojn-umm—and his seemingly innocuous non-Niyyuuan advisors.

Premier and vice premier stood together before a force transparency on the sixty-third level of the central administration facility and contemplated the thriving metropolis of Yieranka spread out before them. Midday in Fiearek-iib meant it was midnight in western Saadh. Fighting there would be on hold, as without the assistance of modern means of illumination, the use of traditional implements of warfare rapidly reached a level of diminishing returns.

"What you, really, make of these exceptional developments?" the vice premier asked her only superior. Though they often differed on matters of policy, what was happening half a world away easily superseded any domestic concerns or local politics.

The premier gestured gracefully with one arm. "Remote threats are often the most dangerous, my friend. Believing themselves inoculated by distance, those are ones the comfortable all too often ignore. I been giving the matter more attention than I admit to in official briefings. For the moment, these atypical events half a world away not matter of immediate concern to Fiearek-iib." He turned away from the reassuring panorama of power and accomplishment. "Important thing is to ensure it never will become matter of immediate concern."

"How can we do that without we become directly involved?" the vice premier wanted to know. Though in parliament they waved in opposite on many issues, on this they were agreed. Therefore, she flattened her crest and lowered her tails in deference and sought to share the wisdom of one she respected, if often disagreed with.

"Keep close watch on intelligence reportings not only from area of present conflict, but in nearby realms also." His eyes, one whitened and opaqued by an inoperable disease and for which he idiosyncratically refused replacement, inclined toward hers. "If one examine close and dispassionately what has happened in Saadh, an interesting pattern of a kind begin to emerge. Intelligence experts mostly agree it start with Toroudian siege of Jalar-aad-biidh. A few others say it start with arrival in Kojn-umm of four mismatched aliens."

The vice premier's mouth contracted to a point. Despite her advanced age, she was still considered very attractive; almost as famed for the flash of her still-taut frill as for her perceptiveness. "I know almost nothing of these aliens save what little I have encounter in the media. How could they be in any way central to such an upheaval among Niyyuu?"

The premier's expression wrinkled slightly. "Apparently, because they want go home. But nobody in astronomical establishment knows where any of their three homes are. It is reported government of Kojn-umm is very fond of them, and in no hurry see them depart."

"So to pass time they involve themselves in traditional local disputes?" The vice premier was openly dubious. "How that bring them closer to their homeworlds?"

Her superior sighed, air whistling through his perfectly round mouth. "There is much here Intelligence Section do not understand. I myself can claim no revelatory insight. It hard enough determine what drives smaller realms such as Kojn-umm and Toroud-eed without trying also comprehend the motivations of unfamiliar aliens."

"Then what course we set for beloved Fiearek-iib?"

He glanced back toward the peaceful midday setting that glowed beyond the barrier. If one tried hard enough, one could almost smell the newly opened hagril blossoms of the nearby Saralas world-forest.

"I suggest armed forces of Fiearek-iib begin maneuvers of traditional military elements four ten-days early. Will generate early holiday for populace, who will be thankful and not look too deeply into reasoning behind it. Also start initiate conversations on private diplomatic level with all neighbors—not only in continent of Paanh, but across planet. Continue active monitoring of situation in Saadh. Otherwise, unless and until existence of formal alliances against Charuchal-uul can be proven conclusively, Fiearek-iib and neighbors stay out of growing conflict."

The vice premier was silent for a long moment before responding. "Do you really think, my friend, that armies that are fighting among themselves can work together long enough to defeat traditional forces of realm as large and powerful as Charuchal-uul?"

The premier considered. "If this growing confusion of attackers can keep from destroying one another in process, then perhaps. If that happen, and it is end of it, then little will have been changed, save for treaties and commercial agreements. But if it continues . . ." His words trailed away.

As always, the vice premier was quick to jump on unspoken implications. "What you mean, 'if it continues'? If Charuchal-uul defeated, there would be nothing to continue. Charuchal-uul dominates Saadh. If it fall to this motley blend of contentious assailants, it will take latter some time just to digest their triumph."

One eye shining, he turned to her anew. "Ambition is a craving that is never sated. Something drive these events that is different from all that have preceded it."

She speculated aloud. "The aliens?"

"Possible. Possibly a combination of factors, a coming together of unique circumstances. We must be ready for anything."

The implications of what he was saying were daunting. "Surely you not think crazy Kojnians and Toroudians could even imagine attacking Fiearek-iib!"

"I not have thought them capable of attacking Biranju-oov, either. Now all three continue appear fight among themselves, yet give every indication of moving against Charuchal-uul: separate but unequal. An outlandish way to run a war."

She gestured deferentially. "In this matter, I and my backers will support you in whatever responses you deem appropriate."

He could not smile, but indicated his satisfaction in typical

Niyyuuan fashion. "I wish I knew of some, beyond what I already have tell you. We must remain aloof, observe carefully, prepare for all possible occurrences no matter how outrageous. And one thing more."

"Speak it, and I will see it carried through," she told him.

When he turned back to the panoramic view for a last time, it was not to gaze down at it, but beyond. "Have Intelligence find out everything, absolutely everything, that they can about these four visiting aliens of whom Kojn-umm has become so enamored."

Coordinated from four different directions, the grand assault on Charuchal-uul was like nothing seen on Niyu in civilized times. Needless to say, the media swarmed the offensive, in more of a frenzy than the combatants on the widely spread battlefields. Rendered lax by centuries of confidence in their own power and the knowledge that any alliance strong enough to seriously challenge them would be considered illicit on the face of it, the Charuchalans hardly knew where to counterattack first. Caught unawares by the need to fight on multiple fronts, their response was momentarily paralyzed. Defenders of ancient walls and fortresses fought bravely, even heroically, in the time-honored Charuchalan manner, but those in the south and east were overwhelmed as the government initially concentrated reinforcements in the north. When a portion of those were hastily dispatched on forced marches to help in the south, the northern forts and ports were taken by contentious battalions of Kojnians, Toroudians, and the marine forces of Biranju-oov, all simultaneously battling one another for ultimate control of the battlefield.

It was all over so quickly that the proud Charuchalans hardly knew whom to surrender to first.

News of the startling conquest of Charuchal-uul spread around Niyu as fast as modern communications could carry it: which was to say, instantaneously. Much discussion and not a little passionate argument swirled around whether or not the unprecedented cooperation of the armed forces of not two, not three, but five different realms constituted a formal alliance requiring a coordinated response from the rest of the planet.

Part of the problem in deciding how to proceed arose from

the very real fact that events had been allowed to progress to the point where even a coalition of all the powerful realms of the remaining continents would be hard-pressed to defeat the troublemakers. Especially since rumors abounded that defeated Charuchal-uul, instead of being plundered for commercial concessions, had been offered the chance to minimize its losses and concessions by becoming the sixth member of the fractious and unlikely partnership. Making traditional war on realms of modest power such as Toroud-eed or Divintt-aap was one thing; marching and sailing by traditional means across half a world to confront them while they were acting in concert with five other maybe-allies, one of whom was now still-great Charuchal-uul, promised to be costly in both expense and blood.

So extensive realms such as Huoduon-aad and Gobolin-ees held back from issuing direct threats while their governments consulted among one another and tried to figure out the best way to respond to a political-military situation that was without precedent. As they did so, they were quite aware that the rapidly changing situation in Saadh and Ruunkh demanded a response as quickly as possible, lest the perceived controversy continue to escalate.

Intelligence reports were eagerly perused in the corridors of power in Huoduon-aad and elsewhere. Many of these were detailed, some conflicted, others packed with absurdities clearly designed only to justify the expense accounts of their respective perpetrators. But a few stood out in the way they focused on a certain confluence of specifics.

Most notable among these was the observation that nothing out of the ordinary had ensued until an apparently innocuous alien cook and his three equally implausible companions had grown unusually intimate with the military command of the midsized realm of Kojn-umm. That this was a matter of some significance was gradually recognized by the more perceptive among the concerned. As yet, however, they had not the faintest notion of what to do about it.

This time the conference was held not in some flimsy portable structure hastily erected on the field of battle, but in the great hall of Sidrahp-syn-sun, in the traditional capital of Charuchal-uul. With its spiraling buttresses and frescoed, bubblelike roof, the ten-story-high vaulted ceiling reminded an awed Walker of a gothic cathedral as it might have been designed by an alien Dali. Even though he had been told that the structure had no religious significance, and its elaborate preserved frescoes depicted alien scenes taken from life on a world other than his own, walking its length still engendered deep and profound emotions in him. For once, Braouk did not have to bend to clear ceiling or overhang.

Subsequent to being stunned by the leniency of their baffling brace of vanquishers, the Charuchalans had been almost painfully eager to accommodate any requests. As opportunistic as any Niyyuu, they sensed, in making a willing offer to cooperate, the chance to recover their own projected losses at the expense of others. Since tentative agreement had already been reached allowing them to keep all of their territory and most of their commercial advantages provided they participate in the peculiar alliance-that-was-not, the present summit had been called to discuss other matters. Being a conference now of associates, albeit continuously argumentative ones, and not a triumph of conquerors over the defeated, the mood was markedly more upbeat than its gloomy predecessor.

Representatives of all sides met beneath a vast thousand-year-old dome that was entirely covered in bas-reliefs of gilded copper alloys inset with semiprecious stones. From below, it was like looking up at a bowl of Heaven, the entire procession of Charuchalan history up to the time of the building's final construction being depicted on that fabulous curved surface. Walker wanted to lean back, relax, and study each and every bit of it at leisure, but knew he could not do so. As an important member of the delegation from Kojn-umm, it would not do to appear too awed.

Speeches echoed as greetings were exchanged. Beneath the dome's perfect acoustics, Niyyuuan voices grated harsher than ever on other ears. Disdaining diplomacy, Sque dealt with the din by placing the tips of no less than three tendrils apiece over each of her aural openings. Braouk, typically, elected to tough it

out. Walker and George had no choice but to endure, since neither of them possessed the extra limbs necessary to cover their
ears while still allowing them to manipulate objects in their
vicinity.

There were no seats, no tables. It was the Charuchalan fashion to conduct such gatherings while standing, the theory being
that when the majority began to grow tired of the effort, it was
time to terminate the proceedings. As no one had been allowed
into the conference armed, modern conveniences were permitted in the ancient structure. Anxious to be consumed, enthusiastic refreshments darted to and fro among the participants,
waiting to be grabbed out of the air. The interior climate was set
at maximum comfort—for Niyyuu, of course. A few select
commentators were allowed to record the proceedings for later
broadcast. To Walker, the gathering had more the feel of a sophisticated party than a formal conference fraught with political
and military meaning.

As minor issues were debated and resolved, attentive automatic recorders faithfully took down everything that was being
said. A general atmosphere of good fellowship prevailed. A
few senior military figures made bold to discuss which realms
should be the subject of the new association's first expedition,
even as their soldiers continued to skirmish among themselves
at scattered locations both without and within Charuchal-uul's
extensive borders.

It was left to senior Charuchalan general Deeleng-hab-wiq to
move directly beneath the center of the dome, stand in the middle of the mosaic stone floor, and call for attention. Turning a
slow circle, he addressed the entire assembly.

"Guests and enemies, honored soldiers of Charuchal-uul and
fighters of other realms: unusual times are upon us." Someone
made a crude but fitting joke, and the massed exhalations of appreciation ruffled Walker's hair. Unperturbed, Deeleng-hab-wiq
continued. "We have seen development of extraordinary tactics
that not so much defy tradition as avoid it." Unexpectedly, he
halted in his slow turning to stare directly at Walker. "Perhaps
significant visitor from unknown world has appropriate defini-
tion for it?"

Though used to speaking in front of others—indeed, even shouting in front of them—Walker was caught off guard by the sudden attention. Something was digging at his ankle. Looking down, he saw that George was pawing his leg and staring up at him.

"Say something, stupid. Just don't say something stupid."

It was a potentially pivotal moment in their relationship with Niyyuu other than those from Kojn-umm, Walker recognized. He cleared his throat. "Where I come from, we'd call the strategy that's recently been employed by the forces of Kojn-umm, Toroud-eed, and others an end run. When the forces arrayed against you, both military and cultural, are too strong to break through, you have to find a way around them."

Though the source and inspiration of the analogy was unknown to them, his explanation was clear enough. Murmurs of understanding were exchanged among the assembled.

Senior General Deeleng-hab-wiq was not finished. "Much has been learned from this experience. Though my realm has suffered, it not done so as significantly as would have been case in more ancient, unenlightened times. Instead of penalty, vanquishers of our traditional forces offer us chance to gain back what has been lost, by joining with them." He spared a glance for the ubiquitous hovering recorders. "While we continue forcefully resist their incursion, of course. Fight against, fight together, all at same time. Is unique way of looking at traditional warfare." Stepping away from the center of the intricately inlaid floor, he approached the human, halting less than an arm's length away. The narrow skull inclined slightly to one side, tall ears tilted forward, and moonlike eyes met Walker's own.

"We have learn that this unique perspective originate not with traditional strategic thinkers of any attacking forces, but with foreign visitors from Seremathenn, and beyond. As is natural Charuchalan way, admiration follows."

Walker shuffled nervously. Cheers after a good tackle on the field he was used to. Standing here, in resplendent alien surroundings, subject to the mixed curious and complimentary stares of dozens of ranking Niyyuuan soldiers and politicians, was another matter entirely. He fought to conceal his discomfort. A soft, whispered voice from somewhere near his feet helped to steady him.

"Don't blow this," George hissed warningly.

Walker gathered himself. "My friends and I are thankful for your compliment, but the congratulations deserve to be spread among all the relevant commanders."

The senior general of the armed forces of Charuchal-uul dipped his head briefly in acknowledgment of alien modesty. "Individual accomplishments are inevitably recognized by the discerning. Our research clearly indicates that you and yous' colleagues, though deceptively incompatible, cooperate fully on matters that affect yous all. We of Charuchal-uul, though caught off guard by yous' tactics, learn quickly." One hand reached out to stroke Walker's right shoulder. "Not surprising learn that new ideas come from new minds."

Walker could only mumble thanks on behalf of himself and his companions.

Deeleng-hab-wiq glanced briefly at the attentive crowd. "When seeking the best of new ideas, visitor Walker, we of Charuchal-uul are second to none in our ability to adapt to new conditions. Clearly seeing, if this unprecedented yet not formally allied consortium of realms is to continue to grow and succeed, leadership concurrent with the new ideas that inspire and drive it is required. The thing is decided." Taking two steps back, he gestured ceremoniously.

"The supreme military council of Charuchal-uul, in concert with full parliamentary sanction and approval of the military and governmental representatives of the other relevant realms, have determine to designate you, Marcus Walker of Earth, as chief determiner of strategy and tactics for all future endeavors involving the armed forces of those realms so indicated."

At his feet, George grinned toothily. Feeling a vast presence close behind him, Walker turned to see Braouk looming over him. A massive tentacle came down to rest on his shoulder while an eyestalk curved around either side of Walker's head as the Tuuqalian stared at him in stereo. The big alien rumbled in the human's ear.

"An important development, in our personal seeking, to progress. Thus think I, while observing this honor, so timely."

Conscious of multiple pairs of penetrating Niyyuuan eyes on him, Walker swallowed hard and mumbled, "But I'm just a commodities trader—and a cook!"

13

Stunned and benumbed, Walker was not the only one present to object to the unexpected and startling announcement. Visibly shocked, Saluu-hir-lek stepped out of the circle of dignitaries and into the center. Behind him, Viyv-pym looked more confused than Walker had ever seen her.

"What foolishness is this?" the commander of the forces of Kojn-umm demanded to know. He was so angry his ears were quivering. "I, Saluu-hir-lek, defender of Jalar-aad-biidh, have overseen every military advance since first pursuit of Toroudian attackers! Nomination of alien advisors as heads of Kojn-umm forces was for show only. Any dominant position is rightfully mine." Though utterly alien in appearance, Walker noted, the general made noises like any outraged sentient seeing a lifelong dream evaporate before his eyes. The irony was that of all those notables assembled under the great dome, none supported the general's assertion more strongly than did the lone human present.

"It's true what Saluu-hir-lek says. My friends and I were 'made' heads of the army of Kojn-umm for certain reasons that need not be detailed here. The general was the one who was really in charge throughout."

Though he made mollifying gestures, Deeleng-hab-wiq did not back down from his declaration. "All of us, most certainly those whose traditional forces have been defeated, recognize the skill and experience of Saluu-hir-lek of Kojn-umm in directing combat operations. But careful study has shown from whence the original strategy comes that has allowed for the establishment of such unusual combinations of forces. Did not arise from you, Saluu-hir-lek." The representative of Charuchal-uul looked back to Walker. "Is not difficult for the interested to assess that unnatural proposals arise from unnatural sources."

"It not matter!" Saluu-hir-lek was livid. "I the one who directed combined armies. I the one who oversaw movements of forces as well as actual assaults. Besides, is madness to give actual as opposed to sham ability to make operational decisions at such a level to this . . . this . . ."

It was fascinating to watch a Niyyuu sputter, George observed. At such rare moments their round, muscular mouths resembled leaky hose spigots. It reminded him also very much of angry cats, though the Niyyuu were only passingly feline. Standing next to him, Walker was handling it rather well. There was something to be said for being stunned speechless. But if you couldn't talk, you couldn't say something foolish. It was hard for a mute to be imprudent.

"This non-Niyyuu?" the commander of great Charuchal-uul's forces finished for the general. "That precisely the reason why agreement to do so was so swiftly reached among affected governments. Biranju-oov, for example, give every indication of balking if someone like youself named to such a position of power. Same true for commanders of traditional army of Toroud-eed. And I may say with some confidence, of Charuchal-uul as well." His attention fixed on Walker.

"But this creature from who originate distinctive military strategy that lead to unprecedented consequences among the Niyyuu, he *not* Niyyuu. His advisors not Niyyuu. Not even Sessrimathe. All are complete strangers to our society. Furthermore, have no external interests beyond the immediately personal." Deeleng-hab-wiq did not look at the irate general of Kojn-umm as he said this. He did not have to.

"Alien Walker person not act on behalf of some hidden, unknown power waiting to take advantage of new and confusing situation here. So he not favor any local faction above another.

Not Divintt-aap over Dereun-oon. Not Biranju-oov over Charuchal-uul." Now he turned and stared hard at the apoplectic general. "Not Kojn-umm over Toroud-eed."

Anxious to maintain harmony, Walker stepped forward. "Listen, nothing I and my friends did or said or advised was for personal gain. At least, not in the sense your people generally think of such things. We just want to get home."

Deeleng-hab-wiq gestured understandingly. "All who decide this matter know that. Such knowledge contribute to our decision appoint you key position."

Walker spread his hands helplessly. "But I don't *want* it."

The voice of the commander of Charuchal-uul's forces fell slightly, sounding like two steel screws being rubbed against one another. "You not consulted," he replied quietly but firmly.

"Actions have consequences, that cannot be foreseen, every time," Braouk intoned solemnly behind the anxious human.

At Walker's feet, George whispered upward. "You're stuck with it, Marc. When a dog's made the leader of the pack, he's got no choice but to fight to keep it. Otherwise some subordinate will rip him to bits at the first opportunity, if only to protect his or her own status."

At this, Walker glanced reflexively in Saluu-hir-lek's direction. But the general of Kojn-umm was not looking at him. He continued to glare at Deeleng-hab-wiq as if Walker himself was wholly unimportant to the disagreement at hand.

But not Viyv-pym. She was watching her human charge closely. If she was seeking evidence of deception on his part, she was looking in the wrong place.

"This is a thing settled." Deeleng-hab-wiq was not to be moved.

Eying the other assembled dignitaries, Saluu-hir-lek saw that their resolve was no less strong. Enraged, frustrated, and full of fury at having had his supreme command usurped not only by an alien, but by an alien who did not even want the honor, he whirled and pushed his way through the crowd. Viyv-pym hesitated. But she was Kojn-umm. Irrespective of any personal feeling she might hold, she owed her allegiance to her realm. Also her enviable position. Turning, she hurried to catch up to the rapidly departing Saluu-hir-lek.

The commander of the traditional armies of Charuchal-uul, now a part of the seething mélange of realms and forces that continued, on a much lower level, to fight among themselves so as to avoid the stigma of being considered formal allies, turned back to Walker.

"The soldier from Kojn-umm has ambition. Perhaps too much ambition for a traditional Niyyuuan fighter. Our species has found a way to let us aggressively settle disputes between different traditional territories without adversely impacting overall planetary development. Yous' successful alien tactics have cast new and confusing ideas into ancient cultural mix. This making many uncomfortable. But new ideas, even uncomfortable ones—especially uncomfortable ones—cannot be ignored. They must be dealt with." Taking a step back, he wrapped both long arms around his upper torso.

"We of the assembled traditional fighting forces of Toroudeed, Biranju-oov, Divintt-aap, Dereun-oon, Charuchal-uul, and perhaps even Kojn-umm await you next advisement."

Having stood openmouthed for so long, Walker became aware that his palate was drying out. He swallowed again, licked his lips. "I—I'll have to consult with my . . . advisors."

"Of course you will. A suitable residency has been prepared for yous here in capital." Dropping his arms, Deeleng-hab-wiq once more approached the human, coming very close. "Is hoped yous will find Charuchalan hospitality as satisfactory as what yous have experienced elsewhere." Lowering his head, he brought it close to Walker's own and whispered.

"Perhaps also you might be persuaded prepare special meal for uppermost level of capital government? Is said that you performances with Niyyuuan cuisine are quite remarkable."

Not knowing what else to say and utterly overwhelmed by the unexpected events that had overtaken him, Walker could only mumble a response. "I'll see what I can do. I don't have my trained assistants here, and I'd be working with unknown instrumentation, and—"

"Whatever is required will be provided," Deeleng-hab-wiq declared importantly as he straightened. He did not elaborate on the request. "Until yous have a proposal for all to consider, yous must relax and regain yous' energy."

Raising one hand, he gestured. A small but well-armed escort appeared. As he and his friends were led away, Walker wondered at the need for it. Was Deeleng-hab-wiq worried that a disgruntled Saluu-hir-lek might react violently to the decision that had been made on the aliens' behalf? Or was it simply the Charuchalan way?

Exiting the enormously impressive traditional building, they were bundled into a transport large enough to accommodate them all, including Braouk and their armed escort. Rising above normal traffic, the huge craft settled into an altitude reserved for travelers on official business, and accelerated.

While George kept his nose pressed to the transparent shell of their craft to better enjoy the passing view of the imposing capital city of Charuchal-uul, Braouk sprawled his bulk in the back, massive tentacles pressing up against the sides and floor of the vehicle. That left Walker to tread in the turbulent pool of his own thoughts until a wandering tendril crept across his shoulder. Turning in his typically too-narrow Niyyuuan seat, he found the glistening, argent, horizontal eyes of Sequi'aranaqua'-na'senemu staring back into his own. As she clung firmly to the supports of the seat behind him, another of her ten tendrils snaked forward to join the first.

"So the bumbling, primitive human is given nominal over-lordship over the decisions of a powerful cluster of alien forces. Truly, the universe is replete with wonders."

"I don't want it," he mumbled by way of response. "We weren't looking for anything like this, and I don't want anything to do with it. Let Saluu-hir-lek have the control." He grew thoughtful. "I bet I can talk Deeleng-hab-wiq and the other commanders into reconsidering. I mean, I understand their line of reasoning, but if I object strenuously enough, if I show them that I'm really not the individual mentally and emotionally equipped for the kind of task that they—"

"That does not matter." As was her manner, she did not hesitate to interrupt before he was finished. "Do not trouble yourself with concern over everyday decisions involving military matters. What is important is that these forces that have gathered more or less together regard you as an honest broker of opinion. What matters is that, despite individual misgivings, they are likely to respond positively to any request you might care to make." Glistening a deep red that was almost black, tendrils writhed. Light flashed from the shards of metal and plastic and thin slivers of gemstone that decorated the sinuous, flexible limbs.

"Regarding specifics, do not worry. As always, I am here to proffer advice and good counsel. I have some small notions on how best we should proceed given these most recent developments."

He smiled at the utterly alien shape that clung to the superstructure of the seat behind him. "I'd be surprised if you didn't, Sque. You're always thinking forward, always one jump ahead of everybody else, so I'm sure you've been—" His words faded away and his eyes widened ever so slightly as he gawked at the eternally cool, utterly composed K'eremu. "My God. You saw this coming, didn't you? All of it. You've seen this coming right from the beginning, when we pushed Saluu-hir-lek to pursue the army of Toroud-eed right after their retreat from Jalar-aad-biidh." His voice rose perceptibly. "And all the time, you didn't say anything. You kept it to yourself." His hand moved sharply as he gestured first toward the dog staring at the window, then at the muscular alien mass sprawled in the rear of the transport.

"You've been using us, manipulating us, right from the start of this. Just like you manipulated us to get free of the Vilenjji ship." He slapped his forehead and rolled his eyes. "What could I have been thinking? Or not thinking. I've been so wrapped up in surviving our time here and trying to think of ways to move on that I forgot to pay attention to what you've been doing, to how you operate. You're a scheming little bag of worms, Sque."

The K'eremu bore the human's outpouring of anger and angst in silence. When he finally ran out of steam, her two extended tendrils lightly stroked his shoulder in the Niyyuuan manner.

"I applaud you. Realization of reality never comes to some. Better to achieve enlightenment late than to forever dwell in the darkness. You are correct in your assumptions—but only to a certain extent. Yes, I did foresee certain possibilities and work to bring them about. For them to have the best chance of success it was required that you assume center stage. You are the one who came to Niyu with the lofty reputation, and your body shape and size is far more agreeable and familiar to the natives than is that of the K'eremu. You are also more diplomatic and self-effacing than I. I can recognize the usefulness of such qualities in lesser life-forms even when I do not possess them myself.

"You loudly decry my maneuverings. Let us consider for a time-part how damaging the results have been to you. They freed you from Vilenjji captivity, assured your good treatment on Seremathenn, and most recently have seen you anointed the chief of strategy for a powerful, possibly unprecedented consortium of the natives who are our present hosts." The slender pink speaking tube danced and swayed. "Yes, you surely have done badly from my maneuvering, human Walker. The misery you have suffered as a result must know no bounds."

"Dammit, Sque, it's not that, and you know it!" Taking note of his shouting, George finally turned from the transparent side of the speeding transport. With one hand, Walker removed the pair of caressing tendrils from his shoulder. "It's this not telling us what's going on, what you have in mind, that's so infuriating. If you wanted me to end up as the tactical head of this bad-tempered coalition of traditional Niyyuuan forces, why didn't you just say so? Why didn't you tell me what you were planning?"

"Look inward, Marcus. Take a good look inside your being, if your kind is capable of such candid introspection. If I had apprised you of such intentions back on the old stone walls of Jalar-aad-biidh in Kojn-umm and you had not panicked outright, what would have been your most likely reaction?" Startling him, she proceeded to perfectly mimic his voice. It was yet another ability she had not previously demonstrated. " 'Oh, Sequi'aranaqua'na'senemu, what a clever idea! Oh Sque, I can't wait to put my life on the line in multiple attempts to fool the Niyyuu as to our true purpose! Oh, yes, Sque, I will be able to portray myself as totally uninterested in the outcomes of all subsequent conflicts!'" Her voice returned to normal.

"It was vital to the success of the enterprise that your innocence as to its ultimate potential objective be at all times preserved. I think you will agree that such has been the case, and that events have developed propitiously. We are now in a position to demand, as opposed to filing polite requests for, assistance from the Niyyuuan astronomic community in locating our homeworlds. This would not be possible without our successive military triumphs, albeit on the low-grade traditional level. One squad of Niyyuu equipped with modern weapons could disperse all the assembled armies of all the six realms we have brought together. But that, fortunately, is not the Niyyuuan way."

He was quiet, trying to digest everything she had said. As usual, no matter how fervently he detested her manipulation of him and his friends, no matter how much he hated being used, he was finally forced to admit that the results just might have been worth all the sneaking and subterfuge. They now found themselves in a position that should greatly enhance their chances of finding a way home. And she was right about something else as well: despite not wanting to admit it, he had to confess to himself that if she had clearly and unambiguously laid out her intentions back in Kojn-umm, he would automatically have rejected them. Not only because he would have believed in their ultimate failure, but because of the potential danger.

At that thought he performed what could only be described as a follow-up double take. "I could have been killed! At any time since we left Kojn-umm, I could have been killed. Or Saluu-hir-lek might have figured out what was going on and had me assassinated. Or the forces of one of the realms we were opposing could have had me killed." Rising slightly, he leaned toward her over the back of his own high Niyyuuan seat. "*That's* why you didn't want to put yourself forward as the promoter of the eventual strategy that was devised. That's why you've stayed in the background and out of the way. You figured that if anything went wrong with your scheming, as the public face of it I'd be the one who'd get killed." His head snapped sharply to his left. "What are *you* laughing at?"

Off to one side, George had fallen off his narrow seat and was rolling back and forth on the floor, teeth exposed, his feet pawing at the air. "Slickly snookered by Sister Seafood! And not for the first time, either. Humans never learn. You're so wrapped up in your own vanity and glory, that—" The dog dissolved in laughter.

Having hoped for at least moral support from the canine quarter of the quarrelsome quartet, it was fair to say that Walker was less than pleased with his companion's ebullient response.

"You are of course correct in your assessment." His accusation found Sque as serene and unruffled as ever. "Surely you must admit that for any of us mismatched fellow travelers to have a chance of returning all the way home, it is imperative that I, of all of us, must remain whole and unharmed."

With an effort, Walker controlled his anger. "I do apologize if my desire to go on living conflicts with your overall assessment of how best to deal with our present situation."

The K'eremu was as immune to sarcasm as Braouk was to flung stones. "There is no need to apologize. You are not responsible for responding according to base instincts over which you have no control. It is the same with all the lower orders." Then, perhaps relenting slightly, possibly realizing she might be stepping over a line she could barely perceive, she added, "I am of course directing all my considerable mental energies to seeing that all of us, and not just myself, complete that much-to-be-desired voyage."

Turning away from her and ignoring her gently probing tendrils, he folded his arms over his chest. "Don't knock yourself out," he muttered crossly.

Transparent lids flicked down over silvery eyes. "I am afraid my embedded translator is having difficulty with your last comment."

By way of response, an irate Walker supplied a follow-up whose meaning her translator had no difficulty whatsoever conveying unequivocally. The questing tendrils promptly withdrew. No more was heard from the K'eremu for the remainder of the journey.

From the capacious rear of the transport, verse floated forward borne on the wings of alien melancholy. Braouk was reciting.

"Cast adrift here, fighting and killing daily, empty actions. How I long for the endless fields of Tuuqalia, for its vaulted skies and waving fields of surashh, for its dense forests and cool plains, for its—"

Necessity overcoming the need to visually display his displeasure, Walker uncrossed his arms and pressed his palms tightly against both ears. George used his front paws to press his own ears firmly against the sides of his head. For her part, Sque simply ignored their massive companion's latest interminable recitation. Unequipped to translate it, their Charuchalan hosts remained blissfully ignorant of the content of the alien drone, however much it sounded to them as if the largest of their honored guests must be feeling vaguely unwell.

The most honored commander of the expeditionary army of the traditional forces of the righteous realm of Kojn-umm was in an ill humor. He had been ever since the startling anointment of the ungainly human as the chief strategic planner for the nonalliance of quasi-cooperating military forces of six territories. It was outrageous! It was insupportable!

It was also, however uncomfortable, a fact, and one that he was going to have to deal with. In order to do that, he needed information. Believing he possessed enough of the latter, he had been taken by surprise by the unity of the other realms' decision. He would not make the same mistake again.

Hence his impatience when the citizen he had summoned to his presence finally appeared before him.

While she was not intimidated by the prospect of a private conference with the general, neither did Viyv-pym have any idea what Saluu-hir-lek wanted of her. She found out very quickly, as Saluu-hir-lek addressed her directly and in nononsense tones.

"What does this alien Marcus Walker mean to you?"

Her tails twitched involuntarily, a clear sign she did not understand the question. "*Mean* to me? There no meaning attached to relationship. I his appointed guide on and to world and culture of Niyyuu. Same functioning applicable to his three companions. If relationship has any meaning, takes the form of what I am paid by government of Kojn-umm."

His words contradicted his gesture of understanding. "I have had abundant time to observe the alien Walker. Also to observe the alien Walker observing you. Is more there than simple diplomacy."

Initially confident upon being sent for, his guest found herself increasingly bemused. "I confess I not follow the general commander's line of reasoning."

Her unfettered bewilderment was answer enough for his purposes. "Never mind. I've learned what I need know. You are blameless of participation in this betrayal." Coming close, he lowered his rasping voice. "You must understand, Viyv-pym: I had to find out. Do not carry any concern with you now that clarity in this thing is restored."

Having been accused and then found innocent of something without ever once having been informed of what it was, she was understandably bewildered. Her trial was apparently over without her ever having been brought before a court. Given her initial perceptions, she ought to have felt relieved. Instead, she was more confused than ever.

"You are upset because of the human Walker's elevation," she hazarded.

"Upset!" Once again he had to lower his voice. "Upset, yes. This whole matter is absurd, ridiculous, and unreasonable." His flexible arms snapped in the air of the room like whips. "The alien is a cook, not military strategist. But I not fooled." His large, alert eyes gleamed. "I see what being done. Charuchaluul, Biranju-oov, and others wish marginalize me and influence of Kojn-umm on future actions. Better they not relax. When time come, I will deal with their deceit."

"And the human?" Viyv-pym was not entirely sure why she

should care, or why she asked. She knew only that she did, and she had.

"*Eehgh,* the human! It strange, but I not mad at him. It clear to me that he being manipulated for the ends of others. What others, I still not certain. No doubt good cook is ignorant of how he being used. No, the alien food preparator is harmless. I more fear the actions of his companions, especially the small rubbery being with many limbs. She says too little, sees too much. I repeatedly reproaching myself for my neglect of her."

Viyv-pym gestured supplely. "I am Kojn-umm. You my superior. I will do whatever you deem necessary to advance best interests of our realm."

"I know that you will, Viyv-pym. For moment, though, nothing can be done. Is better more useful watch and wait."

"For what?" she asked him as she lowered her arms.

He was staring ferociously, but not at her. "For opportunity."

Their rooms were admirable, overlooking just one of the great sweeping harbors for which Charuchal-uul was famed throughout Niyu. If the level of technological sophistication was not up to that of highly advanced Seremathenn, it was at least the equal of Kojn-umm. As honored guests, they had no cause for complaint.

At least not against their hosts, whose attitude toward them continued to reflect a mixture of admiration, suspicion, and a curiosity that bordered on the fawning. Among two of the visitors, there was still some internal dissension.

Walker was pacing back and forth in front of the floor-to-ceiling transparency that overlooked the view. If he closed his eyes almost shut and let his mind drift, he could imagine that he was standing in a skyscraper looking out over Lake Michigan. Then he would open them again, and his sight and mind would be confronted by alien architecture, alien transport, and a sky that was just a shade too greenish.

"You can't keep interfering in local affairs like this. You're going to make a mistake and get us killed." He halted close to the K'eremu. "Look how your actions have offended Saluu-hir-lek. I've become familiar enough with Niyyuuan expressions and reactions to know that this whole experience has changed him from a friend to someone who wouldn't be sad to see us disappear."

As she listened to the human, Sque was lolling on one of the narrow padded benches that were the Niyyuuan equivalent of a comfortable couch. While her tendrils sprawled loosely around her, her body stayed, as always, upright in the center of the ropy mass.

"What I am going to do, Marcus, is get us home. You do still want to get home, don't you?" He said nothing. "As for offending the ambitious general Saluu-hir-lek, I cannot function effectively if I am forced to waste time concerning myself with the possible personal disenchantments of representatives of the local dominant life-form."

Nearby, George had been running nose patrol over a section of the peculiarly resilient flooring, absorbing and cataloging smells for future reference. Now he looked up briefly at Walker. "You sure, Marc, that it's Saluu-hir-lek you're so concerned about offending?"

Walker's brows drew together as he regarded the busy canine. "I don't follow you, George."

"It's been awhile since we had a visit from our lean and trim original minder, hasn't it? Maybe you're worried our activities might have offended *her*?" He bared his teeth. "Maybe you miss her a little?"

"Viyv-pym is our most active and knowledgeable conduit to the Niyyuu," Walker snapped crossly. "She is our connection to this world and this culture and has been ever since Seremathenn. I miss her because of *that,* yes."

"Uh-huh." Cocking his head slightly to the right, the dog sat down and began scratching himself behind one ear. "Tell me something, Marc. When you kiss her, is it like sticking your tongue down a vacuum cleaner hose?"

A furious Walker began chasing the dog around the largely unusable Niyyuuan furniture while the agile canine toyed with him, remaining just beyond the human's reach. Sequi'aranaqua'-na'senemu did her best to ignore them both as she contemplated their immediate future. Despite a nagging conviction that doing so was a waste of time, she was still determined to do her best to save them both, along with the oversized versifier who was presently sleeping soundly at one end of the large room.

How she missed the reasonableness of K'erem! Of home, of her own kind, each individual secure in the knowledge that he or she was the epitome of evolution. She missed the soothing solitude of her own quiet, carefully landscaped residence, the chance to communicate with others of like mind—over a secure distance, of course—the opportunities for advanced intellectual discourse. None of the latter were to be found here, where she was forced to act always as teacher and never as student.

For all that, for all the inherent physical and mental deficiencies for which they were not responsible, she rather liked her companions. Braouk, with his melancholy manner, ever eager and ready to recount the passionate sagas of his world to any who would listen. If only he would shut up more often. The small quadruped George, whose tail never seemed to stop moving, an appendage as close to achieving perpetual motion as any she had ever seen attached to another intelligent being. Even Walker, forever unsure of himself but unafraid to do whatever was necessary to improve their situation.

She wondered if any of them actually liked her, or if they only pretended to do so in order to keep her superior intellect focused on the business of getting them all home. Not that it mattered. No K'eremu needed to rely on the approval of lesser life-forms to sustain a feeling of self-worth.

On the other tendril, it was doubtful any peaceful, solitary K'eremu had previously found itself in her position. To her discomfiture, she found that she did care if her companions liked her or not. Her tendrils drew in more tightly around the base of her body. No doubt, with time and proper meditation, the unnatural feeling of caring what a motley lot of lower life-forms thought about her would go away.

When the human, out of breath from chasing his smaller but much quicker companion, finally halted, she confronted him. "What difference should it make to you, Marcus, or to any of us, if we intervene in local affairs? Our hosts are barbarians who dwell under the slimmest veneer of civilization." Tendrils rose and fluttered, describing distinct patterns in the air.

"They slaughter one another under the pretext of restraining themselves. The fact that they forbid the use of modern weapons in these bloody ritual exercises between individual tribes shows only that they have an interest in preserving their species, not in improving it. Then there is the obscenely ubiquitous media coverage. No other marginally civilized race of my acquaintance views intraspecies warfare as an excuse for crass entertainment."

His quarrel with George forgotten, Walker looked uncomfortable. "One other does," he muttered uneasily. "Except that it doesn't restrict its use of weapons to the archaic." He did not have to elaborate.

Sque's speaking tube emitted a succession of small bubbles. "I might have suspected as much."

He waited for inevitable indictment, the twist of· the verbal knife, the perfectly minted coin of sarcasm. When it was not forthcoming, he blinked and peered down at her. "That's it? You don't have anything else to say?"

Tendrils bobbed and weaved, like an anemone preparing for a prizefight. "What could I add that would embellish the depressing reality of your kind? If your culture is not so unlike that of the Niyyuu, then I should not have to explain why I feel no compunction at manipulating the latter. There is no beauty, no entertainment, no satisfaction to be found in the killing of one's own kind. It is an abomination that all sentient species should have shed. Yet it lingers on in remote, out-of-the-way places."

He found himself nodding slowly. "You're correct, Sque. I have no right to criticize your actions here. The K'eremu, I take it, don't fight among themselves?"

"Only with sharp phrases and pointed words. These cut deeply enough." A knot of maroon-hued coils, she dropped off the couch and slithered past him, stopping at the transparent wall. George trotted over to join her in gazing at the busy metropolitan harbor below. A silence ensued during which the only sounds in the room were the barely audible whisper of the air recycler and the somewhat louder breathing of the dozing Tuuqalian in the back.

"If Fortune is with us, we will not have to concern ourselves with the affairs of this wayward world and its argumentative folk much longer."

Walker looked down at her in surprise. "You've heard something!"

The upper portion of the K'eremu's body arced back, and metallic eyes gazed up at him. "Learning things is as much a matter of listening well as it is of cultivating sources. One picks such bits of possibility out of a society even while its majority is occupied with an activity as wasteful as war. All I am saying is that in the near future there may occur a development or two favorable to that end which is of interest to us all. Should these eventuate, we will need to act together, with one voice." She drew herself up to her full four feet.

"That means my voice, of course, but I am certain you both already understand that."

"I don't understand it," George objected out of principle. "But I'll go along with anything that'll take us a step closer to home."

"Everyone needs to be prepared to fulfill their part." She looked past them both, straining to see past the high, uncomfortable furniture. "Stir that lump of sensitive Tuuqalian flesh from its extended slumber." With several tendrils, she gestured in Braouk's direction. "I will advise you."

"What if these developments you're referring to don't pan out?" Walker asked her.

Glistening eyes turned back to him. "Then your intelligence level will have been raised up an infinitesimal fraction from having paid another time-part's attention to me. Go wake the brute."

Not having anything better to do, Walker did as she requested. Carefully, as always. There were occasions when the Tuuqalian had a disconcerting tendency to wake up swinging.

14

Called at Walker's request—but at Sque's direction—the meeting took place a ten-day later. The representatives of half a dozen different realms and their traditional fighting forces gathered in a bubble chamber attached to the end of a pierlike structure that thrust outward from a point of land north of the capital city's main harbor. Though the chamber was not small, the immense transport vessels that skimmed past at high speed, heading for the inner harbor, made it seem so. After many ten-days spent in the field marching with traditional forces, Walker had still not completely reacclimated himself to the trappings of modern galactic technology.

Saluu-hir-lek's accusations made him even more uncomfortable. Unexpectedly reduced in stature to just one more commanding officer among many, Kojn-umm's most famous soldier was spitting mad as he stalked back and forth in front of the transparent, curving wall of the climate-controlled bubble. As was the custom in Charuchal-uul, there was no furniture. Everyone present was forced to stand for the duration of the gathering. Though uncertain as to the specific cultural rationale, Walker observed that it was an excellent way to keep the length of official meetings under control.

The occasional appearance beyond the wall of quartets of leaping segestroth, who resembled a cross between giant goldfish and drowning doves, formed an incongruous background to the general's rant. It seemed that whenever Saluu-hir-lek became particularly wound up, four or eight or twelve of the spectacularly highlighted ocean dwellers would execute a series of their impressive leaps as they traveled back and forth between the harbor and deeper ocean waters beyond.

Walker's discomfort was caused by the fact that he and his companions were the subject of the general's loud complaining. George remained by his side while Braouk stayed as far from the see-through walls as possible. The Tuuqalian, it developed, could not swim. In contrast, Sque hugged the place where the nearest curving wall met the floor, hoping for an early end to the gathering so she could spend some time crawling over the spume-soaked rocks outside.

As Saluu-hir-lek raved on, Walker would look past him to the rest of the official delegation from Kojn-umm. Sometimes Viyv-pym met his stare; other times he found her looking away. He could not tell, as he might have been able to with a human, what she was thinking. With mixed success, he tried to convince himself that it was not important.

Like a pair of dancing snakes, the general's arms kept twitching in Walker's direction. "Look at him! Who this creature to whom you give such power? A visitor from world that not even part of civilization. Such decision run counter to everything in Niyyuuan history." His attention wandered to George, panting softly near the human's feet. "And his companions. What we know of them, of their real motives? Maybe really come here only to make trouble."

"As it has been told to me," the general Afyet-din-cil of Biranju-oov countered, "they originally brought here to make telugrivk. With sweet garnish."

Saluu-hir-lek's furious stare was insufficient to overcome the hacking laughter that the other officer's observation sparked. Telugrivk was a complex dish whose preparation Walker had mastered during his first days on Niyu, and for which he had become widely admired among those Niyyuu fortunate enough to have tasted it.

"It's true we may have acquired some small influence," Walker responded. "But we didn't ask for it, and we certainly didn't go seeking it." He looked toward Deeleng-hab-wiq. Thus far, the commander of the traditional forces of Charuchal-uul had remained placidly in the background. "It was bestowed upon us. And we don't really want it. Not that kind of power, anyway. What we want is a way to return to our homes. One that will allow us to do so without having to spend any more time than is absolutely necessary at stops along the way." Spreading his hands, he moved his arms in as near an approximation of the relevant Niyyuuan manner as his far stiffer joints would allow.

"I don't see any problem here. We want to leave, and some of you"—he eyed the silently simmering Saluu-hir-lek—"want us to leave. Just give us the resources that we need to do so properly and we'll depart without another word. Any perceived problems caused by our presence will disappear. We've only done anything we have done up until now because no one would give us the help we need."

Now Deeleng-hab-wiq did step forward. "We would prefer that you remain among us, Marcus Walker. Having positioned yourself as you have, you cannot just leave us. Besides"—he eyed his own attending subordinates—"what you request would not only be extremely difficult, but costly."

"The cost can be met."

All eyes turned to the new speaker. Pushing her way to the forefront of the milling group was a Niyyuu Walker had not seen before. She was tall even for one of her kind. Clad in a triple wrap of dark blue, crimson, and silver chiffonlike material, she advanced with a flowing grace unmatched even by Viyv-pym. Even Sque was moved to pause in her yearning contemplation of the wave-washed rocks outside the chamber to contemplate the newcomer.

Satisfied with the impression she had made, the new arrival announced herself. "I am Jhanuud-tir-yed, vice premier of the realm of Fiearek-iib." Murmurs arose from those in attendance who had not recognized the newcomer immediately upon her formal entrance. When the whispering died down, she continued.

"I have come from halfway around world to attend this meeting. I represent not only Fiearek-iib, but others as well." She proceeded to coolly reel off the names of an adequate number of powerful realms to intimidate even the fiery Saluu-hir-lek. That done, she turned her attention to Walker and his now-attentive companions.

"We too wonder at real motivations of strange visitors. You come among us armed not with weapons or proclaimed ambitions, but with curious knowledge drawn from elsewhere." One arm rose and described an arc through the air. "Yet now one of you is in position to determine strategy for combined traditional forces of six realms. Six realms that fight among themselves, yet redeploy together. This is a new and atypical thing in Niyyuuan terms. It is worrisome. It concerns government of Fiearek-iib and its friends. Is even talk that should such an anomaly continue to spread, some might have to break with tradition and make use of modern weapons to stop it."

That shocking statement produced little gasps of disbelief as a number of small round mouths contracted involuntarily. What the vice premier was suggesting was nothing less than a dissolution of the compact that had allowed the various realms of Niyu to settle disputes and safely engage in therapeutic warfare for thousands of years. Among the assembled, only Saluu-hir-lek, Walker managed to note, did not appear distraught. But then, Walker knew better than most the depth of the general's deepest ambitions.

He became aware that the imposing visitor had once more turned back to him. "To forestall such potential upheaval, has been determined by my government and that of those of our neighbors of like mind to do what we can to remove principal source of much of possible contention."

"That'd be us," George pointed out succinctly from the vicinity of Walker's ankles.

"Yes." She glanced down at the dog. "I am authorized by government of Fiearek-iib and its allies to offer whatever financial and material support is required to help yous return yous' homes. But in return, is something we want."

"Sure," Walker replied, without having the slightest idea what he might be letting himself and his friends in for. "If you don't mind my asking, what might that be?"

The voice of vice premier Jhanuud-tir-yed of Fiearek-iib became that of an enthusiastic commoner. "Exclusive rights for representatives of our media concerns to record and later broadcast entire account of yous' attempt to return yous' homeworlds."

The shrill uproar set off in the chamber by this seemingly innocuous request was potentially damaging to ears more sensitive than those of the Niyyuu. Walker knew he shouldn't be surprised. Among certain of their hosts, media rights to a unique narrative were as significant as the conquest of one traditional army by another.

Deeleng-hab-wiq finally managed to restore a semblance of order. The energetic braying and heavy breathing subsided. "What the honored representative from Fiearek-iib demands must be debated. But at first hearing I think is probable suitable mutual agreements can be reached and practical arrangements made." He turned back to Walker. "Is becoming clear that despite wishes of many, yous cannot be held here. Therefore government of Charuchal-uul will also contribute to yous' homeward journey." That said, his tone changed from the officious to the sympathetic.

"But all resources of Niyu insufficient return yous home if is not known coordinates of respective homeworlds."

Not even the commanding figure of Jhanuud-tir-yed had an answer for that. But Sque did.

Scuttling away from the wall, the K'eremu positioned herself between Walker and the vice premier. "One is always grateful for a confluence of favorable circumstances. I requested this meeting through the human Walker to inform all the relevant parties of certain information that has recently come into my possession. I certainly did not expect also to encounter the means by which it might be acted upon. For that I would thank Fate—if I in any way believed in it." Raising her voice, she looked to her left and commandingly waggled several uplifted tendrils. "It is time—come in!"

Yet another new figure came forward from the back of the crowd. Walker reacted with fitting surprise the instant he recognized the newcomer.

It was the Kojnian astronomer Sobj-oes.

She offered greetings in the traditional manner of her realm, with a double-finger caress that stroked him from neck to waist. "Hello, Marcus Walker. It good see you once again."

"But I didn't..." He looked sharply down at the K'eremu. "What's this about, Sque? Why didn't you tell me Sobj-oes would be joining us here?"

"Because the justification for her to do so only came to light very recently, Marc." She blew a conciliatory bubble. "There is no reason for anyone, however individually interesting, to interrupt their work and extend themselves for the purpose of delivering non-news."

The implications inherent in the K'eremu's response were as obvious to George as they were to his human companion. Letting out a loud, joyful bark, the dog bounded forward, rose on hind legs, and rested his front paws against the astronomer's slender legs.

"Earth! You've found the coordinates for Earth!"

Walker felt like barking—or at least shouting with happiness—himself. The feeling of utter elation lasted about as long as his friend's shout.

"I afraid not so." The impression of deep regret in the astronomer's voice was profound.

George slumped, dropping his forepaws from the Niyyuuan's lower limbs, his head lowering. Downcast, he turned and walked slowly back to rejoin his friend. But if Walker had been less quick to respond with excitement, he was also less ready to give up hope. Sque had as much as said that Sobj-oes would only come this far if she had something significant to report.

"But you *have* found something?" he pressed her. Though they would not personally be affected by the astronomer's response, the assembled delegates and notables, from Deelenghab-wiq to Jhanuud-tir-yed and even Saluu-hir-lek, listened with unmistakable interest. So did Viyv-pym, perhaps with feelings more mixed than most.

"As you know, Marcus Walker," Sobj-oes began, "I promise you that night long ago in Kojn-umm that I and a few trusted associates would work in our spare time to try and help yous find yous' way homeward. This work has not been easy. Certain select portions of electromagnetic spectrum very crowded with communicatings of all kinds. Difficult, sometimes impossible, separate unintelligible from understandable, natural from artificial. Search for yous made more challenging by conflicting standards, lack of specifics, other difficulties." One sinuous arm rose to point at the attentive Sque.

"She and I secretly stay in touch these past many ten-days. Exchange information. She make many suggestions. Some very useful."

Walker glanced down at the K'eremu. Her reply was as calm and self-possessed as ever. "You had complex native inter-realmic relationships to deal with. I did not want to distract you—certainly not with false hopes."

He would have replied in a suitably acerbic manner, but was too keen to hear what else the astronomer had to say. "What *have* you and your associates managed to find out, Sobj-oes?"

She eyed him warmly. "As I already say, too sadly not coordinates your own home, Marcus Walker. Not actual specific coordinates any of yous' homes. But just possibly, after distilling from very large volume of information by using unambiguous knowledge provided by Sequi'aranaqua'na'senemu as workable sieve, may have found indications of occasional visitation to certain far-reaching region by one of yous' species." She paused to gather herself. "Are unverifiable but highly suggestive signs pointing to intermittent passage through specified area of occasional ships from world called Tuuqalia."

The roar that rose from the rear of the meeting bubble thunderously affirmed that the largest individual in attendance had not, after all, been sleeping soundly through it all. As an excited Braouk rose to loom over the assembled delegates, many of whom suddenly found one reason or another to shift their position within the chamber, Sobj-oes the astronomer hastened to calm him.

"I say again: relevant indicators do not provide location of this world. Only that representatives of your kind may have been recorded transiting the fairly extensive region in question."

"It is a beginning." Despite the astronomer's bombshell, Sque was, if anything, only a little less composed than usual. "However imprecise it may be, we now have a destination. Our course is clear." Tendrils writhed. "Travel to the place where the outsized saga-singers may have paid a call. In that vast but infinitely reduced section of space, seek additional clues to the location of their world. Even allowing for the distances the Vilenjji cover in their search for novel species to market, any region visited by the Tuuqalia must necessarily be nearer to K'erem. And to Earth," she added with only the slightest of tactless pauses.

"At least it's a trail to sniff." George was sitting on his haunches, eyes half-closed, contemplating the possibility they might at last actually have secured a line on the first phase of a way home.

A way and a means, if Jhanuud-tir-yed and the other senior representatives present were to be believed, an elated Walker reflected. In his excitement he barely managed to ask the obvious next question. "Can you show us?" he asked Sobj-oes.

Nodding, she gestured with one sinuous arm. General officers and senior bureaucrats alike made room, forming a compact, curious circle around her. Even Saluu-hir-lek was intrigued.

Removing from her waist pack a small device that would never have been permitted inside a traditional Niyyuuan military encampment, the astronomer coaxed it to generate a three-dimensional map of the galaxy. Rapidly zooming in, she froze the image on a system containing six planets and a pair of asteroid belts.

"Niyu," she explained for the benefit of the nonnatives present. Another command to the device caused the scale to expand to show hundreds of systems, related astronomical features, and a respectable chunk of starfield. "The always-changing, everfluctuating area of space those who dwell within its boundaries loosely refer to as galactic civilization." Once more the image dissolved and re-formed as the scale expanded. Expanded until the region affected by civilization had been reduced in size to a small blotch amidst the blackness. Like the electrified wing of some dark phoenix, several inner bands of one arm of the galaxy filled the refulgent, illustrated space. A minuscule point of light, a microscopic nova, flared approximately halfway out on one arm.

"The region where mention of Tuuqalia has been detected."

Breathy exclamations of surprise mixed with trepidation and concern rose from the assembled. The point of light was located very, very far indeed from the area demarcated by civilization.

"I have traveled to many worlds," Jhanuud-tir-yed declared somberly, "some of which lie far distant from beloved Niyu. But this representation speaks to distances beyond my experience." She looked over at the astronomer. "Your measurements are accurate?"

Sobj-oes gestured unequivocally. "They checked many times, by better scientists than I. At such distances is tolerated some allowance for error. But given distance involved, potential error is not significant."

Stepping forward, Deeleng-hab-wiq let the two fingers of his right hand pierce the projection. Slowly, methodically, they traced the space between civilization and the region highlighted by the point of light. The expanse was daunting.

"I not historian, but I think no ship of Niyu has ever traveled so great a distance. Certainly not in direction indicated." Vast yellow eyes settled on the attentive Walker. "Know, visitor human, that we Niyyuu not a bold species by nature. We not explorers of the Great Dark. Leave that to far-wandering sentients like the Sessrimathe. The Niyyuu like their world, like being closely linked with civilization. We not the kind to take chances such as this. As you know well, even our chosen manner of internecine warfare is conservative."

With one long, flexible finger, the contemplative Deeleng-hab-wiq stirred stars. "As regarding that, visitors have often forced us to think in new ways. Perhaps now is time to think in new ways regarding bold voyage such as this." Whereupon he added, to show that he had not lost sight of what was really important, "Rights to recording of such an important journey cannot be exclusive. Must be shared. Information must be pooled. This too important an event for one realm, even one such as Fiearek-iib, to control. Related rights should belong to all realms of Niyu."

"That reasonable enough," the vice premier reluctantly conceded, "*if* all realms contribute to costing."

Interest rapidly gave way to negotiating as the assembled delegates began to argue among themselves over which realm's media representatives were best qualified to accompany and document the unprecedented attempt to return the visitors to their homes. Though the debaters were utterly alien, Walker noted that their mind-set was not.

After a while, the ear-grating drone gave way to more calculated discussion as matters of principle were subsumed in debate as to who should pay what actual costs.

"As initiators of the proposal, the government of Fiearek-iib and its friends will underwrite a suitable vessel," Jhanuud-tir-yed insisted, "as well as appropriate crew. Others may participate in proportion to their fiscal contribution." This pronouncement set off another round of strident discussion, until it was interrupted by a single loud·interjection in a distinctive accent.

"No."

At the declamation, voiced in excellent and suitably grating Niyyuuan, debate faltered as one group of participants after another turned to stare at the speaker. Viyv-pym especially appeared taken aback.

Walker held his ground. "No," he repeated, more softly this time, growling out the single Niyyuuan syllable from the back of a throat that over the past months had grown positively calloused from wrestling with the local language. At his feet, George looked up at his friend as if he had suddenly developed a bad case of cat.

"I am afraid I not understand fully what you negating," the dignified but bemused vice premier of Fiearek-iib finally replied.

"You said 'a' ship. One ship won't be sufficient." Pointing, Walker indicated first Sque and then, gesturing over the heads of the assembled toward the back part of the chamber, the massive Tuuqalian. "We need at least three ships. In the event that our respective homeworlds lie great distances apart and in vastly differing directions, the expedition needs to leave Niyu prepared to cope with that possibility."

The murmuring that arose from the assembled in response to

the alien's assertion was more sedate and considered than that which had preceded it, perhaps because this time those involved were not arguing about one realm or another gaining a financial advantage over its neighbor.

"There would be other good reasons for proceeding in the suggested manner," the representative from Toroud-eed pointed out. "Embarking on such an unparalleled journey, it would make sense not everyone have to return if, for example, one ship encounter trouble."

Such thoughts percolated rapidly through the group. "Ships would be traveling far beyond boundaries of known civilization," the representative continued. "If encounter unexpected hostilities, three properly armed ships much better positioned defend selves than lone one."

A flurry of energetic, thoughtful responses greeted both observations. By the time discussion had begun to die down once again, Walker's rationale for the proposal had been completely submerged in other issues.

George nudged his friend's leg. "Once a trader, always a trader—eh, Marc?"

Bending low, Walker whispered to his friend. "I just thought it would be smarter, and easier, for us to make any demands here instead of dozens of light-years out in unfamiliar space."

"Very sensible." Sque had moved to stand close behind them. "A primitive craving, greed is, but occasionally a useful survival trait. Having three ships at our disposal will certainly do our chances of finding a way home no harm."

Walker looked down at her. "They won't exactly be at our 'disposal,' Sque."

The K'eremu waved a pair of tendrils at him. "Give me one ten-day to finalize details." It was an assertion Walker would not have chosen to bet against. In his short and increasingly implausible life, the K'eremu was as sure a thing as he had ever come across. If only, he thought mildly, he could find a way to convince her to come home with him. For just a little while. So she could study the commodities board for a few weeks, perform a quick analysis or two, and then leave him with just a few negligible recommendations.

It was never to be, he knew. Sque was interested in returning only to K'erem. In the many months they had spent together, she had barely learned to tolerate him. Knowing her as he did now he knew that her impression, and opinions of, his species were unlikely to extend to a desire to remain in their presence any longer than actual survival required.

A pity. He would have loved to have seen what she could do with juice concentrate futures.

Some time later, Jhanuud-tir-yed emerged from a conference that had been winnowed down to only the most important figures present. Walker noted that as chief representative of Kojnumm, Saluu-hir-lek appeared less than happy at having been excluded from the deliberations of the august group. Waving one arm hypnotically, the vice premier of Fiearek-iib approached the four guests. (Unable to remain quiescent subsequent to the astronomer Sobj-oes's revelations, Braouk had rejoined his companions.)

"It has been decided. Yous will be provided with support in yous' attempt return yous' homeworlds in the form of three of Niyu's finest ships. All three are the most up-to-date and best equipped. Crews will be drawn from vessels operated by all contributing realms. You will have only the best at your service." She gestured significantly at Walker.

"You official position achieved here on Niyu will continue be maintained on board until such time as you voluntarily leave assigned ship. This decision agreed upon by all participating parties out of respect you accomplishments among us—and also as way of settling arguments among representatives of different realms. As you stated in you military strategy, as alien and not citizen of any realm, you able deliver impartial decisions regarding same."

Walker was not so divorced from Niyyuuan society that he was unconscious of the honor. "With my friends' advice and aid, I'll do my best not to betray any trust you place in me."

Both of the vice premier's hands came up. Twinned fingers stroked Walker's chest. "I sorry I not personally have opportunity get know yous better. Yous a most, most interesting fouring of different types. But better yous go than stay." Was that a twinkle in one oversized, golden eye? "Better for yous—and better for us." She stepped back.

"Will take time prepare designated vessels for such unprecedented journey. Until then, a stopping has been called to all traditional fighting. I would personally wish yous return with me to Fiearek-iib to experience hospitality of my realm." She gestured in the direction of the local hosts. "But Charuchalans claim right of eminence. You will stay here until ships are made ready depart this system. Expect by time yous have dealt with several hundred requests for talkings from media, yous be ready leave even for dead, airless moon."

With decisions having been made and harmony more or less achieved, the delegates began to break up into small individual groups. Simultaneously relieved and excited, Walker felt a touch at the back of his pants. Turning and seeing Sque looking up at him, he knelt slightly to be nearer eye level with the K'eremu. He did not try to hide his elation.

"Well, Sque, I'm still not sure how it all happened, but I guess we're finally going home."

The K'eremu was rather more reserved. "Braouk is going home—maybe. You, and I, and the furry thing on four short legs, are going with him. I would say that with much luck and if the Fate I do not for an instant believe in is on our side, we might be fortunate enough in the course of this journey to encounter the tiniest inkling of where your homeworld or mine happens to lie."

Walker's enthusiasm dimmed measurably. "Always the optimist, aren't you, Sque?"

"Always the realist. You still have no true conception of the size of known space, Marcus Walker. Not even of this infinitesimally small portion of it. Yet I will allow that indications of even peripheral Tuuqalian presence in the region where we hope to go is at least a positive indicator. It forms a destination of a sort, however ephemeral."

Nearby, George muttered, "With unrestrained zeal like that I don't see how we can fail to keep our spirits up."

"Not to fear." With enviable deportment, the K'eremu proceeded to adjust several strands of the polished, treated bits of metal that decorated her slick-skinned person. "No matter how disheartening the circumstances may become, you will always have the enlightening presence of myself to uplift your dismal, backward selves. Now you must excuse me, for I have a date with a particularly inviting damp hole in the seawall outside." And without another word, she pivoted on her tendrils and scuttled off through the rapidly dispersing crowd.

15

Though restricted to the use of the facilities intrinsic to the extensive old-time bivouac area that was serving as temporary home to the visiting forces of Toroud-eed, Biranju-oov, and others, Saluu-hir-lek did not complain. As a leader of traditional military, he was used to the kinds of minor privations that simultaneously appalled and fascinated those Niyyuu who preferred to encounter such throwbacks to ancient times only in the media and while surrounded by the comforts of their own dwellings. Since it was his profession, it troubled him only occasionally that while he was restricted to often-primitive amenities, some of which dated to hundreds of years earlier, his alien nemeses were luxuriating in the most modern conveniences the capital city of Charuchal-uul could provide.

He could enjoy them as well, he knew. All he had to do was resign his commission. It raised his spirits to know that the grateful Council of Kojn-umm would never accept it. Back home, in his own realm, he was a venerated hero. Here, in more cosmopolitan Charuchal-uul, he was but one of several important foreign military commanders. For someone used to being the locus of attention, it was a sobering experience.

With the defeat of the traditional army of Charuchal-uul and the commercial and political advantages thus gained, the combined forces of Toroud-eed, Biranju-oov, Divintt-aap, and Dereun-oon had voted to stand back and reflect upon what they had accomplished. All of Saluu-hir-lek's attempts to urge them to build on the triumphs they had already achieved had been met with indecision, if not outright apathy. For one thing, his emissaries had been told, the aliens were leaving. No matter how hard he tried, the general could not convince them that while it might have been the aliens who had developed the initial strategy that had led to their present success, it was he, Saluu-hir-lek of Kojn-umm, who had seen them carried out. And it was he, Saluu-hir-lek, who could lead their combined forces onward, to greater and greater victories. To the total domination, in traditional terms, not of realms, but of this entire continent and perhaps others as well.

They hemmed and hawed. The aliens were leaving. And their troops were tired. No one wanted to march home, or travel by slow, traditional transport. More and more there was a clamor for an end to hostilities. And without the visitors to guide them...

The implication was that without the aliens' contribution there was no guarantee of further victories. Nothing an angrily earnest Saluu-hir-lek said could convince the senior officers of the armies of previously defeated realms that they would be able to continue their string of successes without the visitors' participation. In a development that was bitterly ironic, Kojn-umm's greatest traditional military commander found himself a victim of the success of his own subterfuge.

It meant that he would have to go home, too. Carrying with him a considerable degree of accomplishment, to be sure. He had much to be proud of. His successive triumphs had gained much influence for Kojn-umm. He would be hailed in Ehbahr as a greater hero than ever. For most Niyyuu it would have been enough. But not for the frustrated Saluu-hir-lek.

He wanted everything.

There was nothing he could do about it, however. The traditional forces of Kojn-umm could not go on alone, without their quasi-allies. The grand march was finished, done with, over. He would have to take his troops and go home. In triumph, to be sure, but a triumph that would remain personally forever incomplete. What galled him most was that it was clear now that the alien Walker and his duplicitous companions had never had any real interest in the kind of world-girdling conquest that he wanted to pursue. What they had been seeking all along was simply to acquire enough influence to ensure their departure from Niyu, suitably equipped and outfitted to find their way home. Having achieved what they sought, they were prepared to leave him and his greater ambitions in the lurch.

It was not fair. Promises had been broken. Trapped by paradox, he was left stewing in a mixture of triumph and anger.

An orderly entered. No electronics allowed here, in the temporary building that housed his office and that of much of his general staff. Following traditional procedures, information had to be conveyed person to person.

"General, you have a visitor. It claims to know of you by reputation."

Saluu-hir-lek's wide eyes fixed on the equally expansive oculars of the orderly. " 'It'?"

The orderly backed out. "You will see for yourself, General."

The being that assumed the orderly's place stood only a little taller than the general himself, but was far more massive. Its skin was a dark purplish hue and as bumpy and uneven as a streambed. Eyes proportionately larger even than those of the Niyyuu nearly met in the center of the tapering skull. Though outrageous in appearance, the origin of the unlikely visitor was not unknown to its educated host. Leaning back in the flexible, narrow seat that flexed obediently under the modest weight of his slender frame, Saluu-hir-lek regarded his visitor. While he was surprised, he was not in the least intimidated. His guest was exotic, but his kind were not strangers to the Niyyuu. Nor to any species that considered itself a member of a widespread and cosmopolitan galactic civilization.

"What matter," the general asked inquiringly, "brings a Vilenjji to traditional combat forces of Niyu?"

Raising one sucker-lined, flap-tipped arm by way of greeting, the thick-bodied visitor sloughed farther into the room. "I am named Pret-Klob, and am here on business, of course. To restore the natural order of things, one might say." Without waiting to be invited, he settled himself as best he could in the center of the floor. "I have come to recover some missing inventory that was formerly the property of my association."

Saluu-hir-lek was unimpressed. "What has that do with traditional forces of Kojn-umm?"

"I have taken steps to do the necessary economic research. While not precisely in your possession, you have apparently recently spent a good deal of time proximate to the property in question. Additional inquiries on my part lead me to believe you might be helpful in its recovery." The flap that comprised the outer half of the creature's right arm flexed meaningfully. "Should that eventuate, there would be an appropriate commission in it for you."

The general was already bored with the conversation. Though he had never previously met a Vilenjji in person, he knew them well by reputation and via the all-pervading Niyyuuan media.

"I not need yous' money."

The thick cilia that topped the Vilenjji's tapering head writhed actively. "Then perhaps another inducement might better encourage you to assist us. I am given to understand that there has of late occurred a lapse in your original fondness for certain other visiting non-Niyyuu with whom you have been working."

What nonsense was this distasteful visitor spouting? "I surmise you speaking of four aliens formerly attached to my staff. What they have to do with the Vilenjji?"

The flap-tipped arm gesticulated again. "They are the property of whom I speak."

That was unexpected. Saluu-hir-lek was not ashamed to admit that he was taken completely by surprise. His mind worked furiously. Who he was clashed violently with who he wanted to be.

"The Niyyuu consider themselves honorable members galactic society. Within that society, holding of sentients as property considered immoral."

"But only illegal on worlds that have specific directives against it." Unperturbed, the Vilenjji gestured afresh. "Otherwise, the relevant business would not be there for such as my association to exploit. The trick is to practice one's trade while staying clear of those meddlesome, do-gooding species who believe it is their moral right to interfere in the honest business of others. The Sessrimathe, for example. Unless my research is seriously flawed, the autonomous realms of Niyu hold no official legal position on this matter. Such isolated instances as might occur are to be adjudicated on an individual basis."

Heedless of the prohibitions against the use of modern devices inside a traditional Niyyuuan military encampment, the Vilenjji proceeded to produce a marvelous little information generator. When he had finished perusing the material placed before him, Saluu-hir-lek found himself torn between conventional morality and a burning desire for something more basic. Or base.

He had once been very fond of the food preparator Walker. These days, the emotions he felt toward the scheming human were more than merely conflicted.

"You want me help you recover yous 'property'? Property that consist of these four visitors?"

The Vilenjji gestured diffidently. "You may elect to accept the applicable commission for doing so or not. My present resources are limited, but still substantial. I think you would be pleased. There are certain trade goods we can offer you that are not readily available on your world."

Contraband, Saluu-hir-lek mused. There were desirable items that were banned from importation into Niyu. He could not help but wonder what they might be.

"If I assist you in this," he said slowly, "must present image of virtuous soldier only helping scrupulous off-worlders to recover what rightfully theirs. Leave moral implications for others to sort out."

The Vilenjji was perfectly agreeable. "While your reputation is of no concern to us, we of course understand that it is of interest to you. Rest assured we are adept at playing the outraged and offended." His voice, as translated by the device he wore over his speaking organ, grew noticeably edgy. "Recently, we have had much practice."

Saluu-hir-lek pondered the offer while his guest waited patiently. What manner of prohibited goods the dislikeable alien was offering by way of "commission" the general did not know. What he did know was that by reputation the Vilenjji had access to many things that were often as tempting as they were illegal. Then there was the matter of how he had been used, and lied to, by the four visiting aliens. Was he not entitled to some recompense for the insult he had suffered? If he could no longer make use of their singular talents to achieve his personal goals, then there was no reason to champion them or their cause.

They were determined to leave anyway, to embark on an outlandish, unlikely, and probably suicidal quest in search of their unknown and doubtlessly unreachable homeworlds. Dragging three ships of the Niyyuu, their crews, and multiple blinded media recorders with them to oblivion. Was it not his patriotic duty to try to prevent such a disaster? On thoughtful reflection, the government of Fiearek-iib and the others involved in this farce would probably thank him, albeit in private, for saving them the expense of having to provide three ships and their respective complements to try to fulfill the aliens' hopeless and costly request. If the visitors were claimed by and taken away by the Vilenjji, fellow citizens of galactic civilization, could not the governments of the realms rightly claim to be morally guiltless of any consequences? Such was how Saluu-hir-lek rationalized the proceedings.

"I will intercede with pertinent authorities," he responded finally. "Yous have documentation to prove yous' claim, of course?"

"I can supply a surfeit of applicable formulae," Pret-Klob assured him. He rose from his peculiar crouch but did not approach the general's seat. "I will provide the requisite contact information. I understand that our missing property is preparing to depart Niyu. Obviously, this matter of mutual interest must be resolved appropriately and to our mutual satisfaction before then."

With that, the alien turned and departed, lurching away on its foot flaps, leaving behind only promises and a slightly foul smell. As he reflected further on the unexpected visitation, Saluu-hir-lek found himself increasingly troubled by its possible ramifications.

A hastily applied dose of the powerful stimulants he utilized for recreational relaxation whenever combat was not going well was sufficient to cure him of any lingering reservations.

Given how jittery and uneasy he had been those first weeks long ago when he was being held aboard the Vilenjji capture ship, it was amazing how well Walker had adapted to sleeping in alien surroundings. Now, whether on urbanized Seremathenn, in a traditional Niyyuuan military encampment, or aboard a parsec-traversing craft in deep space, he found that he was able to enjoy a deep and relaxing rest anywhere.

Hence the necessity for the hand that had at first touched him lightly on the shoulder to slap, then finally beat on his back before it finally succeeded in waking him up.

"George, dammit," Walker began sleepily as he rolled over. "Haven't you figured out how to let yourself out of a Charuchalan residence yet? If you're bored, you need to—"

A pair of fingers touched themselves to his mouth. They were long, slender, and strong. "No shouting." Admonishing, tense, the voice was familiar, though not in such circumstances. "Cannot tell what capabilities other aliens might have."

He sat up sharply. In the near darkness of the quiet room he could see very little. What light there was came from a distant, pale pink indicator showing that the room's electronics were functioning properly. Hovering above him was the vaguest of outlines; whipcord lean and motionless. But his nostrils detected a certain sweetish fragrance, as of slightly soured roses. It was instantly recognizable. During the preceding months, he had come to know it well.

"Viyv-pym?"

The fingers returned, this time to anxiously stroking his bare left shoulder. "You must rise up, Marcus Walker. Now!" In the feeble light, he saw that while she was touching him, she was looking elsewhere.

As he sat up and slipped off the sleeping frame he found himself, as usual, envying the Niyyuu their superb night vision. The best he could do was stumble and feel around for his clothing.

The fact that he was naked did not trouble him and certainly did not interest her.

"What is it? What's wrong?"

"They coming for yous."

Fighting to blink sleep from his eyes and power up the hard drive that was his brain, he struggled to make sense of what was happening. "What are you talking about, Viyv-pym? Who's 'coming' for me?"

"Not just for you. For you and yous' friends. You must all of you leave, now, tonight." Moving away from him, she checked the door readout against the instrumentation that encircled her narrow wrist. "I not know how much time remaining."

While he finished fastening his adapted Niyyuuan attire, she woke George. Growling, the dog snapped upright on his smaller sleeping platform. When he saw who had awakened him, he was just as confused as Walker. She did her best to explain the reason for the nocturnal invasion as they exited the room and hurried to alert Sque and Braouk.

"I have found out that other aliens come look for you."

Hurrying to keep up with her as George trotted alongside, Walker fought to make sense of what she was telling him. The Vilenjji implant functioned efficiently no matter how sleepy he was. "What other aliens?" He thought automatically of the Sessrimathe. Did they want him back? It was flattering, of course, but he had come to Niyu for a reason and had no desire to return to that paragon of civilization and its well-meaning, if sometimes overbearing, inhabitants.

"Big, purple-skinned, with eyes even larger than those of Niyyuu, wider than those of you small, many-limbed friend."

George uttered a sound that emerged halfway between yelp and curse. "Do their skulls rise to a point topped with little wavy things, like thick fur?" When she indicated in the affirmative as they turned a corner, there was no ambiguity in the dog's subsequent angry exclamation.

So the persistent Vilenjji had tracked them all the way to Niyu, Walker mused. What of it? Why the worry and near panic on Viyv-pym's part? The Vilenjji had no power here. Or was he, as was all too often the case, overlooking something? Certainly the sense of urgency she had conveyed ever since waking him suggested as much.

The last of the four fellow travelers to be unexpectedly roused from a sound sleep, Sque divined rapidly what had happened.

"The Vilenjji have found an ally among the Niyyuu, or they would not pose a threat to us." Eyes that were slashes of silver set in dark maroon flesh looked up at those of the tall female Niyyuu. "You know who it is."

She indicated in the affirmative. "I am sorry have to say these beings have corrupted the general. He is helping them."

Braouk could not believe it. "Saluu-hir-lek, whom we assisted greatly, now betrays?"

As they exited the structure and hurried toward a silently waiting private transport, the ocean of lights of Charuchal-uul's capital city pulsed around them. Other vehicles slid or soared past on silent repellers. An increasingly apprehensive Walker eyed each and every one of them, wondering which might hold implacable Vilenjji and their newly inveigled Niyyuuan cronies.

"I not sure what they promise him," Viyv-pym told the lumbering Braouk, "but whatever the specifics, they apparently sufficient. Under some galactic law-reasoning, he sending Kojnian soldiers to help 'recover' you." She looked back at Walker, who was following close behind. "This alien say you its property."

"More twisting of the precepts of civilization." Lacking true feet, legs, or massive supporting tentacles on the order of the Tuuqalian, Sque was having a difficult time keeping up. As her kind were not built for walking, running was almost as alien to them as flying. Perceiving her difficulty, Braouk scooped her up and bore her along, carrying the K'eremu as effortlessly as he would have an infant.

"It not matter," Viyv-pym responded. As her breathing grew deeper, her muscular round mouth expanded and contracted like a miniature bellows. "Who wields what guns is what matter now. I make what arrangements I could, but I not Charuchalan and it difficult this time of night to make contact with relevant parties."

"Something both the Vilenjji and our erstwhile comrade Saluu-hir-lek doubtless have taken into consideration." Freed from the debilitating need to drag herself rapidly across the ground, Sque's voice had strengthened.

Thankfully, the transporter Viyv-pym had engaged was large enough to accommodate all of them, including Braouk. Not trusting automatics that could be compromised, she had sensibly arranged for a manually controlled vehicle. In addition to the Charuchalan driver, it contained one other inhabitant.

"Sobj-oes!" As they entered the big transport, George bounded into the astronomer's lap and gave her face a friendly lick. Having no tongue, she could not respond in kind. She had to settle for stroking his head with one hand, a compromise that more than satisfied him. He sat there, head up, eyes alert and forward, tail metronoming. "Where are we going? Someplace to hide out until the local authorities can get a handle on Saluu-hir-lek?"

She hacked up a racking cough of amusement. "Someplace, yes." Leaning to her left to peer around him, she snapped instructions at the vehicle's operator. They were beyond concise.

He must know where we're going, Walker thought rapidly. *Viyv-pym and the astronomer must have had enough time to brief him before they got here.*

As the trim but capacious craft accelerated, he found himself seated close to Viyv-pym. "Where are you taking us?" Mindful of George's question, he took a guess. "Local authorities?"

Those bottomless eyes seemed to flow into his. "Not safe. I know that Saluu-hir-lek has been compromised by these aliens. I not know who else. At such times, in such circumstances, all must be considered suspect. Promises of wealth and power render even the most upright susceptible. Also, I have no influence here. This is Charuchal-uul, not Kojn-umm. To ensure yous' safety, must get yous away from here."

"You're sending us back to Biranju-oov?" he wondered.

It was Sobj-oes who replied. Her expression when she looked over at him, or as much of it as he could read, was electric with enthusiasm. "No, Marcus Walker. One hope most fervently that we are sending yous home."

The main port was enormous, as befitted one serving the capital of a powerful dominion. Their transporter hummed right past it. As it did so, Walker could see an impressive ship emerging from the night sky and settling massively to ground. Unexpectedly, George began to laugh, snickering in his suggestive way as he rolled back and forth on the astronomer's narrow, bony lap.

Seeing no humor whatsoever in their increasingly dangerous situation, Walker challenged the dog. "What's so funny? You won't be laughing very long if these Vilenjji catch up with us again."

Composing himself, George scrambled back up into a sitting position. "I'm sorry, Marc. It's just that after all these chronological years and light-years we've traveled, after everything we've been through, here we are being spirited away in the middle of the night again, to be bundled up and rushed off-planet."

"It's not the same," Walker murmured in response. "This isn't Earth."

"Neither is where we're going, remember?"

Angling sharply but smoothly to the left, the transporter entered an access that led to a subsidiary section of the main port. The lights were fewer here, the looming nearby facilities showing ample evidence of age and some neglect. Eying them, Walker had to remind himself that what he was seeing was still hundreds of years in advance of anything on Earth.

Looking like a conjoined cluster of mating white and gold beetles, a transfer craft sat quiescent on its raised service platform. It was not as large as the craft Walker had just seen land at the busy section of the port, but it was far larger than any commercial airliner on his homeworld. A loading ramp led at a modest angle up into a dark opening in one of the craft's bulging components. As the transporter slowed to a halt nearby, a squad of energetic, determined Niyyuu emerged from the ship's interior to greet it. All of the tall, slender, big-eyed natives were armed, Walker noted. And not with spears or swords, but with energy weapons and projectors.

Sobj-oes, for one, was clearly relieved to see them. "Some of yous' crew," she informed him. "Most are volunteers. Spirit of adventure not confined to Sessrimathe only."

As he quickly exited the transporter, Walker studied the cluster of assembled Niyyuuan faces. Even in broad daylight and even given the length of time he had by now spent among them, it was sometimes difficult to tell what they were thinking. But it was clear that these were alert and aware. Their two-fingered grips on their weapons were firm. In this group, at least, there seemed to be slightly more females than males.

Without warning, several of them raised and leveled their weapons. Walker tensed, while next to him, George swiftly scampered around behind the human's legs. The guns were not aimed at him and his friends however, but at a point past them. Behind them.

The second transporter that had pulled into the little-used service and loading area was larger than its predecessor. It proceeded to disgorge several dozen armed Niyyuu. Despite the poor light, Walker had no trouble making out the uniforms and insignia of the armed forces of the realm of Kojn-umm. A number of the soldiers appeared disheveled, as if they had been called to duty in haste and forced to dress themselves on the run. In the forefront, he immediately recognized a familiar and atypically undersized figure: Saluu-hir-lek, looking even more uncompromising than usual. Together with that of his companions, however, the bulk of Walker's attention was reserved for the thick-bodied, robed, and sandaled figure that sloughed along beside the Niyyuuan general.

Not only was it a Vilenjji, it was a Vilenjji he and his friends recognized.

"Spawn of sewage, leaver of slime tracks, death sniffer," Braouk rumbled threateningly. As the seething Tuuqalian started forward, Walker hurried to intercept him. There was no need for that—yet.

The Vilenjji was as imperturbable as ever. Businesslike, to another way of thinking. "I see that the special eloquence of the Tuuqalian remains intact. That is gratifying. I am always pleased to find mislaid goods undamaged."

"Sorry we can't say the same for you." An irate George peeped out from behind Walker's ankles.

Implacable, Pret-Klob trained widely curving oculars on the impertinent quadruped. "And the small furred one's intelligence level has not reverted. I always worry about the permanence of complex neural modifications." The tapering skull came up. "I hereby claim property rights of which my association has been illegitimately deprived." One flap-tipped arm rose to point. "That one, and that, and the two behind them. Property of my association."

As the barely restrained Braouk extended a pair of accusatory tentacles, Sque crawled out to the end of one. Her weight did not even cause it to tremble.

"While different worlds adhere to and live by their own individually promulgated legal systemologies, common galactic law forbids the holding of any sentient as chattel. This is not Vilenj. You have no power here."

"On the contrary," Pret-Klob countered her. "All that is required is that means be available for avoiding prolonged deliberation in legal analysis." His eyes bored into Walker's. "Once off this world and in open space, other rulings take effect. I and the surviving, and new, members of my association wish only to recover what is rightfully ours, originally acquired after much hard work and travail. These efforts at recovery have already cost us much." Without changing tone in the slightest, he concluded, "Our goods may already have suffered significant depreciation."

"I wish I had bigger teeth," George snarled. "I'd depreciate you right down to that frizzy pinhead of yours, and play kickball with your eyes."

"An unlikelihood," the Vilenjji responded impassively as he turned to peer down at his recently engaged Niyyuuan associate. "Every minute of this disagreeable but necessary enterprise is costly and awkward to expense. General, be so good as to proceed with the recovery of what are rightfully the assets of my association."

At a sign from the grim-faced Saluu-hir-lek, the soldiers behind him started forward. Simultaneously, the remainder of the armed crew of the transfer craft drew and raised their own weapons so that they were in line with those of their comrades. Taken aback by this suggestion of serious resistance, the uncertain Kojnian soldiers held their own weapons at ready. In the distance, another ship thrummed as it lifted toward space.

Across the far too small, intervening strip of plasticized ground, both heavily armed groups regarded each other tensely.

16

Heedless of the potent weaponry pointed in her direction, Viyv-pym moved forward until she was standing in front of Walker and George. In a voice that did not shake, she addressed those confronting her. Her words, however, were directed not at a furious, startled Saluu-hir-lek, nor at the hulking alien standing next to the general, but at the troops clustered behind and on either side of them. Despite his nervousness at being confronted by so many lethal devices, as she spoke Walker eyed her with the kind of admiration men in his position usually reserved for females of the species who exceeded their annual sales quotas by six figures.

"Soldiers of Kojn-umm! That yous' commander standing before yous. But this not yous' fight. We do not keep other intelligent beings as property in Kojn-umm. No realm, no commercial concern, no individuals on Niyu keep intelligent beings as property." She paused to let her words sink in. "This foulness of a principle is what yous being asked to support. Not security of beloved home realm in courageous, traditional manner of our kind. Not defense of our homeworld. Nothing but a principle of commerce that as alien to the Niyyuu as is the small-headed creature that presently stand before you.

"By refusing do this dishonest thing yous do not disobey principles of combat for which yous enlisted. Is no proper combat here." One slender arm gestured expansively to take in their surroundings. "This not Kojn-umm. No officer or official of Kojn-umm, no matter how famous or feted at home, have authority here." The arm swung around and down, coming to rest lightly across Walker's shoulders. "These sentients beside me have fought alongside you for many ten-days now. They have helped bring great acclamation to yous and to Kojn-umm. Is not right to betray them for benefit of other alien who has done nothing for either." Her voice lowered.

"Whatever other alien has promised, whatever yous been told, one thing is clear to any soldier who claims Kojn-umm as home: is not right sell honor for profit."

Only the breathy industrial sounds of the nearby main port sifted through the cool night air. Saluu-hir-lek spoke into the darkness. "Kill her."

Long fingers holding weapons tensed on both sides. And— nothing happened. From the back of the force of Kojnian troops someone muttered matter-of-factly, "This Charuchal-uul—not Kojn-umm." Though he whirled around sharply, Saluu-hir-lek was unable to identify the individual who had spoken.

First one, then two more, then every weapon was lowered, on both sides. Crew and indigenous Kojnians regarded one another through the night. An officer of average skill knows when to hold his position and when to attack. A superior one knows when to fall back. Saluu-hir-lek peered up at the Vilenjji.

"I find I without necessary resources to fulfill you request. Therefore it with much regret I say that I must decline you offer." Before Pret-Klob could respond, the general had turned back to the aliens with whom he had shared both the good and the bad for many ten-days.

"If yous go with this Vilenjji, Saluu-hir-lek prevails. If yous leave Niyu, Saluu-hir-lek prevails. Due to financial arrangements, I would prefer first option, but circumstances dictate I recognize second." His eyes came to rest on the unyielding Viyv-pym. "I sorry you attached to political arm of government. You would make fine officer." Pivoting, he gestured to his troops and simultaneously uttered a curt command. In response, they began to holster or shoulder their weapons and shuffle back toward the vehicle that had brought them. The potentially deadly confrontation was over.

Just like that. Only not quite.

Pret-Klob had not moved. If the Vilenjji was armed, he chose not to reveal a weapon. A wise choice, given that the transporter crewmembers who had so forcefully prevented him from recovering his inventory had not shifted their own positions. Instead, he let his stretched oculars scrutinize them one and all.

"Human Marcus Walker, canine George, Tuuqalian Broullkoun-uvv-ahd-Hrashkin, K'eremu Sequi'aranaqua'na'senemu: know for a certainty that this only constitutes yet another expensive delay in the implementation of the inevitable. If you will now come with me willingly, I am authorized, on behalf of my re-formed association, to make a one-time offer and grant you a percentage of the profit of your own individual sales when you are sold."

"That's very generous of you," Walker managed to reply with remarkably little recourse to sarcasm, "but I'm afraid we'll have to decline. We're going home, you see, and letting you sell us someplace would put a serious crimp in those plans." Turning to go, he found himself hesitating.

"Something I don't understand, Pret-Klob. If the Vilenjji are such dedicated businessfolk, and such careful monitors of the bottom line, and these attempts to repossess my friends and I are costing you so much—why do you keep at it? Why don't you just give it up and focus your energies on more immediately profitable activities?"

Pret-Klob gazed back at him. "It is not good to allow inventory to escape. It creates a bad precedent. Most especially, it is not good when the inventory in question, though of variable capacity, is manifestly inferior to the Vilenjji." Efficient translator implant notwithstanding, the other creature's true alienness succeeded in communicating itself to the interested Walker.

"To allow you to go free, after you forcibly excused yourselves from our control, would be to admit your equality with the Vilenjji. This would call into question the very principles on which our trade is founded. That we cannot permit. Hear me clearly, human. There should be no misunderstanding. I and my association will follow you wherever necessary, for as long as is necessary, overcoming whatever difficulties may place themselves in our way, until we have recovered our property. This is an absolute."

Hanging from the end of one of Braouk's powerful tentacles, Sque whispered to Walker, "Do not let his words trouble you, Marc. The Vilenjji are as full of gas as the sixth planet of Asmeriis."

"They don't trouble me, Sque," he lied. Louder, to the Vilenjji, he said, "You do what you have to do according to the principles you live by. We'll do the same. And if we are fated never to meet again, know that I ardently wish you poor sales and inaccurate accounting."

The Vilenjji stared at him a moment longer. Either it was truly impossible to genuinely upset one of his kind, or else they had developed the ability to wholly internalize their irritation to a degree unmatched by any species Walker had yet encountered. Conscious of the fact that the vehicle that had brought him to the port was now almost loaded with its complement of put-out Kojn-umm soldiery, he turned on his sandal-clad foot flaps and lurched heavily in its direction. Insofar as Walker was able to tell, the Vilenjji did not look back.

Not until the big surface transporter had cleared the port perimeter did the armed crewmembers who had put their lives on the line for the sake of the visitors finally secure their own weapons and prepare to enter the transatmospheric transfer craft. A cheerful George was the first one up the ramp, already chatting amiably with and making friends among the delighted crew. Braouk followed, carrying Sque, who avowed to any who would listen that from the very beginning of the confrontation she had known exactly how it was going to turn out. Walking just ahead of them, the astronomer Sobj-oes was unable to escape the K'eremu's unrelenting paean to her own infallibility.

Walker lingered, waiting on Viyv-pym. It was left to her to inform him of something he expected but still did not want to hear.

"I not going with you, Marcus Walker. I not qualified to be of crew."

His head tilted back only slightly, he stared into her wide, brilliant, golden-yellow eyes. "Surely you can't go back to Kojn-umm, Viyv-pym." He gestured with his head in the direction taken by the departed troop transport. "Just because Saluu-hir-lek paid you a backhanded compliment doesn't mean he won't find a way to deal with you once you're both back in your own realm. He may not be human, but I know how guys like that work. We have the same types in my business. They don't forget something like this."

"I need not return Kojn-umm," she assured him. "As someone with off-world diplomatic and commercial experience and expertise, I have been offered a succession of admirable positions by both Biranju-oov and Charuchal-uul. Should I wish take advantage of it, opportunities even in Fiearek-iib are open to me." A long-fingered hand indicated the city that lay just beyond the main port. "Many excellent choices are mine." The hand swept downward, and both long fingers came to rest against his sternum.

"When I first save you from Vilenjji and bring you here from Seremathenn to make food presentations for notables of Kojn-umm, I not think it end quite this way." The delicate fingertips brushed his chest. "Good journeying to you, Marcus Walker. I have learn much from you. I hope you have learn some small things, maybe, from me."

"I know that I have, Viyv-pym." Placing the two middle fingers of his left hand against her lower neck, he let them drag gently down her lissome front. Then, impulsively and without thinking about it, he put both arms around her and pulled her close. Though she resisted slightly at first and was taut with lean muscle, he outweighed her by more than a third.

As he put a hand behind her head and drew it down toward his own, a single, not-so-subtle thought ran through his mind as he kissed her. *What in the hell do you think you're doing?* For one thing, she had no lips, and therefore could not properly kiss him back. He didn't care. He very much wanted to kiss her. If only, he told himself fatuously, in the spirit of scientific experimentation.

Taken completely aback, it took her a moment to respond. When she did, it was perhaps in a similar spirit. Or maybe it was nothing more than an instinctive reaction to what he was doing. In any case, the ring of muscle that encircled her small, round mouth contracted, and she inhaled forcefully.

It was not like his first kiss, nor even like those he had enjoyed on successful outings with members of the opposite sex of his own kind. But his lips were bruised for weeks afterward.

The ironic thing was, if he ever did want to boast of it to his buddies, no one would ever believe him.

Jhanuud-tir-yed turned away from the latest multistory media projection that was currently dominating the central atrium of government central in the capital city of Fiearek-iib. Other functionaries, passing around and through the image, were enthralled by the great expedition. As for herself, during the previous ten-days the vice premier had seen and experienced quite enough of the aliens. That they had nearly failed to depart in the intended fashion was a fact known only to a few. With care, it would remain that way, nothing more than an imperceptible bump along the road to what everyone hoped would be a glorious footnote in Niyyuuan history.

Things could have been worse, she knew. They could have been much worse. No one was happier to see the four visitors finally depart Niyu than the venerable vice premier. Given the way the visitors had manipulated the traditional forces of Kojn-umm, Toroud-eed, and several other realms, it was a relief to see them go. While most of the attention had been focused on the bipedal human and the massive Tuuqalian, it was the smaller pair of visitors who had kept Jhanuud-tir-yed awake at night. That seemingly charming four-legged thing—what had it been called? George, yes. A single naming for a singular creature. And that arrogant, pompous jumble of tendrils and glitter who called herself Sque. The vice premier hadn't trusted the K'eremu from the first time she had observed her lurking in the background, letting her more affable companions do the preponderance of the talking.

Now they were gone. Now life on calm, complacent Niyu could get back to normal. And regardless of the eventual outcome of the possibly doomed expedition, of one thing she was certain with regard to the aliens.

It had been worth three ships to get rid of them.

*   *   *

Walker did not know what Sque or Braouk thought of the Niyyuu vessels. Their own species were space-going, sophisticated, and afflicted with their own systems of engineering aesthetics. As for George, the dog volunteered readily, "I don't care what they look like as long as they start up when someone turns the key and go when somebody steps on the accelerator." But Walker thought his first sight of the ships, as they came into view on one of the transfer craft's monitors, was beautiful.

There were three, just as Walker had insisted upon and Jhanuud-tir-yed had promised. Though not nearly as massive as the Sessrimathe ship that had rescued him and his friends from Vilenjji captivity, they were large enough to inspire awe. Burgeoning clusters of conjoined propulsion components and living quarters, illuminated by if not quite ablaze with internal lights, they floated in orbit awaiting the arrival of the transfer craft.

It was half an hour longer before Walker was convinced that their motion relative to that of the three waiting starships had ceased. Concerned, he went in search of Sobj-oes. He found the astronomer forward, chatting with one of the officers who had volunteered to be a part of the expedition. To the human's relief, and somewhat to his consternation, she had a ready explanation for the apparent delay in docking.

"It the media," she informed him. "All those assigned to this voyage clamoring for best position to make first recordings." She indicated the image on the nearest monitor. "This the beginning, an important moment. Each individual desires compose best possible imaging, most dramatic lighting." She inhaled breathily, her red-and-black-painted mouth contracting to a tiny opening. "Is not science. But is necessary."

"My friends and I could do without it," he confessed. "We're pretty tired." He found himself wishing Viyv-pym was aboard, to intercede with the media on his behalf. But Viyv-pym was gone for good, back on Niyu.

I have been away from home for a very long time, he reminded himself firmly.

"I'm glad you're coming with us," he told her. Sobj-oes was

not Viyv-pym, but she was at least a sympathetic and familiar face.

"I would not miss it." The astronomer was a taut bundle of anticipation and excitement. "We will be visiting a portion of the galaxy far outside familiar boundaries. Opportunities should abound to observe previously unrecorded phenomena, visit new civilizations." Her luminous eyes caught the light as they stared back at him. "What scientist worthy of the designation not leap at the chance to experience such things?"

"This is as much a leap into the unknown for you and the rest of the Niyyuu on this voyage as it is for my friends and I. We're going because we have no choice but to keep going. You have something to return to. Doesn't it bother you that you might not come back?"

A two-fingered hand reached out to stroke his right arm. "Any scientist embarking on long journey knows they might die before end of journey is reached. If no one willing to take that chance, no science ever get done."

A new voice interrupted them. "It is always encouraging to hear a mature understanding of the nature of understanding Nature voiced by one of the lesser orders." Sque arrived in what had become her favored fashion: born aloft on one of Braouk's tentacles, her scorn preceding her. "I myself look forward to the acquiring of new knowledge."

"And I sing," the Tuuqalian rumbled, having to bend low as usual to avoid banging the upper part of his body and his stalk-mounted eyes on the ceiling, "of new spaces encountered, rarely seen."

As well he should, Walker knew, since his homeworld was the one they were heading for, and the only one thus far of the three that the displaced travelers desperately sought whose location was even feebly surmised. He steeled himself inwardly. If only one of the four of them made it home, that would be an impressive accomplishment in itself. Guided only by a faint perception of distant possibilities, they were flinging themselves into the unknown.

Three of them were, anyway. Where was George?

He found the dog curled up among piles of last-minute

loaded supplies in the transfer craft's storeroom, sound asleep.
Kneeling, he gently stroked his friend's back until George
awoke. The dog yawned, stretched, and quivered, pushing out
his front legs as he looked up at Walker.

"What'd you wake me for?" he asked irritably.

"Oh, I don't know." Walker sat down beside his friend.
"Maybe because we're about to embark on a journey into deep
space that even our crew has never attempted before. Maybe because we may never see a civilized world again. Maybe because
this is yet another pivotal moment in our lives. God, what I
wouldn't give for a double latte right now. With nutmeg. And
cinnamon."

"You've managed to get hold of three starships. Don't get
greedy."

Walker shrugged and smiled. "I'm a commodities broker. It's
my nature to always want to trade up."

George rolled over onto his back and began contorting his
spine in ways few humans could match, scratching his back
against the oddly tactile surface of the package he had chosen
for a temporary bed. Walker looked on with envy.

"Doesn't any of this bother you, George? The fact that we're
heading out into a part of the greater galaxy unknown even to
the Niyyuu? That we're going beyond the bounds of what they
consider to be known civilization?"

Ceasing his twisting and scratching, the dog rolled over onto
his belly. Panting contentedly, he looked up at his friend and
companion. "You know what they say, Marc. 'Knick-knack, hy-
perwack, vector a dog a zone, this old mutt goes spacing home.'
Better wandering infinity with a full fridge, even if it's an alien
one, than stumbling around cold and starving in the snow in a
dirty alley back home."

A glance at one of the transfer craft's omnipresent monitors
showed that they had at last resumed forward motion again and
were finally about to dock with one of the three waiting starships. Walker straightened.

"I wish I had your casual sangfroid, George. I guess no matter
what happens, I'll always be the nervous type." He sighed.
"Sobj-oes says there's no getting away from it: for the duration

of the voyage we're going to have to tolerate the Niyyuuan media who've been assigned to this excursion."

George rose to all fours. "No problem. If they get too pushy,
I'll just start barking at them. Their translators can't handle
that."

Walker's smile widened. On the monitors, beyond the starships, several thousand worlds beckoned. With luck, one of
them was small and blue and gauzily streaked with gossamer
white. But first they had to see home a very large poet.

"I'm glad you've been with me through all this. I don't know
how I could've gotten through it all without your company.
You're a good dog, George."

"And you're a tolerable human, except for the usual odor."
Shaking himself, the dog started for the main hatch. "Let's go
deal with the media. They're going to be with us for a long time.
Make them no promises, or I'll pee on your leg."

"Canine eloquence," Walker quipped as he matched the dog's
pace.

"I'll believe humans have a better way of communicating,"
the dog countered, "when I see the evidence of it in the way
they run their civilization."

"Maybe," Walker mused as they exited the storage area and
turned toward the center of the transfer craft, "things will have
changed for the better by the time we get home."

"Don't hold your breath." The dog snorted. "Regarding either
possibility."

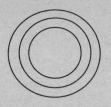

Read on for a preview
of Alan Dean Foster's
next book

The Candle of Distant Earth

Available in bookstores everywhere
from Del Rey Books

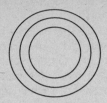

For the eleventh time, Ussakk the Astronomer pored over the most recent collated readouts while trying to decide how best to kill himself. Whichever method he chose, it would be faster and cleaner than what was coming. While the last time the Iollth had ravaged Hyff had been well before his birth, abundant records were available to illustrate in gruesome detail their appetite for destruction. Given the history of their visitations to Hyff, it was remarkable that any of the populace would continue to resist. Yet invariably, outraged at the periodic demands for tribute and treasure, some did. And just as invariably, they died deaths that were as horrible as they were futile.

That much could be tolerated, if not for the disagreeable Iollth habit of slaughtering out of apparent boredom the occasional batch of innocent civilians.

Ussakk felt he would be as fated to be among the latter—that is, if the authorities did not kill him outright as the bearer of bad news. He sympathized in advance with their probable reaction. There was always the hope among his people that the Iollth would tire of their cyclical visits to Hyff, that they would seek to enrich themselves at the expense of others elsewhere and leave the Hyfft to their peaceful, widespread communities and to the tending of the crops of which they were so proud.

A fool's dream, Ussakk knew. So long as the Hyfft fashioned beautiful objects out of rare materials, so long as their mines produced rare and unsynthesizable raw materials, the Iollth would return: to plunder, and not to buy.

The astronomer knew they could not be put off with excuses. A hundred years ago, the Great Government had decreed that the production of objects of beauty and the mining of gems was to cease. Despite the temporary harm this inflicted on Hyfftian culture, it was hoped the absence of such things would discourage the Iollth. After all, one cannot ransack that which does not exist. It was a defensive maneuver predicated on a rational reaction.

Unfortunately, the Iollth did not respond in a rational manner. In their fury and frustration, their unopposed ships laid waste to a dozen of Hyff's largest communities. Tens of thousands died. After that, there were no more attempts to discourage the visitors with clever subterfuges.

Occasionally, there came together bands of Hyfft who were still determined, somehow, to resist. Sadly, having evolved from sedate bands of farmers who had known nothing but greater and greater cooperation that had eventually resulted in the development of the present state of high culture, the Hyfft were emotionally and psychologically ill-equipped for warfare. Even thoughts of acquiring an armed starship from one of the other space-traversing species who paid the occasional rare visit to Hyff fell by the wayside when none among the Hyfft could be found who were bold enough to leave the Nesting World long enough to travel between the stars to arrange the actual acquisition.

Though technologically advanced, the Hyfft could not find it within themselves to manufacture weapons. Psychologically crippled, they could not muster enough individuals to make use of such weapons even if they managed to buy them from elsewhere. Located far from the fringes of galactic civilization, they did not attract the attention of those who might have offered them protection.

Besides, it was rationalized, the Iollth did not threaten genocide. They came only to plunder and ravage, and that only once every hundredth-passing or so. Hardly sufficient reason for distant species with a surfeit of their own problems to take the time and expense to interfere. Especially when most of Hyff never even suffered beneath the heavy foot of the visitors, except to witness and weep over their sporadic depredations via relayed images.

That the fast-moving signatures Ussakk had detected emerging from deepspace belonged to the Iollth there was no question. The infrequent and uncommon traders or explorers who occasionally found their way to Hyff always arrived singly. There *was* one atypical report from three hundred-passings ago of two such vessels arriving simultaneously in orbit around Hyff, but that was only the result of coincidence. They had not been traveling in tandem, and were as surprised by each other's appearance in Hyfftian space as were the Hyfft themselves.

No, without question, a triple signature could signify the imminent arrival of nothing other than the dreaded Iollth.

As the senior astronomer on duty, he had the obligation to deliver the bad news to the local Overwatch, who would then pass it along to all the individual elements of the Great Government. Composed of hundreds of local Overwatches, the Great Government would then dictate an appropriate response. The best that could be hoped for, Ussakk knew, was that the Iollth would take what they wanted, murder for entertainment as few citizens as possible, and be on their way after causing a minimal amount of damage to Hyfftian civilization. It might be, he reflected as he began to make inviolable recordings of the relevant readouts, that with luck he would not be expected to kill himself.

As soon as the necessary recordings had been prepared, he stored them in his body pouch and prepared to leave his post. There was no thought of transmitting such sensitive information electronically. It was his responsibility, his personal *cura,* to deliver it in person. Coworkers were bemused by his nonresponsiveness as he departed. Such glumness was not usually associated with the bright and chipper senior astronomer. But no one pressed the limits of what was culturally acceptable. Though concerned, they left him to his private dejection. That was just as well, since if they had asked what was troubling him, he would have been compelled to answer.

Let them dwell in happiness and contentment a little while longer, he decided as he exited the observatory and ambled toward the nearest conveyor. Horror was now in the neighborhood and would arrive on their mental doorsteps soon enough.

The Escarpment of Lann dropped away behind him and his speed increased as the terrain leveled out. Racing toward the city, he was forced to slow repeatedly as his vehicle bunched up behind other conveyors. Each held, at most, no more than a single family. Hyfft did not travel in groups. On a world as heavily populated as theirs, even though that population was evenly dispersed, personal privacy was at a premium. So was courtesy, which was why the anxious Ussakk waited his turn until one by one, those in front of him reached their exit points and left the main conveyor route. Only then did he accelerate again.

There was no road, the conveyor route being only a line on a map that was duplicated in actuality by perfectly spaced sensors buried in the ground. The route Ussakk was following ran through fields of *pfale,* whose dark green fruit burst from the center of a spray of bright blue-green leaves. Enormous in extent, this particular field was nearly ready for harvesting. For a moment, the color and anticipation took his mind off the dreadful news he was about to deliver. *Pfale* was famed for its piquant taste, and for the ability of master cooks to turn it into a variety of elegant dishes usually supplemented with a quartet of *semell* condiments. Descended from wholly herbivorous ancestors, the Hyfft were masters of vegetarian cuisine.

An alien observer might have wondered why the agitated astronomer did not simply accelerate his levitating personal conveyor and pass the slower travelers in front of him. He could easily have done so, to the right or to the left. But such a move would have been an unforgivable breach of manners. On Hyff, one politely waited one's turn. The queue was a way of life, and woe betide any who violated it. Rules such as waiting for those in front to finish whatever they happened to be doing were not merely a matter of unspoken courtesy; they had been officially codified.

Exceptions were tolerated only for extreme emergencies. Unable to see how delivering his bad news a few morning-slices earlier would make things any better, Ussakk preferred to take his time and follow custom. Officialdom might soon berate him as the harbinger of doom, but no one would be able to accuse him of being impolite as part of the process.

The family ahead of him finally turned off, allowing him to accelerate afresh. Once within the outskirts of the city, he was able to take advantage of the much greater multiplicity of available conveyor routes. Like most urban concentrations on Hyff, Therapp was not large. With few exceptions, the majority of structures were built low to the ground in traditional fashion. Such buildings might cover considerable stretches of ground, but that was how the Hyfft preferred it. They did not like heights, and they favored open spaces.

Therapp's administrative center was housed in one such complex, which extended for several *midds* from the center of the city and across the meandering river that cut through it. Slotting his conveyor in a public receptacle, he quickly swapped it for its much smaller in-house counterpart. Within the vast structure, municipal workers dashed to and fro along clearly designated routings, never so much as nudging any of the pedestrians they passed. Without the internal conveyor, it might take him half a day to walk to the sector he sought.

Like the spokes of a wheel, the adjuncts to the office of Overwatch Delineator fanned out around a central core. As custom dictated, there were twenty-four such offices. Today the office of Delineator was held by number nine. Tomorrow it would be ten, and so on until next-month changeover. In this way the city's administration had twenty-four heads, among whom both responsibility and credit could be divvied up collectively. With only one day in charge each next-month, no one official had time to accumulate power over another. Occasionally, number twelve might swap day-work with the official occupying office twenty-one. Like everything else on Hyff, the system made for an administration that was both civil and efficient.

Today's Delineator was Phomma, of office nine. An unlucky number, Ussakk reflected as he stepped off his conveyor and snapped it into the nearest unoccupied recharger. Unlucky, because she would be the one to have to receive and deal with the dreadful news he carried with him.

When he entered, office nine was occupied by a pair of subordinate administrators engaged in debating the merits of expanding the city's southernmost recreation facility. Both looked up at his entry.

"Devirra li Designer," declared one. "Zubboj vi Procurer," added her companion.

"Ussakk ri Astronomer," he responded. While on business, the Hyfft did not waste time on extended formalities. They were an efficient folk. "To see today's Delineator."

The Designer's reply was prompt and inflexible. "Delineator Phomma qi Administrator sa Nine is not seeing visitors or supplicants until last two afternoon-slices. We respectfully suggest you return to request a meeting at that time." Small, dark, fast-moving pupils regarded him hesitantly. "Unless you already have arranged a meeting time for this morning."

"No, I haven't," he replied, "but I must see the Delineator immediately. It is a matter of global importance."

"Global?" Long, feathery white whiskers twitching to emphasize his amusement, the Procurer eyed his fellow subordinate administrator. "From an astronomer I would expect nothing less than galactic." They shared a casual touch, he clicking his prominent incisors against hers.

Ussakk was as well-mannered as the next person, but today he had no time for sarcasm. "You are more right than you say. The Iollth are returning to Hyff, and will be here within a two-day."

Later, though he could easily justify it, he regretted his bluntness.

A look at his face—eyes staring evenly, whiskers unquivering, short round ears perfectly erect and forward facing—being all that was necessary to convince them that the visitor was not joking, the change in attitude among the pair of subordinate administrators was shocking in its abruptness. The Designer's hairless eyelids fluttered once, twice, before she collapsed. Trembling visibly, the Procurer bent over her and began to tug on her short arms in an attempt to reestablish normal breathing.

He was so badly shaken he could not sustain his grip, leaving it to Ussakk to take over and maintain the procedure until the psychologically stunned female finally regained consciousness.

"I apologize," he murmured. "I did not mean to cause shock. That is why I did not use public channels to communicate the information, for fear it might get out before it could be appropriately reviewed. But it must be delivered now, here, so that means of dissemination to the rest of Hyff can be decided upon, and propagated accordingly." His tone, normally relaxed and carefree as that of any of his kind, was unnaturally solemn.

His seriousness seemed to steady the Procurer. "Go on in, quickly," the subordinate administrator told him as he resumed working the Designer's upper arms.

With an acknowledging twitch of the whiskers to the right of his nose, Ussakk hitched up the cross-straps of his formal work attire, turned, and strode toward the inner wall. Sensing his approach, number nine of twenty-four ceremonial panels slid aside to admit him to the circular inner office.

It was beautifully appointed, the citizens of Therapp and the surrounding district being proud of their accomplishments and those of their local artisans. A conical central skylight of synthetic crystal flooded the interior with sunshine lightly tinted gold by the swirling, stained panel attached to it. Directly beneath the skylight, a round desk sat embedded in the mosaic stone floor. There the Delineator of the Day of Therapp sat and worked. Placing the desk slightly below floor level compelled each of them to look up at approaching citizens. In this manner, humility was enforced on the Overwatch's principal public servant.

Delineator Phomma qi Administrator sa Nine looked up and chittered a polite traditional greeting, followed by, "I specifically asked staff to grant me a two day-slice period of privacy. You must have considerable influence to have gained admittance in spite of that." Her long, drooping whiskers inclined toward him as she spoke, the aggressiveness of their posture belying the civility of her words. Unusually, he noted, they were tinted a pale red.

"I am Ussakk the Astronomer, and I have no influence: only bad news."

"Proceed forward." Rising from her seat, she stepped away from the trio of readouts that floated in the air before her. They started to follow obediently until she thought to wave them away. "What news can simultaneously be so bad and so influential?"

He descended the six short ceremonial steps, each corresponding to one of the whiskers that dominated the Hyfftian visage. "This morning I regret to say that I was forced to reconfirm certain previous significant observations made by my facility's instrumentation. Three starships have entered our system from deepspace. Though it has not happened in my lifetime, I know from history that infrequent visitors to our world invariably arrive in only one such vessel. One time, by coincidence, two such marvelous craft arrived at Hyff." He blinked meaningfully. "The presence of more than that can mean only one thing."

As an educated person, the Delineator Phomma knew what it meant, too. To her credit, she neither fainted nor shook. But moisture did begin to appear at the lower edges of both eyes. She wiped it hurriedly away.

"This leaves no time for advance lamenting. That will have to come later." Turning, she moved purposefully back to the seat she had been occupying when he had arrived. Her hovering tripartite readouts had to move fast to hold their positions in front of her eyes. This time she did not dismiss them. "The Great Government must be notified immediately. You will provide all details. Work must be started to minimize the inevitable panic that will greet the official announcement." As her hands moved, the four short fingers on each waving instructions at the readouts, she glanced over at him. "Who else knows?"

Ussakk considered for a moment. "Only the two sub administrators whose permission I had to seek to enter here. Their personal reactions," he added thoughtfully, "were as might have been expected. Otherwise, not even my colleagues at the observatory know. Yet."

She chirruped an acknowledgement. "Then this can be handled appropriately. Or at least, as well as can be hoped." He thought he saw tears begin to rise again, but the Delineator shut them down before they could dampen the neatly trimmed brown fur under her eyes. Leastwise, the formal face paint that streaked and speckled her plump cheeks did not run.

"If you do not require my presence any longer," he murmured, "I should be getting back to my work."

She replied without looking up at him, her hands busy with the readouts. "Your work is here now. As Delineator of the Day for the Overwatch of Therapp, I am requisitioning your services to city administration. When your coworkers have been notified, they can monitor the approach of the . . ." She could not choke the name out, did not want to get the name out. "Of the incoming vessels," she finally finished.

Ussakk was appalled. "I am an astronomer, not a bureaucrat or civil servant. I answer to the Great Science, headquartered in Avvesse. Of what possible use could my extended presence be to the city government of Therapp?"

She paused in her work to study him. His whiskers quivered slightly under her suddenly intense stare, but he held his ground. "It is clear you are not a politician, either. Very well; if you need a reason, I feel that your continued presence in an urbanized area will in itself help to provide some small modicum of reassurance to the general populace."

His small black nose twitched. "How can that be?"

"By showing that you have not run away." She returned to manipulating the readouts. "In the coming days, that may prove critical. I don't suppose you can tell by the angle of approach of the Iollth ships where they intend to put down on Hyff?"

He reminded himself that this was not a fellow scientist he was talking to. "Angle of approach means nothing. They may decide to go into extended orbit around Hyff before choosing a place to—put down. Or they may decide to land at three different places. History shows that—"

"I know what history shows," she barked irritably. He took no offense at the sharpness of her response. Helplessness bred frustration, and frustration bred anger. He felt like doing some yelling and screaming himself. As a scientist, he realized the futility of such reactions better than most.

A tenth of a day-slice later, she waved both hands simultaneously, and the readouts that had been hovering before her vanished. With a weariness not even her elaborate ceremonial makeup could dispel, she turned back to him.

"The appropriate authorities have been advised. The Great Government is now in motion." Eyes as red as her whiskers met his. "All continental representatives are to meet here tomorrow. That is as fast as travel allows. Each of the eight continental Overwatches will determine how best to respond should an Iollth vessel set down in their territory. If all three approaching craft send their landers to one place, a worldwide response will be coordinated." The tearing started again, and this time it did not stop. "As we have throughout our history, we can only hope to minimize the destruction."

Stepping forward, Ussakk took her in his arms. The fact that she was the day's Delineator and he a research astronomer, and that they had never met before this moment, meant nothing. The Hyfft were a species as emotional as they were demonstrative, among whom close physical contact was not only common-place but expected. Anyway, Ussakk was glad of the opportunity to embrace someone.

He needed the warming physical contact as badly as she did.

They traveled to Therapp from all over the continent of Vinen-Aq, Delineators who under the newly imposed regulations of emergency had found their terms of office extended indefinitely beyond the usual one day. It was not certain that each was the best of their kind to deal with the crisis at hand, but there was no time to process extended evaluations. If you were Delineator on that dire day, you found yourself chosen.

Having come from far and wide, they assembled the following morning in the circular chamber of Therapp's administrative center. Informed of Ussakk's discovery, his scientific colleagues had promptly dropped all other work to devote themselves to the single task of monitoring the approach of the three ships. That left Ussakk free to exhibit himself to the general public. True to Phomma sa Nine's observation, his presence did seem to have a reassuring influence on public opinion.

That did not prevent some panic from spreading as word slipped out. At least by the time it did, the efficient and fast-moving Hyfftian authorities had been given a breathing space in which to prepare. The worst of the panic was quickly contained. But nothing could stop the consequent rush of city dwellers toward the countryside. Every conveyor route out of every conurbation was soon jammed with desperate, would-be refugees. Even so, the lines were orderly. The few seriously unbalanced individuals who actually ignored the designated routes in favor of taking off across private property were quickly apprehended and suitably chastised.

The Hyfft might be prone to panic, but they did so in an orderly fashion.

Within the chamber, designated Delineators from dozens of Vinen-Aq's largest communities milled and conversed. There was no yelling, no piercing echoes of raised voices. Administrators were not allowed that kind of emotional release. But the general conversation was certainly borne along by an uneasy edge.

Nestled in one ear, a communicator kept Ussakk in constant touch with his associates at the observatory. Every similar installation on Hyff had likewise abandoned its regular work schedule to focus on the incoming craft. Thus far there had been no attempt at communication. If history was any guide, Ussakk knew, that would come once the Iollth had settled themselves in orbit and chosen the unfortunate location or locations for their landing. In the past, they had been known to destroy a city center or two from orbit, just as a preliminary object lesson. Or perhaps for entertainment. On that aspect of Iollth psychology, there were few details.

All across peaceful but tense Hyff, ten billion individuals now spoke one thought with one mind, albeit usually in private so as not to offend their neighbors. *Please don't let them land here.* In silently wishing this, Ussakk unashamedly had to admit that he was no different from his less scientifically inclined fellows.

No one thought of mounting an active resistance. Confined to their planet and happy to be so, at peace among themselves for thousands of years, the Hyfft possessed no weapons of advanced destruction: nothing more offensive than nonlethal police gear. Nor did they need any such—except when the Iollth came calling. Discussion of developing such weaponry, which was certainly within the technical ability of Hyfftian science, had come to naught. The one time such a thing had been tried, over a hundred years earlier, an Iollth landing craft had actually been destroyed. Its three companion vessels had escaped to orbit, one badly damaged.

Safe high above the surface of Hyff, their mother ships had proceeded to kill some two hundred thousand Hyfft. After that, their subsequent visitations had met with no further resistance.

Wandering among the dense crowd of visiting, apprehensive Delineators, Ussakk had the opportunity to eavesdrop on numerous ongoing discussions. All he could do was listen, having nothing tangible to contribute. He would much rather have been back at the observatory, even if there was nothing to do there but monitor the rapid progress of the three incoming starships and agonize about possible landing sites.

There was one good thing. Given the speed at which the Iollth vessels were traveling, they should arrive by tomorrow, thus putting an end to all the increasingly nerve-wracking speculation. He felt himself to be as ready as any of his kind for whatever might come. His elderly parents had been sent out of the city, to a (hopefully) safe refuge deep in the agricultural countryside. He was not mated and not courting. He had no offspring. If anyone was suitable for sacrifice at the hands of the Iollth, it was him.

But he didn't want to die.